A PLUME B[OOK]

THE ROMANCE READ[ERS']

JULIE L. CANNON is a true native Georgian, tracing her ancestry back to the Cherokee Indians. She lives in Watkinsville, Georgia, with her husband and three children. She is the author of three previous novels: *Truelove & Homegrown Tomatoes,* *'Mater Biscuit,* and *Those Pearly Gates.* Visit her website at juliecannon.info.

Praise for *The Romance Readers' Book Club*

"Julie Cannon weaves prose like a master artisan! The lyrical text is magical, the story line—a rich Southern tapestry of pathos and joy— is filled with characters as delightful and delicious as a prized pecan pie. Don't miss it!"

—J. L. Miles, author of *Roseflower Creek* and *Cold Rock River*

"Sweet, tender, and funny. A delightful read!"

—Augusta Trobaugh, author of *The Tea-Olive Bird Watching Society*

"Julie Cannon has written a masterpiece of fiction that, while set in the South, will wind itself in the hearts of people everywhere. Tammi Lynn Elco is a multidimensional and unforgettable character. This is a long-overdue topic and a must-read for those who love to laugh and cry and sneak romance books when no one's looking."

—Susan Reinhardt, author of *Not Tonight, Honey: Wait 'Til I'm a Size 6* and *Don't Sleep with a Bubba*

The Romance Readers' BOOK CLUB

Julie L. Cannon

A PLUME BOOK

PLUME
Published by Penguin Group
Penguin Group (USA) Inc., 375 Hudson Street, New York, New York 10014,
U.S.A. • Penguin Group (Canada), 90 Eglinton Avenue East, Suite 700, Toronto,
Ontario, Canada M4P 2Y3 (a division of Pearson Penguin Canada Inc.) • Penguin Books
Ltd., 80 Strand, London WC2R 0RL, England • Penguin Ireland, 25 St. Stephen's
Green, Dublin 2, Ireland (a division of Penguin Books Ltd.) • Penguin Group
(Australia), 250 Camberwell Road, Camberwell, Victoria 3124, Australia (a division of
Pearson Australia Group Pty. Ltd.) • Penguin Books India Pvt. Ltd., 11 Community
Centre, Panchsheel Park, New Delhi – 110 017, India • Penguin Books (NZ), 67 Apollo
Drive, Rosedale, North Shore 0745, Auckland, New Zealand (a division of Pearson
New Zealand Ltd.) • Penguin Books (South Africa) (Pty.) Ltd., 24 Sturdee Avenue,
Rosebank, Johannesburg 2196, South Africa

Penguin Books Ltd., Registered Offices: 80 Strand, London WC2R 0RL, England

First published by Plume, a member of Penguin Group (USA) Inc.

First Printing, January 2008
10 9 8 7 6 5 4 3 2 1

Ⓟ REGISTERED TRADEMARK—MARCA REGISTRADA

LIBRARY OF CONGRESS CATALOGING-IN-PUBLICATION DATA

Cannon, Julie, 1962–
    The Romance readers' book club : a novel / Julie L. Cannon.
        p. cm.
    ISBN 978-0-452-28899-7
    1. Grandmothers—Georgia—Fiction. 2. Granddaughters—Georgia—Fiction. 3.
Book clubs (Discussion groups)—Fiction. 4. Teenage girls—Sexual behavior—Fiction.
5. Religious life—Fiction. 6. Georgia—Fiction. 7. Domestic fiction. I. Title.

    PS3603.A55R66 2007
    813'.6—dc22
                                    2007009449

Printed in the United States of America
Set in Horley Old Style
Designed by Eve L. Kirch

*This book is for Lynne Fortson Milner, a friend
closer than a sister, who discovered the world of
men and romance right alongside me.*

Acknowledgments

I am deeply grateful to Jenny Bent, my literary agent, for helping me hone and publish this book. Her faith in me and her passionate response to the story made *The Romance Readers' Book Club* a reality.

I am indebted to Trena Keating and Allison Dickens, my editors at Penguin, for their patience while reading the voluminous drafts, and for their skill and talent with a red pen. They are truly amazing artisans.

Special heartfelt thanks go to my wonderful and supportive fellow writers and traveling companions, the Dixie Divas. They are: Karin Gillespie, J. L. Miles, and Patricia Sprinkle.

I feel gratitude beyond what I can articulate to Tom Cannon, my life partner and love, whose endless acts of selflessness and support make my writing life possible, and to my children, Iris, Gus, and Sam, who love me whether or not the scene works. Finally, my humble song of thanks goes to my fellow author, God, who tells the greatest story of all time, an epic narrative with words and love that touches hearts and changes the world.

The
Romance Readers'
BOOK CLUB

CHAPTER 1

There's not much time. In half an hour they'll be leaving for the Wednesday evening fellowship supper and prayer meeting at Promiseland Church. Granny Elco is busy chopping carrots and celery in the kitchen at the back of the house, and as long as Tammi hears the steady *whack! whack!* of her knife on the cutting block, she has the boldness to slip out onto the dusky front porch and over to a small white Philco radio, the sole means through which the outside world is permitted entrance into the farmhouse.

Crouching in shadow, Tammi fiddles with the tuning knobs to move the station from WGPL, a religious station out of Hillsboro, to a black station in Bonaire. She turns the volume so low she has to mash her ear right up against the vibrating speaker.

When the sensual rhythm of this other world fills her ears, Tammi squeezes her eyes shut. Her heartbeat quickens at her neck and wrists, and the notes envelop her body, jump-starting her backside to pulse along with the beat. She wriggles in pleasure while she bites at the sheer gloss on her lips, tasting a hint of Bubblegum Bonne Bell. This, too, was done in secret, and the tube hidden away at the back of her panty drawer.

No longer a child, and not yet a woman at fifteen, when Tammi feels the stirring of her budding hormones, she tries to be content biking along the dirt road from the big house to Aunt Minna's, or dangling her feet in the trickle of water that is left in Viking Creek. Whenever she runs out across the pasture where Pepaw keeps his herd of cows, she stops and talks to them. Their faces wear empathetic expressions, and she melts into warm brown eyes that let her pretend they know exactly what she's saying and how she's feeling.

Only now, at the tail end of the autumn of 1974, October 31 to be exact, the usual sheen on their hides is missing, and their pointy hooves are splayed out on top of a pasture dry as shoe leather, scarcely puckering the crusty earth where once little half-moons followed the herd as they shifted their feet on steaming beds of moist red clay and dung. Tammi loves the cows, and when she hears the county agent say that the state's eight-month-long drought is forcing many farmers to sell their cattle, she gets a terrible feeling.

Most of the citizens in Rigby, Georgia, including Tammi's Pepaw, Melvin James Elco, are farmers, and if you were to be a fly on the wall during their conversations with one another or their pleadings with the Heavenly Father, you'd hear them say that the worst thing about the drought is that there's no hay stored up for winter.

Tammi had felt the weight of the drought early on, in that part of her that lived for Pepaw. Small at first, a mere catch in her breath as she stood with him watching the cattle hover, eternally thirsty, at the water trough, while ants scuttled soundlessly in and out of the cracks in the red clay, and the little blue-black iridescent bodies of desperate flies buzzed listlessly in the searing heat. But it had increased steadily, till now it was a constant nudging presence, making her flinch each time she walked out the front door, feeling the blast of fiery breath from rays so fierce they blistered the fields, stunted the grass, and turned green cornstalks to brown dust. Tammi sometimes prayed for miraculous things: gully-washers and floods with two-foot-high waves. But usually it was the same little prayer every night after she climbed into bed: that God would release one of those long, gentle, soaking thundershowers that had lasted for several days in the summers of her past. This seemed a much more reasonable request, one certainly not requiring too much of His dynamic power, not enough to siphon any mystical force away from starving African children or from saving those souls ensnared by the devil.

As far back as June, Granny had stood at the window with pinched lips all drawn up like the tied ends of a balloon, saying, "If you want to find out how dry that ground is, Tammi Lynn, just get yourself a shovel and try to dig a hole. I guarantee you'll run slap out of a handle before you find good, moist dirt." Tammi only nodded. She knew no words of consolation for someone who had actually cried in late August because there were no muscadines plump on the vine, no fuzzy pods of okra for gumbo. Even September felt like a sizzling skillet, everything just stunned senseless with the heat.

As October crowned, everyone held their breath awaiting cool, refreshing fall air; but the searing, relentless sun remains a given, bearing down on the hapless rooftops and fields of Crawford County, blistering the tops of the pine trees, turning their crowns a brownish yellow. No apple blossoms dot the orchard with the promise of juicy Winesaps for a fall treat.

Granny is one hundred percent certain God has abandoned Rigby on account of unconfessed sin, but Pepaw, a good-natured man who feels that he has received from God the earthly wisdom to buy an irrigation system, simply smiles and tells Tammi not to fret. When he mentions this purchase to Granny, she folds her arms across her scrawny chest. "And where will we get the money?" she snorts. "What we need to do is get to prayer meeting tonight to repent and beseech the Lord for rain."

Promiseland Church sits on the end of Sprayberry Road, past the cattle barn and the Ejibwah Indian mounds and right before Bob's

Handi-Pantry, where you can go to buy coffee or aspirin if you don't want to drive all the way into town to the Big Star.

Pepaw leads his wife, his son Orr, and Tammi through the gravel parking lot and up the brick steps, across the dim vestibule, then down two steps into the fluorescent light of the social hall. The tables have centerpieces of cornucopias spilling over with an assortment of papier-mâché vegetables. There are real pumpkins, though, alongside the fake eggplants, corn, and peppers. Purposefully, the pumpkins are not carved into jack-o'-lanterns.

Setting Granny's tray of crudités down next to a dome of lime Jell-O, Tammi notices that someone has brought a bucket of Kentucky Fried Chicken. The chicken and Miss Eva Claire's double-fudge brownies will go fast. At potlucks the young people have to go last, so Uncle Orr always gets things for Tammi.

Orr is in his late thirties, but according to the doctor his mind is stuck at around seven years old, and he has kept the guileless character of that age, too. Plump, and with a mostly bald head, he resembles a large toddler.

Tammi is tall and gangly, with long hair the color of molasses hanging in silky sheets from a center part. Generally she wears a wide smile that reveals the gap between her front teeth and highlights the smattering of freckles fanned out across the tops of her tawny cheeks. She has a slightly upturned nose and beguiling eyes, golden brown like a cattail in the sun.

Through the years Tammi and Orr have changed roles off and on: from child and adult, to peers, to adult and child, and then to companions who turn to each other because they have to. Given to the irrational fears of a small child for whom the world is a big, scary place, Orr depends on Tammi to be his filter. She explains things to him when she can. Soothes and distracts him when she cannot. But that said, there are times when he surprises her, when his insight is sharp and profound.

Tonight Orr drains a cup of spiced cider and sits down across the table from Tammi. "You're sad," he says, looking hard at her.

"Yep," she says. "Sad and bored."

"Want me to give you a Indian sunburn?"

Tammi laughs. He's so serious. She knows better than to argue with him. Besides that, he *is* making her laugh. Orr pushes up her sleeve and twists his hands on her forearm.

"I wonder where all these folks got the cockamamie idea that Halloween's evil!" Tammi hisses into his ear. "No dancing, no card playing, no drinking, no trick-or-treating. I swear Orry, I'm getting sick and tired of the way this—"

"No swearing, either," he whispers.

Tammi slaps her knee and laughs, a short loud burst of "ha!"

Across the social hall, Granny turns her long stringy frame as a unit and pierces Tammi with a glance. Her old raisin eyes peer hard through those glasses that are so incongruous with the rest of her. They're black cat's-eye bifocals left over from the sixties, when she had her first and last eye exam. She's no slave to fashion. If it works, why change? Even then, she'd gotten the frames off a sale rack, as one of the sparkling faux diamonds had come out of the right eyepiece. The rest of her is no-nonsense; long gray hair pulled back into a bun, pointed nose, and narrow face. She wears drab dresses for the most part and serious support shoes with stockings.

Tammi smiles and mouths "Sorry" to Granny, but as soon as her back is to them again, she scowls. Then she gets a wonderful idea. "You and me are going to sneak off and go trick-or-treating tonight, Orry," she whispers. "After prayer meeting."

"What?"

"It's Halloween."

Orr looks puzzled.

"Trick or treat! You know, wear costumes and knock on doors for candy. We'll play tricks on the folks who don't give us any."

"Tammi," Orr says, his eyebrows raised high. "It wouldn't be very Christian of us to play tricks on people."

"Silly." Tammi pats his hand. "Not *bad* tricks. Funny stuff like rubbing Crisco on doorknobs or throwing eggs at windows."

The Reverend Goodlow clinks a spoon against his coffee mug. A wiry man with big pink ears, he bows his head to say the blessing, at the end asking the Lord to take pity on his flock and quench their thirsty fields. "Alrighty, brothers and sisters," he says, opening his eyes, "dig in."

"What you want, Tammi?" Orr says.

"Get me . . ." says Tammi, her mind on costumes she can whip together in a hurry. ". . . a chicken leg, deviled egg, Miss Perkerson's beans, and a brownie."

Prayer meeting should be over by eight o'clock, she calculates, and they'll be home by eight-thirty. She'll be a hobo and Orr a scarecrow, costumes easy enough to assemble and sneak by Granny in.

Tammi has butterflies in her stomach as she grabs tea and a fork. Orr holds a small mountain of food on top of two nested plates.

"I don't want to play tricks, Tammi," he says when he sits down.

She kicks his ankle gently underneath the table and swipes a pinched thumb and forefinger across her lips. They're sitting at a table with the Hickmans and the Geters, two elderly couples Tammi's known for as long as she can remember. The wives quilt, garden, cook, and clean all day if you go by their conversations.

"You surely have shot up, Tammi," Mrs. Geter remarks. She's a stout woman with a red-cheeked face and brown eyes with nice smile wrinkles at their corners.

"Yes, ma'am," Tammi says. She definitely bloomed over the summer. Got a set of firm pear-shaped bosoms that she enhances with an exercise Aunt Minna showed her. In her room she presses her palms together between her breasts, like she's praying, and squeezes to a 1–2–3 pulsing rhythm.

"How old are you now?"

"Fifteen."

"She's still three inches under me," Orr adds.

"Well, that's nice." Mrs. Geter doesn't look at Orr as she speaks. Some folks are uncomfortable around him, referring to his condition as "tetched in the haid," which loosely translated means "mentally afflicted."

Mrs. Hickman asks Tammi if she can sew yet, and Tammi tells her about the apron she made in last year's home economics class. "What's Mrs. Ransom teaching you girls this year?" Mrs. Hickman looks concerned.

Tammi has to stop and really think. The truth is she's never been excited about domestic skills, and she blocks them out of her mind as soon as class is dismissed. Mrs. Hickman, however, with her potato-colored homespun dress and orange hand-crocheted vest over that, clearly believes in home economy.

"We're learning to fix a Thanksgiving meal." Tammi forces a smile.

"How lovely. Now, is she teaching you to do *cornbread* stuffing?" Mrs. Hickman's face gets serious. "I make mine with cornbread."

"I put water chestnuts in mine," Mrs. Geter says, and the two women begin an animated conversation about Thanksgiving dinner that somehow turns to one about the drought.

Tammi tunes them out, absentmindedly nibbling a deviled egg as she muses on her plans for Halloween.

CHAPTER 2

O rr was almost as excited as he was on Christmas Eve. Tammi dabbed big brown freckles on his cheeks with a Magic Marker while he bounced on his seat atop an antique trunk at the foot of her bed. She set an old straw hat on his head and tied a red bandanna around his neck. "Okay, Mr. Scarecrow," she said, "ready to go get us some treats?"

He nodded. "But I don't want to play tricks on folks."

"Yeah, okay, Orry," Tammi whispered. "Now, listen. We have to get by Granny without her suspecting a thing. When we get downstairs, take that hat off and just hold it down behind you, out of sight."

"Okeydokey."

"And don't look at her. Don't say a word to her."

Everything was quiet as they crept into the dark hallway and down the stairs, sliding outside into a night illuminated by a full moon. Tammi looked over her shoulder at the big house. "It'll be fun, Orry," she said. "Don't worry." Taking a deep breath, she led him down a path that ran alongside Minna's house, then over a moss-covered log bridge and along the smooth bank of Viking Creek till they got to the third house along the water's edge, tiny and made of tar paper. It belonged to Orr.

"Now," Tammi said, pulling a pillowcase wrapped around a flashlight from underneath her shirt, "we'll need this once we get in the woods."

Down a dirt trail that led from Orr's house to the woods. They walked by the light of the moon. When they were far enough into the thick of the trees, creeping along on top of dry, crackling leaves, Tammi turned on the light. The air was cool this late, nine o'clock, and she was glad she'd thrown on Pepaw's tattered shirt. "Isn't this fun?" she asked Orr.

"Fun."

"Now, listen." Tammi pushed a floppy felt hat up off her eyebrows. "We're going to do our trick-or-treating where the folks live that don't go to Promiseland."

"Why don't they go to church?" Orr stumbled over a root.

"Hush and get on up here beside me and the light so you won't trip." They walked along quietly for a spell, shoulder to shoulder.

Suddenly Orr stopped. He grabbed Tammi's arm. "Why don't they go to church?"

She didn't know how to answer him. She'd often thought about the folks she knew from school who didn't go. Granny said they were walking in darkness, blinded by the follies of sin and the pleasures of this world. These thoughts put a queasy feeling into Tammi's stomach.

"They don't go because their folks don't make them go," she said, suddenly feeling like she was standing on the edge of a cliff with the bones in her knees missing. She had to find a way to ignore the little voices in her head telling her to turn around and go home. She caught a taste of smoke from a lingering brushfire and felt for a moment only the boundless joy of their daring adventure.

Orr sniffed the air, too. "These folks living up here better be careful burning stuff in the middle of a drought," he said. "Pepaw says it's too dangerous and that the fire department ought to out-law fires." They'd reached the backside of a handful of mobile homes in a horseshoe formation, and Tammi could see TV sets blinking on and off in several of them. However, there were no happy groups of children wearing pointed black hats or draped in sheets milling about, the way she'd always pictured Halloween. Shoulders back, she marched into the clearing with Orr. "Here we are," she whispered.

"I know!" Orr said, gesturing at a smoldering metal barrel behind the nearest trailer. "We can be good citizens and check to be sure the fires are out."

"Later." Tammi stuffed the flashlight into the rope at her hips that was holding up a pair of baggy trousers. She drew a deep breath, eyeing a trampoline with a crumpled base holding a mountain of leaves. "Let's walk around front and see if there's any jack-o'-lanterns."

"They're the devil's work," Orr said underneath his straw hat.

"You don't really believe that, do you? Those happy, shining pumpkins?" Tammi grabbed his arm and shook it. "How could they possibly be evil?" But even saying this, she wasn't certain herself. "Now hush and come on." Her heart hammering, she took Orr's arm and pulled him around to face some steps.

"Alrighty, Orr, march right on up there and knock on the door." She nudged him with her knee. "And say 'trick or treat' when they open it."

"Come with me," he begged.

"Nah. I'll be right behind you." Tammi put her hands in her pockets and stared. She was disappointed. Maybe God was telling her something. What if Granny was right, and participating in this holi-day *was* the same as inviting the devil to gain a foothold in your life?

Tammi felt better when she looked up and saw Orr's expectant face. "What're you waiting for?" she asked.

Orr clutched the pillowcase tighter, marched up to the tiny stoop, and banged his fist on the door. "Aren't you coming, Tammi?" he called over his shoulder.

Tammi swallowed the lump in her throat and hurried forward, not so much for honoring her word to Orr or even as a dare against Granny and the Reverend Goodlow as for a pressing need to break free, an unnameable stirring and declaration of the hunger at her core. "Remember, say 'trick or treat,' " she whispered into Orr's ear, stepping slightly behind him.

Tammi blinked when the door swung open and the high-pitched yipping of a tiny dog assaulted them.

"Who's that?" came a smoker's husky voice.

"Trick or treat," Orr sang out happily, thrusting his pillowcase low and open.

"What?" An old woman's anxious face looked Orr up and down. A floppy mint-green bathrobe hung from stooped shoulders, and a cigarette dangled from her bottom lip. "What you want?" She narrowed her eyes. Suddenly a dog that looked like an overgrown rat shot out from behind her, growling, his body shivering from head to foot and his toenails clattering on the linoleum.

"He's dangerous!" the woman warned. "He bites!" The dog's pop eyes made him look like he wanted to tear them both limb from limb.

"Come here, you pretty little thing," Orr crooned, dropping to his knees, patting his thighs. The bristling creature made a happy noise and jumped into his lap.

The woman's jaw went slack. "Well, I'll be. Mookie don't like nobody."

"Dogs love Orr," Tammi said.

"Who are you, girl?"

"Tammi Lynn Elco, and this here's my uncle Orr."

"Ain't he a little big for trick-or-treating?" She pointed her cigarette at Orr.

"He was born with his cord wrapped around his neck," Tammi explained. "He's never been trick-or-treating before, and I figured I would give him a new experience."

"That's real sweet of you, girl. I don't get many visitors. I'm Dell Terhune."

"Mighty nice to meet you, Miz Terhune," Tammi said.

"Ain't no young'uns been trick-or-treating around here in ages. We're all old folks that live up here."

Tammi wanted to say something kind to the woman, excuse herself and Orr, and get on home. "You certainly have a lot of books," she said, inclining her head toward a mound of paperbacks on the floor.

"Getting ready for my yard sale. Come on in and have a seat."

"You have candy?" Orr was holding Mookie like an infant now, rubbing noses in an Eskimo kiss.

"Reckon I've got some of them peppermints from the Shoneys around here somewheres." The old woman said.

"Hush up," Tammi hissed, nudging Orr's arm.

"I want candy," he said. "You said we'll play tricks if we don't get candy."

Mrs. Terhune frowned.

"No, no!" Tammi laughed and slapped her knee. "I was just teasing him! We'd never do a thing like that."

"We're here for candy." Orr pushed out his bottom lip. "Tammi, you said we'd—"

"I'm going to *buy* you some candy, silly," Tammi said, jumping to her feet. "It's been nice meeting you, Miz Terhune. Reckon we'd better get ourselves back home. Come on, Orry."

"Set a spell longer and I'll hunt them peppermints."

"Why are you selling all those books?" Tammi asked out of politeness.

"Well, I done read 'em all forty-'leven times, and I reckon I got my enjoyment out of 'em, anyway."

Tammi leaned forward to see the cover of the top book. *Knights of Desire* was embossed in gold letters. There was a picture of a brawny, bare-chested man with his arm encircling a woman whose head was thrown back in what appeared to be ecstasy. Her parted lips screamed passion. Tammi looked at the way the woman's hand touched the man's pectoral muscle, and a feeling washed through her that she couldn't name.

"Go on and have a look through them books," Mrs. Terhune urged.

"I like books," Orr said. He nuzzled Mookie's belly. "Let me see, too."

Tammi ignored him and got down on her knees to spread the books out across the floor like playing cards.

"Look at that one with the horsey!" Orr exclaimed. There was a cover with a woman clad in a sheer white gown, riding a horse. The woman's gown left nothing to the imagination. Her nipples were big as silver dollars. "Pretty horse," Orr said. "Can we read it, Tammi?"

"Them are women's books," Mrs. Terhune said. "Romances." She laughed and it turned into a smoker's cough that bent her forward.

"These books don't look very Christian, Orry. Leave them alone," Tammi whispered, hearing her own voice, all at once surprisingly like Granny's.

"But—"

"Anyway, we *can't* read them. Look how fat they are. Just one would take weeks. We'd better get home."

"Please wait," Orr said. "Pretty please. We've got to get our candy."

"Don't go," Mrs. Terhune said. "Mookie's in heaven. Beat all I ever saw. It's like he's cast a spell over that there dog."

For a moment Tammi debated; so far they hadn't sinned. It didn't count as trick-or-treating since there were no carved pumpkins, or witches and ghosts, and they hadn't gotten any candy. Still, she decided she wouldn't tempt evil.

She hesitated a moment too long and her eye caught the cover of *Island Pulse*, which featured a barely clad couple underneath a palm tree, entangled in each other's arms. The woman's eyes were closed, and her tongue caressed her upper lip. Tammi reached for the book and brought it to her lap. She turned it over. *A story burning with forbidden love . . . virile bodies . . . passion unleashed like you've never read before.* Tammi could feel the quickened beating of her heart.

"Mmmm mmm." Mrs. Terhune shook her head slowly from side to side. "That's a good one, girl. Read it five times. Take a gander at page 37."

Tammi turned the cover, ruffled by the first few blank pages, the title page, and on to page 37.

"I could 'bout tell it to you by heart." Mrs. Terhune cackled.

Tammi skimmed the words, searching for what, she wasn't sure, until she got to a part where a man named Cody was crushing the mouth of a woman named Tatiana with his own. Tatiana's hands swept over the taut muscles of his golden torso, and she was desperate for more. Her reddened lips were tremulous, and his loins were quivering in eagerness for some unnamed part of her. Shamelessly, Tatiana pressed her pulsing pelvis toward Cody in raw hunger as he sank into her tender, yielding flesh with one powerful thrust.

Tammi gasped, held her breath to read on feverishly, puzzling over a sentence that called Cody a unicorn rampant. Orr set Mookie on the floor and sidled over to elbow Tammi, but she was unaware of him as she read on silently, a feeling stirring inside of her—that shaky, new-of-late feeling that was demanding attention.

"I want this." She pressed the book against her chest, meaning more than she could understand.

Mrs. Terhune smiled at her desperate tone. "You can have it." She pointed her fuzzy slipper at the rest of the books. "Take all of 'em. Likely nobody's going to buy 'em, anyway."

Mookie was dancing around Orr's feet, begging him to scratch his ribs again. "You're a fine fellow, yes you are," Orr cooed.

Tammi smiled. "Thank you very much, ma'am," she said. "But I can come back—and pay you for them."

"No, they can be your trick or treat. Put 'em in that bag he's toting so you can carry 'em home."

"You serious?" Tammi held her breath.

"I surely am."

"Thank you very much!"

Orr turned to Mrs. Terhune. "Peppermints?"

"Yes! Let me go hunt some up."

While Mrs. Terhune was scratching around in her kitchen, Tammi looked over the pile of things for sale. They were things Granny would call white trash: stacks of yellowed *National Enquirer* newspapers, a macramé owl hanging, a ceramic kitty with jeweled eyes. She thought of what Granny would say if she knew where Tammi and Orr were.

Tammi's palms began to sweat when she imagined Granny reading those things on the back covers of the worldly books. Maybe I shouldn't have them, Tammi thought, setting *Island Pulse* on the floor. She would not tempt evil.

"Aha!" Mrs. Terhune scurried back in with a palm full of dingy, cellophane-wrapped peppermint lozenges. She dumped them, along with the books, into Orr's pillowcase. "Now you've both got treats!"

Walking back home through the woods, Tammi felt like she'd begun to unravel a mystery. "We'll start us up a book club, Orry," she said when they reached Viking Creek. "You and me."

"What?"

"Let's hide these books and plan our *secret* club. You've got to cross your heart not to tell anybody."

"Deal," he said, galloping up the cinder-block steps onto his tiny porch and swinging the door open for her.

"First we'll read *Island Pulse*. Let's find us a good hidey-hole."

"I've got me a secret place under here." Orr slid his pine table over and pried up a floorboard. A nice-sized hole let out a waft of mildew as Tammi deposited the pillowcase next to a worn baseball glove and a *Women of Promiseland Church Cookbook* from 1962.

In the big house, Tammi couldn't fall asleep. Thoughts of the novels sent a shivery pleasure through her. She would learn things now. But was defining these feelings she'd been having lately worth the risk that Granny might find the worldly books?

Of course it was! Knowledge was power, and these books contained knowledge she could actually feel. There was really no question, then, because Tammi had always known she was meant for more than just the practical and passionless existence of a housewife in Rigby, Georgia.

CHAPTER 3

Tammi's father passed away when she was six months old. Her mother, Loretta, remained single for less than a year, catching the eye of Junior Elco, son of the owner of the antique shop where she worked.

It was brutal living in the Elco family compound under the scrutinizing eye of Constance Elco, Junior's mother. Tammi felt like the redheaded stepgrandchild, and she made it a game to stay clear of Granny. "Out of sight, out of mind" was her mantra as she roamed the woodlands and the fields. This was easy when she was small, but as she grew, Granny began to work Tammi like a field hand, spouting sayings such as "Idle hands are the devil's workshop."

Melvin James Elco Senior was the antithesis of his wife. When he laughed—and he was almost always laughing or smiling—his entire face lit up something powerful. Tammi couldn't have adored her Pepaw more if they'd been blood kin.

The spring Tammi turned ten she was to be Mary Magdalene in a Good Friday Easter drama at Promiseland. She could not have said what her folks talked about on that fateful drive. It was as if someone had erased everything right up to the moment when she was dimly aware that her stepfather had turned too sharply, so that the car sailed through the dusky air, coming to rest upside down in the ditch.

Tammi moved through the next several days feeling like she was in a big black hole, dropping, dropping, dropping. Granny locked the doors of Elco Antiques, and the reverend came to sit with her and Pepaw, somberly discussing funeral arrangements for Junior and Loretta. Dr. Floyd stopped by the house to check on Tammi's scrapes and bruises, assuring her that her mother's passing had been instantaneous, painless. Painless for her, maybe, but not for Tammi. It felt as if there was a hole torn in Tammi's soul.

Summer came, passing slowly. Tammi traveled through the days like she was moving in a dream, waiting to see what would happen without her mother there as a buffer between herself and Granny. Tammi was terrified of conversations regarding the wreck, as she fancied she could feel an undercurrent of resentment and blame in Granny's tone during what mundane words they did have together.

Tammi wanted desperately to believe that the wreck was nobody's fault, but the reality that it had been her play they were driving to was as immutable a fact as the moon rising each night.

She worked at her chores furiously, more for the purpose of numbing her mind than for pleasing Granny. Granny watched everything from her own grief, and she was working harder than ever, too. Yanking weeds from the garden, slamming the iron down onto clothes like she was pressing out the devil, scratching gravel as she gunned the Cadillac engine before roaring down the driveway on her daily trek to oversee Elco Antiques.

Granny's weekend bird-dogging trips to scout the countryside for antiques were the only times she would wear anything but a wide-eyed, remote expression. She loved antiques, adored finding that rare and priceless treasure moldering in some ancient barn or dilapidated house, and bringing it home to refinish and restore.

At the tail end of that summer, Tammi got a bad case of poison ivy. What began as a small itchy patch on one wrist soon spread to her arms and legs. At first she felt something like gratitude for the distraction, some misery to throw herself into other than grief. But then it spread to her trunk and up her neck, and into the impossibly tender spaces between her toes. Nights were agony, and Tammi could tolerate only the merest whisper of fabric against her skin. She'd dug an old sleeveless undershirt out of the rag bag, worn so thin it was like a spider's web. Wearing this, and a pair of cotton panties, she lay immobile on top of her sheets, the oscillating fan caressing her little breast buds and the fine blonde hairs on her arms and legs. She kept a hairbrush on her nightstand to rake her welted flesh, knowing this was only temporary relief at best, and really not so much of that. The heat magnified the itch beyond measure.

Tammi didn't say a word about her affliction, believing nothing could penetrate or eclipse that shroud of grief surrounding Granny. She was used to being ignored by her; and truth be told, it felt more than a little deserved. Pepaw had been busy harvesting corn in the lower pasture and was not home before Tammi shut herself away in her room at dusk.

After a week of nights spent tossing and turning in torment, Tammi slipped from her bed and hurried down the hallway to the lavatory for a stack of washrags to dip in ice water. She crept past Granny and Pepaw's closed bedroom door, tiptoeing downstairs so fast her feet were a blur. The kitchen smelled of the stewed onions they'd eaten for supper. She opened the door of the freezer, light spilling out so that from the corner of her eye she spied Granny's shape seated at the table.

Granny was sitting in her usual chair with her hands cupping her chin as she rested her elbows on the tabletop, eyes transfixed on something lying in front of her. It was the large gilt-framed portrait that hung above the mantle.

"Hi," Tammi offered casually, as if it were nothing out of the ordinary to be standing in front of the Frigidaire at 3:00 A.M. while Granny sat in the shadows.

Granny looked up at last, her eyes fastened on Tammi. "Lord God in heaven," she spat, "you're indecent!" Tammi was unprepared for the venom in her voice.

"A woman's body is to be kept covered!" Granny persisted. "This is an abomination!"

"I—I'm sorry, but I can't hardly bear to wear anything," Tammi whispered, a pink flush of embarrassment creeping up her neck. "I've got poison ivy."

"And you think that excuses you?" came Granny's shrill reply. "You'll be *developing* soon, Tammi Lynn. Getting your womanly curves. It's time you learned that men have no resistance, and it's your responsibility to cover yourself."

Tammi stood silently, looking at a drugstore calendar hanging above the phone. She could not get her breath.

"My mother," Granny said, lifting the large portrait with hands clenched so hard it was shaking slightly. "She raised me right. Her words were pearls of wisdom, of righteousness. Till the day she died. She knew the value of purity. I wish you could have known her."

Tammi felt like a mouse in Granny's sharp talons as she stared for a long moment at the grim, austere faces of the Reverend and Missus Zachariah Graves. She shifted her feet. Clearly, Granny expected some kind of response. Taking a deep breath, Tammi gave it a stab. "She sounds like a lovely woman." She smiled lamely because she thought she ought to after saying something so corny.

Granny seemed to take it at face value, however, and her voice grew softer. "Everything is resting on my shoulders now that your mother and Junior are gone. Guess I have to do my share of bending the twig."

Tammi knew this comment stemmed from one of Granny's favorite expressions: "As the twig is bent, so grows the tree."

"Now, run along and cover yourself properly." Granny's voice took on a whole new air of purpose now.

"But . . ." Tammi all but wept as she chewed her lower lip. "I'm itching so bad I feel like I'm gonna *die*."

"Our Lord said we must die to ourself daily, Tammi Lynn. If I scratched every itch I had, why, there's no telling what or where I'd be!"

Tammi had a fleeting notion that Granny was crazy, talking gibberish. Then she realized the old woman was mixing the Bible with metaphor in her strange fashion. Tammi could think of no rebuttal for these words, though she felt sure God would be compassionate. He would be tender on a person suffering such as she was. He knew how fiercely she itched. Sadly, she realized that Granny, who settled only for unquestioning obedience, would never accept this as an excuse.

Tammi trudged back upstairs to her room, stripped, and lay naked underneath the fan. It was miserable without the icy rags, but she would endure. Outside the window she could see the sky sprinkled with stars. She closed her eyes and swallowed the lump in her throat as she thought of her mama up there in the heavenly realm.

The color drained from Tammi's face half an hour later when she heard footsteps hit the strip of Oriental carpeting at the top of the staircase. She leaped out of bed to pull on her high-necked, ankle-length nightgown just as Granny stepped inside, cradling a pasteboard box.

"I came to tend to your rash." Granny plunked the box onto Tammi's nightstand. "You're decent now, anyway. You're a good girl to mind me, Tammi Lynn."

Bewilderment snatched Tammi's words away as Granny ordered her to lie down on her back. Moonlight slanted in through the open window and fell at Granny's feet while she rustled through the contents of the box, coming up with a pink bottle. She shook the bottle vigorously. "You need some of this calamine lotion on you," she said. "Says it dries up the weeping of the rash."

"Weeping" was the perfect description of what the poison ivy was doing, Tammi thought, watching Granny shake pink liquid onto a cotton ball. She bit back a whimper as Granny dabbed the first bit of cooling lotion onto her feet. Her hands were rough and brisk against Tammi's skin, but not unpleasant as she moved upward to her ankles.

Tammi let out a long, slow breath as the itching began to subside. Now she wanted to say something that would let Granny know how wonderful this was, being fussed over, soothed, *touched*, but she didn't know how to say it. This kind of intimacy between herself and Granny was so alien to her that she couldn't imagine how to begin. If Granny was a different type of person, Tammi might have sat up and pulled her into a hug.

Tammi stared intently at a water stain on the ceiling as Granny used two fingers on her left hand to delicately tug the hem of Tammi's gown upward so that the fabric bunched at her hips.

"You're covered up with this, aren't you, child? Now, you're definitely going to have to stop that scratching. Put some socks on your hands before you go to sleep." Granny continued to anoint the welts, all the while humming tunelessly under her breath. She stopped at the top of Tammi's thighs and stepped sideways so that she could minister next to her face and neck. She bent over so close that Tammi could see the downy white hairs on her earlobes, as well as a long white scar running diagonally across her chest that she'd never noticed before.

"Oh, what happened to you?" Tammi whispered, reaching out wonderingly to touch the scar. Granny flinched, dropping the sodden cotton ball onto the sheet. A pink stain spread across the sheet as the old woman quickly straightened herself, pulling the lapels of her robe together tight, a faraway look creeping into her eyes.

"Don't worry yourself about it," she said tersely, setting the calamine on the nightstand, picking up the box, and walking to the door. She stopped in the hallway and looked back. "Don't forget to put some socks on your hands."

After Granny's footsteps faded Tammi stood up to slip out of her gown. She got a pair of white cotton bobby socks from her dresser and placed them on the bed next to her pillow. She lay back down and sprinkled lotion out of the calamine bottle from her hip bones up to her neck before it was empty, smearing the milky liquid with her fingers. It dried to a thin film like skin, and crackled whenever a muscle moved. She turned off the lamp and let the rhythmic whir of the fan caress her body.

She slept that night with her hands dutifully inside the socks, and when she woke, it was the first time in days that she didn't itch.

She had naively supposed things would get better from there on, that all their old tensions would quickly fall away. But that was not the case. There were still many tough times over the years, though eventually she and Granny did settle into a kind of routine—a carefully choreographed dance of life in which Granny was constantly vigilant over Tammi's physical and spiritual welfare, while Tammi earnestly attempted to walk the straight and narrow.

But all too often she found herself stumbling off on a sidetrack, whispering under her breath as she peered sideways at Granny, "Hopefully she won't notice this. Surely I'll get away with it."

CHAPTER 4

Trick-or-treating with Orr was Tammi's biggest rebellion to date, the worst breach of her unspoken pact with Granny, which was, "You walk the straight and narrow, and I'll continue to keep a roof over your head."

Tammi lay in her bed in the predawn darkness of that November first, her heart hammering and her stomach a fluttery knot as she visualized the suggestive cover of *Island Pulse*.

Groggy from no sleep, she stumbled to her closet, frowning at the lineup of calf-length skirts and modest blouses. No wonder her life was so dull! She craved to look like the popular girls at Rigby High, the distant and untouchable girls who pointed and whispered about her when they weren't ignoring her. Those girls wore hip-hugging blue jeans, pink frosted lipstick, flirty blue eye shadow, and mascara so thick their lashes looked like spider legs.

Since Tammi's mother's passing, Granny's oldest daughter, Minna Elco Burbuliss, had been Tammi's only source of knowledge when it came to the frivolous, feminine things in life. Minna was trained as a beautician, though she hadn't worked since her husband's death. She had lots of time to devote to her looks and knew all about the current clothing styles in Milan and New York from the stacks of fashion magazines she pored over. Occasionally, Tammi would finish her chores early and slip over to Minna's for a little girl talk, sitting on the sofa, watching Minna paint her nails or wax her legs, adoring each gesture.

Tammi shrugged into her least offensive garments—an ivory blouse underneath a corduroy jumper—and made her way down the steps to the kitchen.

"Morning, gal," Pepaw said. He sat at the table in coveralls, a shock of gray hair like a rooster's comb, one furtive eye on the percolator, listening to the radio deejay's dour report on the weather—no rain in sight.

"Good morning, Tammi Lynn," Granny said, turning bacon in a skillet at the stove. "Eggs are ready."

Tammi was too excited to eat. "All I want's coffee," she said, "I'll go feed the chickens first."

Granny flew over to turn down the volume on the radio. "You'll set down and eat first," she said, shooting Tammi her finely honed *Don't you defy me, girl, because you know who'll win* look that time had proved was strong and effective.

"Yessum." Tammi sat down across from Pepaw and forked up squishy clumps of eggs, depositing them into the napkin on her lap and working her jaw as if she were chewing. She waited several minutes, her mind wandering to the fact that this was the same as lying. Add this to last night's grievous sin and she could feel like a regular heathen. Still, it was like setting out to cross a skinny rope bridge hanging over a deep ravine—how could she turn back? She would not give in to her traitorous conscience.

She was standing in the bathroom, her hair damp and toothpaste in her mouth, when she heard the distant rumble of the bus. She spit without rinsing, grabbed her book bag, and flew downstairs and out the door. Wet hair and a minty coating in her mouth made her feel sharp and clear, almost transparent, as she bounded up the steps of the bus and breathlessly took her seat.

Her day at school went as well as she could expect. She managed to keep her eyes open though the temperature outside was still above 80 in the afternoons and the Crawford County School Board had turned the AC units off in mid-October. In PE she told Mr. Arnold she was on her period and had cramps so bad she couldn't stand up straight enough to play volleyball. His face turned red as he looked at the ground and nodded. She sat in the bleachers daydreaming about the romance novels waiting for her.

Tammi fell asleep on the bus ride home, and the half-hour catnap did her a world of good. Walking down the long drive, she rubbed her eyes and focused on the big house at the end. Begrudgingly, she acknowledged that it *was* pretty. Built in 1894, it was an impressive white three-story clapboard with a gray slate roof, chock-full of priceless furniture that Granny collected on her constant buying trips for Elco Antiques.

There was a substantial roof overhang shading wraparound porches, with Victorian corbels attached to the tops of the posts just beneath the porches' ceiling beams. Top-story gabled windows matched those on the first level, and a bay window looked out over the drive, which was flanked on either side by stately magnolia trees.

Each of the bedrooms had its own fireplace and ceilings so high you felt like you might float away. Things Granny claimed Tammi didn't appreciate. She liked to say Tammi would be just as happy in a double-wide trailer on a cement lot, instead of a fine home that was on the historical tour and surrounded by four hundred acres of prime Georgia farmland. And it was true. Of all the homes in the family, Tammi preferred Orr's humble tar-paper shack and comfortable furnishings she could put her feet up on.

Minna's house, a small replica of Elvis's Graceland at the side of the big house, Granny declared gaudy. Nanette, the married daughter who lived in Las Vegas, was said to live in a duplex, and

Carson Elco, who was married to Onzelle, lived in a fine brick ranch home on the other side of Rigby.

Tammi had forgotten the long afternoon of chores Granny had planned for her until she walked inside the front hall and spied the jug of furniture oil, a rag, the broom, and the dustpan lined up along the wall. There was a note fastened to the handle of the broom. Granny's looped letters said she had had to make a run to the antique shop (there was new counter help) and that when Tammi got around to washing Pepaw's lunch dishes to be sure and rinse the tinfoil that came off the pound cake thawing on the kitchen counter.

Granny'd never thrown out a single rubber band or a twist tie, and she used coffee grounds twice, so saving and washing tinfoil was nothing new to Tammi. There was only one thing Granny was extravagant on, and that was her antiques. She didn't bat an eye at spending hundreds of dollars if it was for a two-hundred-year-old table with claw-and-ball feet or the mahogany sideboard that Tammi chose to begin her dusting on. Tammi swiped haphazardly. All she cared about was getting over to Orr's as fast as possible—to the books waiting for her.

The polishing finally done, Tammi returned to the front hall for the broom. She hadn't heard the Cadillac puttering down the drive or shuddering to a stop, and it surprised Tammi when Granny came around the corner, making a beeline for the front porch.

Normally, around four o'clock each weekday, Granny sat on the porch and tuned in to the Gospel Jubilee on WGPL. She called it her siesta and drank a whole pot of strong coffee. As a rule, Tammi steered clear of her during siesta time. She hated the fiddler's twang and the nasal voices of the Glory Clouds Quartet, followed by the Reverend Cotton's fervent words.

Tammi moved toward the kitchen, halfheartedly sweeping the foyer and the bit of hallway that held the Deepfreeze. Sighing, she slipped into rubber gloves and poured a capful of translucent blue

Dawn into a sink of hot water. It was almost five when she dipped the tinfoil into murky water and draped it across the row of drying saucers. She pulled the sink plug, and with a satisfying slap flung the rubber gloves over the faucet, sprinting out the back door to the faint closing twangs of the Gospel Jubilee.

Orr kept the dirt yard in front of his house as smooth as marble. In the fall, this job always consumed him. He would be sweeping frenetically, only to turn his back for a moment and find a new smattering of leaves.

Tammi climbed up on the porch and opened the screen door. "Orry!" she called. "You home?" No answer. She was sorely tempted to get *Island Pulse* and read without him, but she walked back outside and poked her legs through the center of his tire swing, sinking down on the warm rubber to wait. Feet on the ground, she swung from side to side like the pendulum of a giant clock. Waiting was the hardest work there was, and some days it seemed her whole life stood still. Achingly still.

With her chin resting on her chest, in the twilight of half-dreams, she dozed. She slept until a shadow fell across her and she felt hands on her shoulders, twisting her in circles and making her rise higher and higher until her feet were off the ground. She opened her eyes to see Orr's beaming face.

"No! I don't want to get drunk now!" she said in a voice that made him stop immediately. "Where in the world have you been? I practically fell all over myself running to get here."

"I was helping Minna hang up sticky papers," he said. "She doesn't want Priscilla eating flies anymore." He held the tire steady as she climbed out.

"It won't hurt a dog to eat flies. Now go get *Island Pulse*."

"Granny never sets foot down here," Tammi told Orr as they hurried through a stretch of woods to the edge of Viking Creek.

"Now, think of this as going to the movies. Close your eyes and I'll read."

Orr stepped over the tiny rivulet of water left in Viking Creek and climbed up onto a flat boulder in the middle, sitting like he was in church, head bowed and hands folded in his lap. Late-afternoon sunlight slanting through tree limbs as dry and creaky as old bones hit the sweat at his hairline and made him look like he was sparkling.

Tammi settled down on the bank. Ceremonially, she folded back the cover, stared at the title page, and cleared her throat. "*Island Pulse,*" she began, ruffling past several blank pages.

> *Chapter One. Tatiana Kua heard the sound of a man's heavy boots approaching the door of her hut. Her heartbeat quickened as she wrapped herself in the gauzy curtains. She had to hide. If it were Mikolo, she was done for. She had told him she was going to be at the market all day to sell her orchids, and Mikolo had a fierce temper. If it was Cody, they could drink piña coladas, then run along the frothy edge of the surf. Waikiki Beach at this time of day was beautiful —*

"The beach!" Orr clapped his hands. "You've been to the beach before. Remember, Tammi? You brought me that—"

"Yes!" she cut him off. "*You* remember to hush and keep your eyes closed."

> *Waikiki Beach at this time of day was beautiful. Waves lapped at the shore, and not far from the water, thick-trunked palms swayed in a sultry breeze where orchids hung like orange trumpets. Lush tropical rains left the forest floor damp and steamy, perfect for a natural sauna. Perfect for romance . . .*

Tammi placed a finger on the page. "Ain't this somethin', Orry?" she said.

He nodded and she read a description of Tatiana and Cody drinking a slushy concoction of pineapple, coconut, banana, and rum. Beads of water slid down the tall stems of their glasses, and they licked froth from each other's lips, closing their eyes in rapture. Finally they kissed deeply from the depths of their souls. Tatiana trembled with the urgency of her desire for Cody.

Tammi took a deep breath and dog-eared the page to mark their place. For several minutes she and Orr did not speak. Then, when Orr did, he stumbled and restarted and searched for words in vain so that Tammi was frustrated as well.

"I could almost taste that piña colada," she blurted at last. "Don't you think Hawaii sounds a whole lot better than Rigby?"

He didn't answer.

"Alrighty," Tammi said. "We've got just enough daylight to get to the end of chapter one here." She read two pages about Tatiana and Cody frolicking on the pure white sand, and an old man who warned them about an impending hurricane named Iwo, which was going to hit the Hawaiian Islands and dump billions of gallons of water. The last sentence of chapter one was about a threatening sky Tatiana saw through her long silky lashes as she pressed her trembling body against Cody's.

With a great sigh Tammi closed the book. How could she wait to read again? The descriptions of Hawaii, of Tatiana and Cody, from their skimpy island clothes (clothes Granny would never let Tammi wear) to their passionate kisses and breathtaking tingles, were so exciting. Tammi couldn't fathom the freedom these two lovers possessed, and she reopened the book to flip forward to page 37, the page Mrs. Terhune knew by heart, telling herself Orr wouldn't notice her skipping ahead.

"No, we mustn't," Tatiana breathed as Cody lifted the dark, shining sheet of her hair and let it spill through his fingers. "Mikolo

will be here any minute, and he will kill you if he finds us together."

"I would die a happy man, though. And if we do not make love, I will die of heartbreak." Cody's deep blue eyes moved over Tatiana's voluptuous body as he made a noise like he was eyeing a sumptuous morsel of food. "My loins ache for you."

"But I'm promised to Mikolo." She looked into his eyes, her heart clearly breaking.

"I'm a starving man, and I can't resist you one minute longer. Promises can be broken. Come away with me, Tatiana." Teasingly he bit the tip of her finger.

She leaned into him and let him suck her finger all the way into his hot mouth. "Ohhhh," she murmured, her eyes rolling up into her head in ecstasy. "I want you, too! You're all I think about!"

Orr began to fidget. He got to his feet, reaching up high to break a twig from a tree branch over his head, blocking the last weak shreds of light. "Tammi," he interrupted, "is the hurricane coming?"

Tammi looked up with a sudden, violent motion, startled to see where she actually was. She had half a mind to yell at Orr to hush up and then read on silently, but seeing his puzzled face she managed to collect herself. "It's coming, Orr. I imagine it'll be in the next chapter," she said as gently as she could, closing *Island Pulse* and collapsing backward onto the creek bank.

"Why are your eyes shut, Tammi?" Orr asked in a small voice as he sank down beside her, carefully holding his twig.

She couldn't explain. "Well, I reckon that's all for today," she said finally, standing up and stuffing the book between her back and the waistband of her panties. "I've been gone so long Granny's probably had herself a conniption fit by now. It'll be hard waiting to see what happens, but it'll give us something to look forward to."

As they walked along, Tammi pictured Tatiana. Long, lean, brown-limbed, with sleek black hair. She thought about mangoes and dazzling orchids, about Cody's chest and his piercing black eyes and the curve of his buttocks in swim trunks. She swallowed hard, her heart pounding as she pulled in her bottom lip and hurt it with her teeth. "Orry," she whispered, "did you ever realize there's all those islands out there? A lot more beautiful and exciting than Rigby." He didn't answer and she continued. "Know what? I'll bet it's raining in Hawaii right this very minute. Bet they never have a drought."

He stopped walking, shut his eyes, and shook his head. "A drought is bad."

"Yep." Tammi pressed a flat palm against his back. "Come on, we better get you home."

It was hard leaving *Island Pulse* with Orr, as they had made only a tiny dent in the juicy parts of the story. Tatiana's words "craving hunger" gave a name to Tammi's secret restlessness, and Tammi was desperate to know more, to know that these frustrations she felt living here with Granny were normal, to know that the nudging sensations blooming "down there" were normal, too.

Over the following days, Tammi and Orr gulped *Island Pulse*. Tammi began to refer to their reading times together as official meetings of the Romance Readers' Book Club. On their fifth afternoon with the novel, in which they hoped to finish it, Orr waylaid Tammi as she stepped off the school bus and asked if they could read right away.

"Got to do my homework and chores before I can slip out," Tammi said. "You're still keeping it a secret, aren't you? 'Cause if you're not, if you're telling, Orry, I swear I'll stop the club."

"I'm not telling," he assured her.

Viking Creek was cool enough for a sweater now, and since daylight savings brought darkness around six, Tammi could count on only an hour of light. November's sun was weak in the late afternoon, and the leaves that still clung to the trees made pockets of murky shadows on the final chapter of *Island Pulse*.

Today Orr wrapped his hands around his knees and cocked his head. "I hope Tatiana picks Mikolo," he said.

"You just don't get it, do you?" Tammi said. "Tatiana and Mikolo do not possess overwhelming physical passion like Tatiana and Cody do."

"But Mikolo is *nice*." Orr wrung his large hands.

"Yeah, he's nice and honorable, and controls the appetites of his body and all that, but he's about as boring as watching paint dry." Tammi sighed, scratching her nails in the cracked red clay. Rigby felt like those freeze-dried packages of camping food they sold in the Army surplus store —the kind where you needed to add water to get the food to come to life.

"Read," Orr implored, reaching out and touching Tammi's ankle.

"All right. But we absolutely *cannot* end this meeting of the Romance Readers' Book Club without picking our next book."

She began reading the final page of *Island Pulse*, and from the corner of her eye she noticed Orr chewing his bottom lip. When she read the last sentence, which had Tatiana running down the beach with Cody, Orr was clenching his hands into fists.

"Well," she said softly as she closed the book, "what did you think?"

Orr frowned. He blew out a long whoosh of air through his teeth. Tammi stood, stepped over the trickle of water, sat down next to him, and patted his thigh. "Listen," she offered, "I bet old Mikolo will find someone for himself."

"You do?"

"Sure. I mean, he's so good. Pure of heart. 'Course he'll find a true love to share his life with." Although she thought to herself that he would find some insipid little milquetoast who would be demure and subservient, and follow him to a dull, dry little town where the women sat around cooking, cleaning, and being practical.

"Time to choose our next book!" Tammi jumped to her feet. "I say we read the fattest one with the bumpy gold letters. *Texas Toast*, I believe." Tammi put *Island Pulse* underneath her blouse and they walked along together solemnly.

She sat down on Orr's couch while he moved his table to pry up the floorboard. "Does this one say *Texas Toast*?" He waved a book.

Tammi didn't hear him. She sat staring straight ahead, lost in thought, unaware of the fat paperback Orr now placed on her lap. "I just don't think I can tolerate this town anymore, Orrville! It's like the people around here are content to live one boring day after another. There's no passion in Rigby! I'd rather live anywhere than here."

"Don't leave me, Tammi." Orr sat down, squashing himself close to her.

She jumped up suddenly, catapulting the novel to the floor, then bending to pick it up with shaking hands. "Orry, I've just *got* to read some of this right now! Just a teeny-tiny bit."

"Go back to the creek?"

"It's too dark to read at the creek now."

"Mama doesn't even knock," he warned, eyeing her. "Sometimes she brings cornbread and buttermilk for my bedtime snack."

"I know." Tammi sighed. "But I *need* to begin this book tonight. Understand?" She sank down beside him, patting his knee and studying the cover.

He reached out and traced a finger along the ornate gold *T* of *Texas*, then over the powerful muscles of a galloping palomino.

"She's gorgeous, isn't she?" Tammi said of the blonde woman riding sidesaddle.

Orr shrugged. He touched a cow skull near the horse's hooves.

"Well," Tammi said, sucking in a breath, "I'm going to take a chance and read the back cover." She flipped the book over and read a teasing paragraph.

Bart's mouth came down on Clemmie's, searing it like a cattle brand, sending red-hot flames licking through her whole body until she was on fire. The velvet shaft of his tongue tenderly caressed, then wildly thrust itself against her own so that her mouth was consumed with the deliciousness of him, and her nostrils were filled with the scent of sweat and warm prairie sun . . .

"That comes from somewhere in this book. Can you believe it, Orr?" She shook his arm.

He poked his bottom lip out. "I like horses and cowboys."

"They're in here, believe me. Listen at this." Tammi read a sentence in red letters along the bottom of the back cover, "Love can conquer the deadliest of rivals!" She clasped the book to her chest, feeling that mix of scary and excited feelings inside, a sensation like she was standing on the edge of a ravine and could fall off or not. "I just can't stand it much longer." Tammi's voice came in a hoarse whisper as she bowed her head. "I gotta have passion."

She said good night and as she walked back to the big house, Orr's moon-pie face hovered in her mind. She began to pity him for the one thing she used to envy about him —his innocence. His stuck brain only endured the passionate scenes to be with Tammi and to hear about the beach and the hurricane, and now the cowboys. There had to be someone else she could ask to join the club. Someone who could understand passion. "Sorry, Orry," Tammi whispered. But there was no real remorse in her voice as she smiled into the brilliant sunset washing out to a flat, dull pearl.

CHAPTER 5

At Rigby High, Tammi was more or less invisible. Some days she moved through her entire schedule without a word to anybody save "Here" when her homeroom teacher called roll, and "Thank you" when the lunch ladies passed a plate of mystery meat over the stainless-steel serving bar.

Today, for the first time, she felt almost anticipatory about walking through the front double doors. Her pulse sped as she climbed the brick steps, her eyes zipping along classmates she might possibly approach about joining the book club.

Hesitating in the shadowed recess of the guidance officer's hallway, Tammi silently rehearsed her words: *Hi, Margie, would you like to join my book club? Hello, Ann Marie, do you enjoy reading?* Fifteen minutes remained until the first bell rang, and groups of kids were sauntering in through the front doors, clustering around the trophy case near the office, laughing and talking about tonight's football game against Paldrop County. After five minutes, Tammi took a deep breath, patted the fat copy of *Texas Toast* in her book bag, and stepped out underneath the fluorescent lights of the main hallway. *The worst that could happen was they'd just say no,* she mused, making her way to the lockers.

Slowly she opened her locker, stood there stacking and restacking a pile of papers until finally LaDonna Tallchief appeared, dragging behind her a canvas bag on wheels. It thumped and bumped along, coming to rest two lockers down from Tammi's. Tammi stared at the bag. "Bet that's easy on your back," she called. "Feels like my backpack weighs a million pounds."

LaDonna looked up, startled. "This?" she asked, eyeing Tammi hard. "This isn't my books. It's my overnight stuff. My dad's weekend and all." LaDonna rummaged around in the bag and pulled out a worn copy of *Walden*.

"You love to read, don't you?" Tammi asked in one quick breath.

"Yep." LaDonna's answer was offhand. She stuck her nose in her locker.

Tammi paused to pat her fragile confidence. She thought for one brief, dark second of Granny's undisguised contempt for anyone by the name of Tallchief. The Tallchief clan was Rigby's equivalent of the Gambino Mafia family. They had a wild streak a mile wide, and their names frequently appeared in the police blotter. You could pretty much count on the fact that when they decreed war on anything or anyone, it was all over but the shouting. Tammi decided not to pay Granny's assessment a bit of mind. She saw nothing unscrupulous in LaDonna, a girl she admired more than any other classmate. LaDonna was not wild and in your face like most of the other hormone-ravaged teens. She possessed a reserved and serene nature, which Tammi translated into proof that she was older and wiser by eons than her peers, though LaDonna looked to be about twelve years old if you judged by her almost boyishly slender figure and her unpainted face. LaDonna did not appear to hold with any foolishness. Perhaps she'd think the novels silly, even try and convince Tammi of this . . .

"Hey, LaDonna, you wanna join my book club?" Tammi asked quickly.

LaDonna withdrew her head from her locker, tossing a shining sheet of black waist-length hair over her shoulder. Her dark eyes peered curiously at Tammi. "Hm?"

"Um . . . I'm starting a book club, and since you like to read, I figured you might . . . you know, want to join? I've got the first book right here." Tammi paused to exhale, brandishing *Texas Toast*.

LaDonna opened her mouth, her fingers hovering over the words "Tremulous passion of two virile bodies" on the cover as she reached for the book. "Is this dirty?"

"Why would you think that?" Tammi said, honestly curious.

LaDonna wrinkled her brow. She reached for the book and turned it over to read the back cover as Tammi held her breath. It seemed to Tammi that the moment was an hour before LaDonna looked up again.

"Have you really *looked* at this?" LaDonna asked, her eyebrows high.

"It's just a love story."

"It's a 'sensual glimpse into the erotic lives of two very passionate people,' " LaDonna read.

"They're actually just ordinary folks. A man, a woman. In love."

"Be honest, Tammi. This is some hot stuff."

Tammi smiled. "But it's not bad. How could love be bad? Besides, the settings in these are wonderful."

"*These?*"

"Yeah, I've got a whole library of them."

They stood in silence for a small space of time, and then LaDonna said, "I think the librarian reads these things."

"Miss Shipley?"

"Mm hmm." LaDonna giggled.

Tammi looked at her keenly to see if she was making fun of the books. Miss Shipley was a huge, slovenly, and single woman. But LaDonna's face was soft with delight.

"Well," Tammi said. "Think of it—a *librarian* reading them? That right there should be enough proof. You ought to just come and try the club."

LaDonna handed *Texas Toast* back to Tammi and looked away, biting her lower lip and scowling. "Okay," she said finally and Tammi released a long deep breath.

The bell clamored overhead. "I'll call you about the time and place of the meeting," Tammi said, trying to sound casual as LaDonna headed off to class.

Wonder of wonders! Tammi could hardly believe it had been so simple. Instead of slinking into first period, she held her shoulders back and literally glided to her desk. "Morning, Miss Black," she said.

She floated through the day, slowly absorbing the fact that a real book club was finally coming into bloom. There would be someone to discuss the mysteries of passion with, the places beyond Rigby High and Promiseland Church and this tiny dry town. She felt pleasure spreading over her being like warm rays of gentle spring sun—something infusing and pulsing through every moment, with endless possibilities and a joy so heavy she could hardly swallow.

But by the time the dismissal bell rang, the tone of her thoughts had wilted. Winter was coming, and it would be too cold to read down at the creek. Where in heaven's name could they meet?

After washing up the supper dishes that night, Tammi threaded her way through oaks and maples instead of following the creek to Orry's. She tapped expectantly on the glass at Minna's front door.

Presently, Minna poked her head into the foyer from the kitchen, holding the telephone, waving for Tammi to let herself in.

Tammi sat on a faux leopard-skin sofa with cushions that engulfed her, watching her aunt. Minna's phone had a long cord that allowed her to sit down on the kitchen floor with Priscilla, her dog, in her lap, cradle the receiver on her shoulder, and use her hands to pick fleas off the dog's stomach. Today Minna looked like a movie star, with her plummy rouge, fake eyelashes, and a Marlo Thomas hairdo in platinum blonde. Minna had a real hourglass figure. The exact opposite of Granny. "There's trouble brewing big-time in Nevada!" Minna exclaimed after she hung up the phone. "Mama would have a conniption if she knew what your uncle Finch is doing."

"What's he doing?"

"Poor baby sister," Minna said solemnly. "Nanette says they don't have a pot left to pee in. Finch's twenty-two thousand dollars in debt, and his liver's just about give out on him."

"Uncle Finch is sick?"

"Finch Dupree is a lush, hon."

"A what?"

"A drunk. He's lost all their money, and they've got to find somewhere else to live." Minna frowned. "Sister and Leon do, anyway. Finch's in the hospital."

"They could come here," Tammi said.

"Nanette's staying with friends at the moment. Leon has school, you know. Besides, it would be terrible to have Mama and Nanette in the same house together. Even when we were little bitty girls, they went at it constantly."

"They did?"

"Yessum. Yelling, throwing shoes and hairbrushes at each other . . . two of the hardheadedest women you ever saw. You cannot imagine."

Tammi nodded, wide-eyed.

"The only thing Nanette ever did right, in Mama's eyes," Minna said, "was giving birth to Leon. She thinks Finch is the devil incarnate."

"Because he's a drunk?"

"Partly, baby. There's a lot of other reasons in addition to that, but I don't think you're ready to hear them. One big thing, to Mama, is that she thinks Finch doesn't let Nanette and Leon come home to Rigby enough. And he *never* comes. I can't remember the last time I saw him."

Tammi thought this over. Minna's words were interesting news. Certainly a lot more exciting than the drought. But, as little as she saw Leon and her aunt Nanette, it was more like the plot of a movie happening to characters she didn't really know. "Run pop in that Donna Fargo 8-track there, hon." Minna gestured with her elbow to a tape lying on the coffee table. "Yep, Mama'll be mighty tickled if Nanette and Leon have to come home."

Tammi rose to start the music. "I'm the happiest girl in the whole USA" careened around them.

"You didn't come here to talk about this stuff," Minna said. "What's on your mind?"

"You remember, back a while ago, when you told me Granny couldn't set foot in here? Well, without asking you if she could first?"

Minna nodded.

"Is that still true?"

"Child, look at me." Minna held Tammi's shoulders. "I couldn't *live* here if it weren't. Don't know where I'd go, but it would have to be far away."

Excitement flooded Tammi's voice as she described her hopes and dreams for the Romance Readers' Book Club. ". . . and so, I wondered if we could meet here?"

Minna grinned at Tammi with one penciled eyebrow raised. "It will be my pleasure," she said. "Mind if I sit in on a few meetings? I could use a little romance."

"Here she comes. Now, you be sure and behave yourself," Tammi admonished Orr the next evening. He sat on Minna's sofa as Tammi perched on the velvet chaise in her front window, watching a glint from the setting sun on LaDonna's glossy hair. In the shadows behind LaDonna, Tammi saw the ponderous form of LaDonna's older cousin, Parks Tallchief. She couldn't believe it! She'd watched Parks from afar for years. Parks was a wild and sloppy girl. She drank beer and smoked cigarettes, and listened to loud rock music as she came zipping up to Rigby High each morning in a baby blue Trans Am.

"LaDonna brought her cousin," Tammi said, gnawing on her lip. She noted Parks's massive thighs ensconced in faded jeans, her breasts like watermelons taut beneath a black sweatshirt emblazoned with the words LED ZEPPELIN. Despite her bulk, there was a sultry, hip-thrusting glide to her walk. Parks moved along as if she were totally in control of life, like absolutely nothing amazed her. She had bleached blonde hair, and the same Cherokee nose and brown skin as LaDonna. Tammi thought she looked like a brown biscuit with a golden pat of butter on top.

"How do?" Parks said in a nasal whine, heaving herself down onto Minna's sofa.

Tammi wondered at the addition of Parks to the club. She supposed it couldn't hurt just for this meeting, but the big girl was such an unknown factor. She was somebody you'd better steer clear of or stay on the right side of.

"This one's about cowboys," Orr said, holding *Texas Toast* aloft as Minna set a tray of Cheetos and Frescas on the kidney-shaped coffee table.

"You the president?" Parks asked, looking sideways at him.

He cocked his head.

"I'm the president of the Romance Readers' Book Club," Tammi said. "And Orry is the vice president . . . and LaDonna is the secretary and Minna is the hostess."

LaDonna looked startled at this information, but she nodded.

"Huh," Parks said, shaking out a cigarette, lighting up, and narrowing her eyes as she drew in a deep lungful. Minna placed a Howard Johnson's ashtray on the end table at her elbow.

Every eye focused intently on Tammi, and for one fleeting moment she lost her place, her trembly fingers toying with the silky fringe of a pillow. She felt shaky, like she'd gone too long without eating. She imagined herself reading aloud to the group the way the county librarian did for preschoolers—a hand puppet held aloft on one hand as she slipped in and out of dramatic voices.

Oh goodness, that would not work. This was a mature audience. Tammi's instinct told her to *act* as if she knew what she were doing, because if she wanted to be the president of this club, she was going to have to take control. Quickly she drew a deep breath, locking eyes boldly with Parks. "First we'll need to perform some type of initiation ceremony," she said. "Where we swear loyalty to one another and the club." After this declaration, a smooth powerful feeling came down on Tammi. Her heartbeat grew slow, and she knew she could do this.

"All right," she said, dropping to her knees in the shag carpeting, spreading both arms out to her sides and trilling her fingers to summon everyone. Parks stubbed out her cigarette, blew a tuft of pale hair from her forehead, and knee walked to position herself at Tammi's hip. Orr scrambled quickly to Tammi's other side and looped his arm through hers. Minna set her Fresca down and took a place in the circle, glancing pointedly up over her shoulder at LaDonna, who was sitting primly in her chair.

Tammi gave LaDonna an encouraging nod. "C'mon," she said, sounding surprisingly sure even to her own ears.

LaDonna shut her eyes, visibly wrestling with herself before asking warily, "This club's not going to be some kind of cult, is it? Because I just don't think it's right to—"

"Get your little uptight buns down here this instant," Parks ordered, hints of a smile on her face.

"Um . . ." LaDonna drew out the word in a long hum as she raised her hands in surrender, nervously stationing herself between Minna and Parks.

"Okay." Tammi threw her shoulders back. "We're gathered here today to be initiated into the Romance Readers' Book Club, and to swear . . . I mean vow, to uphold its ideals, which are increasing our knowledge about love, romance, and the urgency of desire. We also promise to keep the club a secret, and," she paused to clear her throat, "to support one another in our personal pursuits of passion."

Tammi knew Orr would never agree to anything concerned with blood, so she decided they'd have to place hands on a Bible, then sign their names to paper. "Bible, please," she said to Minna.

Minna frowned. "I don't reckon I've got a Bible, but I believe I've got something even better!" A cloud of White Shoulders perfume spread as she rose and spun around to head for her bedroom. The clip-clop of her high-heeled bedroom mules made her sound official and efficient.

"Reckon what she'll come up with?" Parks's expression was amused anticipation, but LaDonna's eyes were anxious and filled with unspoken questions.

Tammi placed her hand on LaDonna's arm. "Relax. Minna's had tons of experience with passion."

"This feels really weird," LaDonna said. "Vowing and all." She looked about ten years old, her eyes wide, twisting her long hair with one hand.

"Chill, girl," Parks commanded, shifting her bulk from knee to knee. "It's not like we're swearing on the Bible."

"True," LaDonna said. "That would be sacrilegious. I don't believe in swearing on the Bible."

"Why are you scared?" Orr asked LaDonna. "You'll love the club. Me and Tammi already read *Island Pulse*. It had the beach and even a hurricane. Nobody died. Not scary one bit."

LaDonna opened her mouth, then shut it again as Minna swooped back into the circle. "Here we are," she said, waving a Frederick's of Hollywood catalog. "We'll swear on this. The perfect thing for a romance club."

LaDonna looked down at the suggestive cover of the catalog. "That a dirty magazine? It looks nasty."

"No, hon," Minna said. "It's a catalog of lingerie and things."

"Absolutely harmless," Tammi said quickly, placing a trembling hand on the Frederick's of Hollywood catalog. "Put your right palms down and repeat after me."

Tammi was amazed at how smoothly things went after that. Once they repeated the oath, Minna rummaged around in the drawer of an end table and came up with a notepad and pen. She signed her name with a flourish and passed the pad to Tammi.

Tammi scribbled down the pledge, signed her name, then passed the pad to Parks, who enthusiastically signed hers. Parks thrust it at LaDonna, who eventually signed it and handed it to Orr. With great concentration he wrote *Orrville Elco*.

Without a moment's hesitation, Tammi charged headlong into a plan for passing *Texas Toast* around. "Me and Orr'll read the first couple of chapters," she said, "however many we agree on. Then I'll pass it to Minna, and after she reads it, I'll carry it along with me to school and pass it to you, LaDonna. You can read it, give it to Parks, and she can bring it along to our next meeting, where we'll discuss it."

"Maybe you should wrap it up in a brown paper bag," suggested LaDonna. "Like our schoolbooks."

"Uh, sure," Tammi said.

Parks clucked her tongue. "I ain't afraid of anybody seeing *me* reading it," she said.

"Well," LaDonna said. "It is a *secret* club."

Tammi watched LaDonna's face. It was still uneasy. "I'll read y'all the back cover," she said, "and a tantalizing excerpt to whet your appetite." Quickly Tammi flipped *Texas Toast* over. "'Love can conquer the deadliest of rivals,' " she read. "That's the theme of our first book together." She felt the *bam! bam!* of her heart as she cleared her throat and continued.

Take one coarse ranch hand named Bart, allow his potent, virile masculinity to be exerted over Clemmie Gustafson, shake the hormones well, and place the two together on a darkened prairie . . . a delicious recipe for physical passion that threatens to overwhelm them both. Will Clemmie defy her father to dress as a man so she can be near her heart's desire? Beautiful Clemmie must choose between duty and passion for a man whose station in life only makes him more irresistible, and all the more forbidden.

There was a silence in which only Priscilla's muffled pants resounded.

"Well, I'll be," said Parks finally. "That's some powerful words." She shook her head in mock wonder, licking the orange powder from the Cheetos off her fingertips.

"I can't wait to sink my teeth into it." Minna sighed and settled into the sofa cushion. She shut her eyes.

Orr shut his eyes, too. "Are you happy it's about horses, like I am, Minna?"

"Yeah," Minna said, nodding her head in an exaggerated manner. "It's that horsey on the cover *I'm* dreaming about." She laughed so hard she collapsed sideways onto the couch.

LaDonna remained silent, looking like someone who walks into the theater halfway during a movie. At last she took a deep breath. "Parks," she said in little more than a whisper, "it's time we were getting back home. I've got homework."

"No way, José," Parks said, shaking another cigarette from the package. "President Tammi here says we get to hear a sample from the book."

Tammi slowly riffled through the pages like a jeweler selecting the perfect stone for a priceless necklace. Stopping confidently at chapter three, entitled "A Sexy Deception," she began to read.

> *Clemmie unbuttoned her chambray shirt to reveal two orbs of breasts. "Huh," Bart snarled, "thought you was a boy."*
>
> *"You thought wrong," she laughed throatily as she removed her Stetson, unpinned her hair, and crawled over the tall Texas grass, pressing her hips to him. Sunlight made golden glints on her hair as she moved her hand along the outside of his steely thigh.*

Orr sighed audibly. "Where's the horses at?"
Tammi shot him a look and continued.

> *I'm Clemmie Gustafson. But I'm willing to sacrifice that, Bart. To be with you."*
>
> *"You're a Gustafson?" He looked incredulously at the little vixen.*

"Yes! Let us satisfy this desire we have." Her voice was high and trembly over the dusky prairie as her eyes caressed his beautiful pectorals.

"But I'm like a wild stallion, Clemmie," Bart said, his eyes piercing her soul. "I'll never be broken. Never will a saddle be put on this back."

Clemmie reached a hand out and grabbed a wiry hank of his hair, her every nerve tingling with exquisite desire. She licked the rugged skin where his chestnut eyelashes fanned his sun-kissed cheeks, a moan escaping her trembling lips.

"Well, that ought to be enough to whet our appetites," Tammi said, closing the book.

It was not until they heard Minna's mantel clock chime the hour that anyone spoke.

"I may just pop waiting for my turn," Minna said, hugging herself. "Don't you take too long with it, Tammi, hon."

"She has to read it to me first," said Orr, poking out his bottom lip, clearly not understanding that Minna was half-teasing.

"Calm down, Orry," Tammi said. "There'll be plenty of time. I'm figuring we'll meet every four or five weeks or so. Today being November fifth, let's try and meet again on December fifth. That's a week apiece with the book. Sound okay?"

"Fabulous," said Parks.

"Yep," said Orr, and Minna nodded. All eyes turned to La-Donna. She was looking down at her hands folded primly in her lap. "I suppose," she said at last.

"Well, I'll provide the snacks, like Tammi said." Minna was all business now. "Y'all got any special requests?"

"How 'bout some José Cuervo!" Parks slapped her massive thigh and guffawed.

Minna shot her an amused look, but LaDonna sighed and shook her head. "I like lemonade," she murmured in a voice so soft they could barely hear it.

Minna nodded. "How about we pick us a topic to discuss at each meeting? Maybe how to flirt? Or how to pick a good man and spot a bum one? I mean, we could all take turns suggesting topics. Then, between meetings, everyone can think about our topic. I'll start it off since I've had the most experience."

LaDonna eyed her skeptically.

"Well, if experience makes you wise, I ought to be wise beyond my years. My years *are* getting on up there. I'm so old I'm having to hunt blind boyfriends."

Everyone laughed, and LaDonna relaxed visibly. Minna was renowned in Rigby for her worldly ways and quick wit, and Tammi felt a sudden keen pride in her. Now she realized what an invaluable support her aunt would be along this journey.

"So what's the topic for our next meeting?" Parks asked.

Minna paused, her mouth partway open as she considered.

LaDonna had her chin raised in that priggish way, her arms crossed over her flat chest. "Maybe we could discuss respect, or . . . I've got it, modesty!"

After a moment, Minna said in a soft voice, "How about we discuss the 'Dos and Don'ts of Cleavage'?"

Tammi's sense of relief as LaDonna nodded her assent was extreme. "We'll read the first six chapters of *Texas Toast* for our next meeting," she proclaimed. "Let's close with a pledge." She raised her warm Fresca can in a toast and chanted an impromptu "All for fun and fun for all!"

They lifted their voices in unison and became a club, comrades in the pursuit of passion and romance.

CHAPTER 6

L ate that night Tammi lay in bed, drawing in a deep breath of the freshly sun-dried pillowcase beneath her cheek, and glancing out her window over moonlit treetops toward that piece of sky hanging above Orr's house. A conflict raged inside her: Should she or should she not read *Texas Toast* to Orr?

Ever since she realized that she needed other people in the club, that Orr just wasn't getting the nuances of passion and romance in the same way she did, she'd felt uncomfortable about sharing the books with him. When they read *Island Pulse*, he'd been hopelessly lost during the sensual encounters, turning away and drumming his fingers. He'd begged her to read the hurricane parts again and again, and he had had no inkling why Tatiana ended up with Cody. Tammi knew somehow that Orr was not the right reader for these books. And tonight, when he'd gotten himself fixated on the horses, she had been aware of LaDonna's uncomfortable scowl and Parks's impatient huff. It was true that Orr was a child in many ways. Would she share these books with a child?

Suddenly Granny's stern face popped into Tammi's mind. Well, that was no barometer. It was the gospel truth that Granny would not share these books with *anyone*, and Tammi knew for certain that she could not give them up. Not now. She took a deep breath and let it out slowly, wondering what to do.

The dilemmas Orr thrust her into were constant and required great patience to settle. Usually, she just excused all of his eccentricities because of his stuck brain. It tore her heart to realize that he'd never have a normal life, and often she went against her better judgment when it came to indulging him.

After a time she decided that the solution was to orchestrate a certain ad-lib, skimming style of reading the romance novels aloud to Orr. She would skip the steamy parts, filling in just enough to satisfy his feeble brain.

With one deep breath she eased down into her quilt and closed her eyes, waiting for the sweet deliverance of sleep.

It was a cold Saturday afternoon, and Tammi stood on the creek bank, a thick cardigan over her wool dress, as well as over *Texas Toast*, which lay solidly against her navel. There was no sound save the dry snap of a twig as she moved her feet toward the path back through the woods. She wondered if she'd been missed at the big house, if Pepaw were in from the barn or Granny home from hunting antiques.

She'd just finished reading the first six chapters through for the third time, telling herself that this was necessary so that she'd be able to digest the plot enough to regurgitate it in a G-rated, seamless manner that Orr could understand.

In truth, she devoured the words, pouring them as a healing salve on that gaping wound inside of her, the place where hunger lived. But for some reason the words never filled her up or left her satisfied. It was like they evaporated instantaneously and left her needing more and more. Occasionally, when she paused to look at her watch, she had to blink and rub her eyes when she saw what time it had gotten to be, and *where* she actually was, too.

She felt herself slide right through the paperback spine of *Texas Toast*. She lost herself, walking the wide stretches of Texas with Clemmie, feeling the rough, cold hands of Bart on her creamy skin. Shuddering when he took her.

It was like she had two separate lives now. Sitting in the passenger seat of Pepaw's pickup, she was at once his best girl, a young and innocent version of Minna. But if she closed her eyes she could be Clemmie from *Texas Toast*, held protectively in the brawny arms of her man. She even got the two confused occasionally and had to stop and draw a deep breath and consider what was the real world, or at least that world presenting itself to her at the moment—the world that required certain words and actions.

It was all she could do to stop herself after chapter six, and she was torn about relinquishing the book into Minna's hands. Four of her days were up, and she decided that tomorrow was the time to "read" to Orr.

To Tammi's surprise, she was good at skimming over steamy scenes and paraphrasing the plot into one seamless, G-rated narrative. After several hours huddled with Orr, she came to the close of chapter six, and she knew he was satisfied. He hadn't complained a bit. His brown eyes were bright as she closed the book.

"When can we read more?" he asked.

"Not till three weeks or so." Tammi tucked *Texas Toast* back up inside her cardigan, walking toward the big house. Orr followed along, his hands folded behind him, chewing his bottom lip.

"Tammi?" he asked after a spell. "Why do I have to wait?"

"Because that's our club rules. *I* can't read any further, either."

Orr scratched the side of his head. "Okay," he said with great disappointment as they approached a watering trough at the upper pasture. A herd of black Angus cattle hovered at the trough, their flesh sunken in so deep their ribs protruded. They looked listlessly at Tammi and Orr.

"You pitiful creatures. You're doomed," Tammi muttered under her breath, leaning against the barbed-wire fence.

The cows paid no attention, but Orr cried out sharply, "What do you mean, 'doomed'?"

"Lord have mercy, Orr!" she said, looking at him with her head cocked. "You been living under a rock? They've lost seventy-five to a hundred pounds apiece. They should have *gained* a hundred pounds by now. This blasted drought!" She gritted her teeth, looking out across the dusty pastureland and beyond that to a stark wall of trees against a chalky sky.

Orr shook his head indignantly. "Don't swear, Tammi!" She mouthed an apology and the two kept walking. Before long they came to the rain barrel at the corner of the big house. Tammi was thirsty, and her tongue felt shriveled like a raisin. She leaned her face over the barrel. "Dern it!" she hollered down into emptiness, hugging the edges and giving it a swift kick that hurt her toes. She breathed out a soft "Ouch," leaning her forearms on the lip of the barrel and shaking her head. "I swannee, Orr. This is ridiculous. We're *all* going to dry slap up."

Orr inched close, his expression grave. "We can go to Hawaii, Tammi," he crooned, patting her back. "They never have a drought in Hawaii. We can go there and we won't dry slap up. But I don't know if the cows can go with us."

Tammi didn't know whether to laugh or cry. "You're right, Orry. You're the only one around here with a lick of sense."

Tammi did not dry up, however. When she managed to sneak by Granny to head to Minna's on December fifth for their second meeting, she felt full of *something*, on the verge of a tremulous discovery.

The table behind Minna's sofa was a combination bar and entertainment station, where a cut-glass decanter of whiskey sat next to the 8-track tape player and a stack of tapes. Tammi sat leaning into the plush sofa cushions, craning her neck to study this setup carefully. She narrowed her eyes at the whiskey and turned her attention to the tapes: six Elvis, two each of Barbara Mandrell and Tammy Wynette, and one lone tape entitled *Carpenters*.

"Put us on some Elvis, darlin'!" Minna's lilting voice entered the room before she did. "Set the tone for our meeting. I just can't wait!" She kissed Tammi's cheek in a loud *smack!* of lipstick that smelled like strawberries. "You're here mighty early, and I'm glad because you can help me make hot cocoa. What do you think of my new wallpaper?"

"Beautiful!" Tammi eyed the silver paper with swirls of hot pink. It matched Minna's chrome dinette chairs, with their sling seats of pink vinyl. Minna loved to decorate her house almost as much as she loved to decorate herself. Only one thing she fussed about, and that was the fact that she didn't own a television set. No one had run cable out this far into the county yet, and Granny wouldn't allow her to fasten an antenna to the roof.

"Get Elvis going." Minna nudged Tammi's arm, and she realized she'd been sitting there with her mouth hanging open.

"Okay," she said, jumping up to start the music. She'd come half an hour early so she could gather her thoughts on their topic—the "Dos and Don'ts of Cleavage"—but so far all she could think of was her nervous stomach about Orr's participation in the discussion, as well as about LaDonna's feelings on the subject of breasts. She'd heard the boys at school laughingly call LaDonna "A Pirate's Dream—a sunken chest!" The picture arose in her mind of a club meeting filled with hurt feelings and embarrassment. There was a big responsibility when it came to being president, and she was going to have to somehow smooth over these potentially troubling areas. First she had to figure out a way to distract Orr during today's discussion.

"Come on in here, hon," Minna called from the kitchen as Elvis's voice rang out in a plaintive note. Minna was standing at the stove, watching a pot of water. "Hunt that brown box of cocoa mix in the pantry, would you?"

"Perfect day for a warm drink, isn't it?" she asked as Tammi handed her the box.

Tammi nodded. Overnight the weather had turned much colder, wind howling and rattling the stark branches of the oak outside her bedroom window.

"Cold weather always makes me hungrier." Minna tugged at the waistband of her hip-huggers. "Right now I'm dreaming of popcorn. Popcorn drenched with butter. Lots of salt. That'll go good with hot chocolate, won't it?"

"Sounds fine," Tammi said in a soft, absentminded voice, her thoughts zipping around with the fact that there were now only ten minutes till the meeting.

Minna saw her face and said, "What's wrong, hon? You don't look very excited about our little get-together."

"Oh, Minna, I'm worried," Tammi confessed, relieved to unburden herself. "We've got to think of some way to keep Orr distracted during the discussion part. I'm worried he'll say something wrong. I mean, you know, something that might upset LaDonna. She's probably real sensitive about, you know . . ." Here she made a gesture to her own breasts.

"Oh, don't worry," Minna said with one flit of her hand. "We'll figure something out. Just listen at that Elvis! Sweeter than Tupelo honey."

"Sure," Tammi said faintly. She stood there feeling torn about leaving Minna, but urgent to get back to the solitude of the sofa so she could have everything figured out before Orr arrived.

Minna rustled around underneath the counter and got out the big pot she used for popcorn. She set this on a burner, tipped oil into it, and slapped a lid on. "I know!" she said suddenly, her face brightening. "Orr can count out marshmallows. I believe I've got a bag of those miniature marshmallows somewhere in the pantry yonder. That ought to keep him busy here in the kitchen for quite a while."

Tammi hugged Minna hard. "You're brilliant!" she declared, making her way over to the pantry to kneel down and sift through a clutter of cans and bottles. She felt rather than saw Orr come into the pantry to stand behind her.

"Hi, Tammi," he said. "Whatcha doing?"

Tammi glanced up. "Hi, Orry," she said, smiling. "I'm so glad you're here because Minna has a very important job for you!"

He watched as Tammi set five bowls out on the countertop. She placed a tiny fork and the bag of marshmallows next to these. Patting the marshmallows, she felt herself growing calmer. "Like I said, it's very important," she said. "Promise to take your time and get exactly the same number of marshmallows in each bowl. And, if there's an odd number left over at the end, when you're through forking them into the bowls, you can eat them."

"I'll do a good job," Orr said, watching her with serious eyes.

Minna opened the front door and a blast of cold air entered with Parks and LaDonna. They laid their purses and jackets across the chaise, and Minna gave them each a quick hug.

"I reckon it's titty-talkin' time!" Parks laughed, rubbing her hands together. "Speaking of titties," she said, "outside it's cold as a witch's tit in a brass bra doing push-ups in the snow."

LaDonna gave Parks a look of stunned indignity, but Minna and Tammi burst out laughing, saying, "In a brass bra," and "Doing push-ups in the snow," bending double and holding their sides.

Presently Parks spoke. "This here is one great piece of literature." She cradled *Texas Toast* like an infant, her words laced with awe. "I mean, I ain't never been much of a reader, but this was definitely worth it! I read the chapters two times, and I didn't skip a single word." She paused for a breath. "Don't y'all think it was so fine when Bart surprised Clemmie that time she was skinny-dipping in the watering hole? Oh, man. I could just *see* it. Felt like I was right there." Parks lit a cigarette, murmuring, "So fine."

"Yes, dear," Minna said. "It was indeed some good reading."

LaDonna cleared her throat. "Wasn't what I call fine literature." Her voice was flat. "Written by a hack, I'm sure."

Tammi blinked. "But you read it, right?"

"Sure, though I found some of it to be utterly offensive."

"It was beautiful," Parks said fiercely. "I wouldn't expect *you* to like it, though. Let's get the club to take a vote on it. Hey, where's our vice president at?"

"Orr's working in the kitchen," Minna said. "Which reminds me, we've got cocoa and popcorn for later. But right now, I believe there's something important we need to put into our bylaws." Minna looked pointedly back and forth at LaDonna and Parks. "It's this: We'll do all in our power to respect one another's feelings, especially when we talk about personal things. Deal, ladies?"

The two of them looked at her and nodded. Tammi wanted to hug her aunt. It felt as if almost anything was possible as they sat there chatting pleasantly about the beginning of *Texas Toast*: Clemmie defying her father, dressing as a man to join the cattle drive of which Bart was the foreman. Clemmie had to bind her breasts with a wide elastic and tuck her flowing chestnut locks underneath a Stetson hat.

"Man, oh man," Parks drawled, shaking her head. "I sure couldn't fool nobody. There's not enough elastic in the *world* to flatten these melons!" She lightly touched the tops of her breasts. "But LaDonna here would be perfect, 'cause she ain't got nothing but a freckle!" Parks hooted with laughter.

Tammi glanced over at LaDonna, expecting a scowl, but LaDonna only shrugged. *And maybe*, Tammi thought, *Parks looked slightly wistful. Perhaps being well-endowed was no picnic.*

"But that's okay!" Minna said brightly. "I'm okay, you're okay. A cup, double-D cup, you'll learn some men don't give a fig about titties. There are butt men and leg men. Feet men . . . you never can tell what'll get a man going. Somebody out there for *everybody*. I mean it. Here in Georgia, most men might like big, corn-fed women with generous bazongas, but I hear French men think anything more than'll fit in a champagne glass is too much."

"I reckon LaDonna ought to head on down to France then," Parks teased.

"Well, in France, I hear they go topless on the beaches," Minna said. "This one place, St. Tropez, they run around topless there and the men don't pay them a bit of mind. Just no different from looking at a hand or an ear, I reckon. Them being out in plain view all the time."

LaDonna's face reddened. "Well, that's one place *I'll* never go."

Tammi shut her eyes and imagined herself far away in St. Tropez, where she was curiously energized as she envisioned herself frolicking around bare-chested on a sandy beach, shameless before all eyes. I don't believe I'd have a bit of problem with the sun and the water, or the *eyes* on my bare breasts, she mused, snuggling down into the velvety cushions, trembling all over, on the verge of something wild, free, that surrounded her like gauze. Something she was just beginning to peel off. "Well," she ventured out loud at last, "I reckon I'd be willing to go."

This brought a hoot of approval from Parks, but LaDonna gave Tammi an intense stare. "Listen," Minna said to no one in particular, "there ain't hardly a thing taboo anymore in this day and age. 'Let it all hang out,' as they say. Which brings me to our topic—the 'Dos and Don'ts of Cleavage.' Personally, I think a woman ought to show enough, but not too much. Leave the man wanting more . . . something to dream on. I mean, it's not what they see, it's what they think they *might* see. That's my opinion." Minna smiled. "Now I want to hear you-all's thoughts on the matter." She looked pointedly at LaDonna.

"Well," LaDonna said, dropping her eyes, "I don't reckon I have too much to say on the matter of breasts."

"Don't you worry, hon," Minna said softly. "Enhance what you do have. No matter how little. Accentuate the positive. Even if you don't ever grow up top, you've got a figure lots of girls would kill for . . . long, lean legs!"

"Yeah," Parks said, poking out her bottom lip. "I'd trade these big jugs for your figure any day. I've got to wear heavy-duty Playtex Cross Your Hearts to hold these girls down. Think about when I get old . . . they'll be hanging to my hip bones!"

Tammi thrust her shoulders back. That was one issue she hadn't had to face. Her breasts were average size, 34B, and Parks's comments made her look at LaDonna's flat chest with new eyes. "I'm thinking of buying one of those lacy black push-up bras from Frederick's," she said finally, her voice careful and questioning. "I think it says it will lift and enhance . . ."

"Yes, it does," Minna said, "and sexy lingerie is definitely a plus. Men simply cannot resist a hint of sheer lace! We women have no idea what it does to them. Just knocks out all their good sense and makes them putty in our hands."

LaDonna looked at Minna disbelievingly. "It's true, hon." Minna laughed. "I promise. Turns them into animals."

Tammi heard the sound of the Frigidaire opening in the kitchen, and Orr muttering something. "Excuse me," she said, leaping up.

"Orr," Tammi whispered to his back as he stood staring into the refrigerator with naked disgust. "Did you finish the marshmallows?"

He nodded. "Know what, Tammi? Minna doesn't have any sweet milk in here."

"She made us hot cocoa," Tammi said. "With water, but you'll never know the difference! Hey, let's dip everyone a mug and you can sit in here at the dinette and put marshmallows in yours."

Tammi left Orr happily clutching a mug of cocoa. She returned to the girls balancing a long tray full of steaming mugs and a bowl of popcorn. She set this on the coffee table. Parks was finishing up reading a passage aloud from *Texas Toast*.

. . . *Bart eyed the voluptuous creature splashing about in the watering hole. Moonlight made golden glints on the orbs of Clemmie's breasts. She laughed throatily, unpinning her hair and running her tongue teasingly across her lips. Bart had known many women. He'd known passion. He had never known this white-hot energy arcing between himself and Clemmie.*

"That is my favorite part so far," Parks said in a dreamy voice as she scooped up a handful of popcorn.

Minna nodded. "That was good. I especially liked the part where he whipped that rattlesnake just before it slithered into Clemmie's bedroll."

LaDonna raised a finger to object. "I found it hard to believe she could parade around as a man and get away with it for three days. Especially if she's apparently so gorgeous in the face and has an 'hourglass figure,' like the author keeps crowing about."

Now there was an unpleasant silence. At last Tammi spoke. "There's all that prairie dust the horses kick up. Makes it hard to see anybody's face. And remember, she was wearing baggy men's clothes to *hide* her womanly curves."

"Well," LaDonna said in an irritated tone, "I think it's totally unbelievable, even if you do ignore all that. And what's this ridiculous love-at-first-sight hogwash?" Fire flashed in her dark eyes as she sipped cocoa.

"Lord, LaDonna, somebody pee in your Cornflakes this morning?" Parks narrowed her eyes as she drew in a deep lungful of smoke.

"You're so unrefined, Parks Tallchief." LaDonna shook her head.

"Yeah, well, at least I'm not an uptight little high-and-mighty nun," Parks retorted, her lips shiny from greasy popcorn. "How do you know there's no such thing as love at first sight?"

"I just do. You can't possibly know anybody well enough to love them if you've only *looked* at them briefly."

"You never heard of *chemistry*?!" Parks let out a long, low whistle. "You're worse off than I thought. Twice in my life, and I am not even twenty yet, I have experienced the kind of chemistry that leads to love at first sight."

LaDonna rolled her eyes and shook her head. "Lust, maybe," she said. "But not love."

"Please! Stop it, both of you," Minna said, holding her hand up. "Remember, we are respecting each other. But you've given me an idea for our next club meeting topic. We'll discuss 'Is There Love at First Sight?' Now, how 'bout we read chapters seven through twenty? That okay with you, Tammi, hon?"

Tammi nodded. "Let's see, this being December fifth, I reckon our next meeting'll be . . . how about New Year's Day afternoon? We've got a break from school."

They all nodded and fell silent until Tammi stood to lead them in the pledge. "All for fun and fun for all," they repeated solemnly.

After Parks and LaDonna left, Tammi sank down into the warm corner of Minna's sofa to finish her cocoa and to think, for the first time in her life, about the kind of chemistry that was not offered as part of Rigby High's science curriculum.

CHAPTER 7

Tammi's allotted week with *Texas Toast* flew by. On December twelfth, when she had to relinquish the book to Minna, she still hadn't gotten enough of the feeling a certain scene brought her. It teased and titillated Tammi and brought her to the brink of tears with frustration. For the first time, she ached to find a man of her own.

This scene was one where all the ranch hands went to Miss Delia's large Victorian house. A dozen girls lived there, and Miss Delia was like their mama, pampering them: hiring dressmakers to sew lavish costumes, masseuses to rub costly unguents into their magnolia-white skin, hairdressers to create glistening coiffures. The girls slept in until noon, and in the afternoons, when it was just the girls, they lay about on chaise longues wearing camisoles, giggling, wrinkling their noses, and telling secrets to one another. In the evenings they danced and sang, making lighthearted banter with men who were starved for the finer things in life. The girls at Miss Delia's never cooked, never cleaned. They were never somber or bored. Their lives were like one giant party.

This was the exact opposite of Tammi's life. School holidays began on the twenty-first, and Tammi spent what seemed a lifetime moving through her chores, so, on Christmas Eve morning, when Pepaw mentioned that Nanette and Leon were coming in from Nevada for dinner, she was beside herself with the pure novelty of it.

Tammi had to go way back in the recesses of her memory for a picture of Nanette and Leon. Their last visit to Rigby was when Tammi was seven and Leon nine. A skinny, knock-kneed sylph of a boy, she recalled Leon out on the screened porch with her as she pulled the last shreds of wrapping paper from a new Easy-Bake oven. He'd helped her mix up the first tiny Betty Crocker chocolate cake. They ate it while it was still too hot to taste, laughing at the chocolate on each other's noses. She couldn't remember much about Nanette except that she was tall and slender like Granny.

Minna's recent words about Uncle Finch's indiscretions had Tammi's curiosity working overtime. She finished her morning chores and lay across the sofa at eleven, waiting and listening to the grandfather clock in the corner of the parlor—every agonizingly slow ticktock. They were not due to arrive till seven o'clock, and the only entertainment till then would be trimming the boughs of a fir tree Pepaw had set in the front hallway.

"God rest ye merry gentlemen," Granny sang gaily from the kitchen. A pungent clove-ginger smell told Tammi she was baking her treasured spice cake. "Leon's coming! Oh, this is the *best* Christmas gift I can imagine!" Tammi overheard her gushing to Pepaw as he brought down boxes of ornaments from the attic. "It's a miracle! I wish Carson, Onzelle, and their kids weren't out of town. Feels like forever since we've all been together."

Tammi felt a rush of apprehension then, that Granny might mention her stepfather's death and throw a pall over the day, but she did not. Her jubilance over Nanette and Leon's impending visit remained untarnished as she orchestrated the trimming of the tree and set the dining table with her best china. She festooned the banister with fir boughs and hung Christmas cards from a ribbon across an archway. She dressed in a black velvet skirt and white blouse with lacy cuffs, admonishing her husband to drive safely to and from the airport. At six-thirty she turned off the front parlor lights and lit the tree just as Orr and Minna arrived, their arms laden with presents. A moment later, the sound of Pepaw's truck pulling up outside caused Granny to fly out the door, crying, "They're home!"

From the front steps Tammi watched Granny grab Nanette, laughing and pulling her close in a breathless hug. "Merry Christmas! Where is that dear Leon?"

"Boy's helping get the luggage," Pepaw called from the shadows. Tammi stood in silence watching Granny embrace Leon as Orr and Minna came down the steps to surround their sister in a hug. They moved up the steps into the light, talking among themselves in excited voices.

Cousin Leon Dupree! Tammi looked hard at him. She wasn't the only one who had changed. Leon was gorgeous, the spitting image of what she pictured Bart in *Texas Toast* to look like: an aristocratic nose and a chiseled jaw, jet-black hair, glinting blue in the lights from the tree, an upper body that was a V and that sat atop a pert rear end. "Oh!" escaped Tammi's mouth.

"Merry Christmas, Tammi," Leon said, smiling faintly at her. Goose bumps prickled her arms. Her heart stopped beating, and she felt that fluttery pulse where her legs joined. Was this what Parks meant by chemistry?! *Something* was there, and it wasn't her imagination. It wasn't wishful thinking, either. She was relieved to remember that they weren't flesh-and-blood cousins.

"Merry Christmas," she called awkwardly.

The family chatted by the light of the tree for a while until Granny announced that it was time for dinner and everyone trooped in and seated themselves around the long mahogany table. Granny and

Pepaw were at either end, Orr between Minna and Tammi on the buffet side, with Nanette next to Leon on the window side.

It was a lavish meal of roast lamb and potatoes, but Tammi didn't taste a thing. She kept her eyes on Leon in the flickering light of the candles as the adults talked a mile a minute.

"Remember that Christmas you got the Raggedy Ann doll, Nanette?" Minna asked as Granny brought out spice cake and coffee. "I remember crying for a week because I didn't get one."

"You got a little plastic telephone," Nanette said, "and you used to pretend Santa Claus was calling you to tell you that you were exceptionally good and he was bringing you a sleigh full of toys, and I believed it!"

"Did I believe it?" asked Orr.

"You weren't born yet," Nanette said. "Mama was expecting you that Christmas." She turned to Granny. "You were about to bust you were so pregnant. And boy were you moody! Lit into us for even *mentioning* Santa Claus!"

"Oh, I wouldn't say I lit into you. It was more like guiding you onto the right path, the righteous path. Our focus at this time of year should be on our Savior, not Santa! But you always were one to defy me. Marrying that Finch Dupree! Remember? I told you. I said, 'That man is trouble on two legs.'" Granny eyed Nanette significantly.

Tammi saw Nanette tense, but she didn't retort.

"How *is* your father?" Granny turned to Leon, smiling tenderly at him.

"Um . . . he's okay," Leon said too quickly, giving a meaningful glance to his mother.

"Finch must be doing pretty well at his job, hm?" Granny stabbed a bite of cake. "Seeing as he wasn't able to come home with you for Christmas."

"Finch stays busy," Nanette said vaguely. Tammi looked across Orr's plate at Minna, who met her eyes and gave a faint, conspiratorial shake of her head.

But this didn't slip by Granny. She leaned forward and peered hard at Nanette, her smile gone, fierceness blooming in her eyes. "Finch is in trouble again, isn't he?" When Nanette didn't reply, she continued. "Move home, Nanette. I'll give you a job at Elco Antiques. Leon needs security."

Nanette closed her eyes. "Leon," she said slowly, "is in school, Mother. We've got to get him through high school . . ."

Minna sat back in her chair, a teasing smile on her face. "I bet Leon's got himself too many girlfriends back in Vegas to leave."

Leon said nothing. Tammi's mouth went dry.

"Nanette!" Granny said sharply. "Rigby High is a fine school, and Leon can transfer his credits and graduate here. It was good enough for you and Minna. It was good enough for Carson. And Junior." Her eyes clouded over at the thought of Junior, and a solemn quietness spread across the table.

"Let Leon finish his junior year," Nanette said after a spell. "We'll talk about coming home to stay in June. In time for the reunion."

Granny dipped her head forward in one firm nod before draining her coffee and standing to signal the close of the meal.

That night before she fell asleep, Tammi lay in the velvety darkness thinking of Leon. She recalled one of Tatiana's lines from *Island Pulse* that described the way she was feeling to a tee: *I have a craving hunger for you, my every nerve tingling with urgent and unbridled desire.*

Leon and Nanette left early on the twenty-seventh to fly back to Nevada. For as much attention as Leon had paid Tammi during their brief visit, she may as well have been invisible. She drank him in secretly, silently, struck literally speechless in his presence when she made several efforts to approach him.

Tatiana or Clemmie would have known what to say. They would have used their feminine wiles to seduce Leon, undulating their rounded hips, trailing a pulsing finger down his arm . . .

But Tammi had been paralyzed by the steely jaws of her own shyness and inexperience. Her only consolation was reminding herself that Granny would kill her if she caught Tammi undulating anything. Well, Tammi determined that she would keep reading the romance novels. Lines from the books were helping her put names to her raging and confusing emotions, instructing her word by word on the nuances of passion, and she was determined that when Leon came back in June, she would be ready to seduce him, even if she had to do it in secret. Her thoughts turned to those brazen girls at school who pursued boys so effortlessly, their long hair swinging as they slipped a note into a locker or engaged in heavy petting beneath the bleachers on the football field. The same girls who rolled their eyes at Tammi as she passed them in the hallways wearing her clunky skirts and modest blouses. How could she be seductive in the clothes Granny made her wear? She longed for the revealing clothes that Tatiana wore, the flowing skirts that showed a flash of leg, the plunging necklines that invited a man's glance. Maybe that would make Leon pay attention to her.

Tammi was just hanging on until January first's book club meeting and her next chance to read.

It was with a grudging sigh that Tammi stood in the kitchen the Wednesday after Christmas, eyeing a mound of sweet potatoes in the sink, imagining herself flinging them out the back door to roll in the dusty yard while chickens pecked holes in their skins. She was to prepare a soufflé for the potluck at Promiseland. She turned on the water hard, letting a river of red clay run off the potatoes and down the drain before she diced them into a boiler, covered them with water, and slapped a lid on. Tammi turned the burner to high, drumming a wooden spoon on the cabinet as she waited for the water to boil. *Hurry up,* she willed as she glanced out the window to see the sun making its way down behind a stand of pines.

She leaned against the counter and began to imagine herself on the wide Texas plains, where meals were simple: black coffee, cold biscuits, and beef jerky. She heard Clemmie's lilting voice singing a lullaby to Bart as he lay on a bedroll next to the fire, exhausted from herding cattle, his rugged jaw slightly open in sleep. Firelight flickered on his eyelids, on his hard, muscular arms. Now Clemmie bent over him tenderly, and he felt her presence, pulling her hungrily into a passionate embrace. How wonderful Clemmie's life must be! To live from new experience to new experience. To have freedom, wandering along with the man she adored.

When the potatoes were fork-tender, Tammi drained them and used the electric mixer to whir the steaming mass with butter and orange zest. After she slid this into the oven she made her way to the dark corner of the front parlor, collapsing on the sofa, folding her arms across her chest to fall back into the fantasy of Clemmie and Bart, which somehow turned into her and Leon, living on the wide-open prairie, far from Granny's furrowed brow and the eyes of Promiseland Church.

Tammi startled awake at the taste of smoke. Heart in her throat, she flew to the kitchen to yank open the oven, fanning away billows of smoke to look in at the charred soufflé.

She set the smoldering dish onto the back porch and tried to swallow over the lump of fear in her throat as a set of heels came clipping down the stairs. Granny in her dressy coat, handbag slung over one wrist.

Granny's eyes narrowed to slits. Her nostrils flared. "What's burning?" she said in a voice that drew Tammi's neck muscles together in a sharp knot.

"I'm sorry," Tammi whispered.

"You burned the soufflé?!" Granny peered around Tammi to the smoldering dish outside. "Your head has been in the clouds entirely too much lately, Tammi Lynn."

Pepaw smiled. "Ah, Constance," he said, "she's just being a teenager. Ain't no use crying over sweet potatoes. There's plenty more of 'em out there in the dirt."

"Well," Granny said, clearly not sure that she was ready to forgive this offense, but with a sniff she turned on her heel. "Let's get a move on. You know Orr's waiting."

Sure enough, Orr was there beside the shed, in a cast-off sport jacket from Pepaw, his hair sleek and furrowed with liberal Vitalis, a Bible and a half-empty box of Fig Newtons tucked underneath his arm. He grabbed Granny's hand and squeezed it. "Hello, Mama," he said. "You look beautiful tonight."

Granny brightened and leaned over to kiss his cheek, straightening his clip-on tie. "Thank you, dear."

Tammi climbed into the backseat of the Cadillac and felt the cool vinyl seep up through her slip and skirt as she breathed in the familiar balm of Pepaw's Old Spice.

When they got to the big road, Granny glanced at her watch and hit the gas pedal, sending Orr's round head back against the front seat.

"Take it easy, Constance," Pepaw warned.

Granny's eyes flashed as she glanced at Tammi in the rearview mirror. She spoke through her teeth. "We'll not be late," she said. "We may be one dish short, but we'll not be late. I'm praying a little dose of the Word tonight will bring Tammi Lynn back down to earth."

In the soft blue gray of dusk, Promiseland's light over the front door was a welcome beacon as they crunched across the gravel parking lot and up the stairs.

After an uneventful potluck, everyone filed into the sanctuary and Tammi took her customary seat beside Orr, between Granny and Pepaw. The sanctuary had eight stained-glass windows depicting the life of Christ, and a strip of lush burgundy carpeting running down the center of golden oak pews, spreading out like a capital *T* at the front of the sanctuary and covering three steps leading up to the altar rail. Behind that was the pulpit and a baptismal font full of water brought home from the Holy Land in Mason jars by the Reverend Goodlow.

Everyone loved the Reverend Goodlow. He was a hard worker who was the first to pitch in when any of the farmers needed an extra hand. A man who'd sat by the bedside of many an ailing or dying church member; a simple soul, he was happy in his modest home and old model car, his heart wholly resting above. Before their opening hymn was even done, she noted Orr's head drooping forward and his mouth agape in sleep. Poor Orr. He was exhausted because he thought of Clemmie and Bart from the pages of *Texas Toast* as his own personal friends, staying awake nights worrying over their problems like you wouldn't believe. What happened was, inevitably, the author left some shred of plot hanging at the end of each chapter, and though Tammi endeavored to smooth these rough spots during her paraphrasing, the unresolved tensions and conflict just about tore Orr up.

Gradually the drone of Martha Higginbotham reading from Proverbs faded into nothingness, and Tammi's own eyes glazed over with the memory of Clemmie's latest romantic encounter. Tammi's body began to pulse with the rhythm of hoof beats as she envisioned Clemmie's silken hair flying in the wind while her horse galloped toward Bart. She slid from the saddle and ran to Bart to press her trembling lips on his, shamelessly thrusting her tongue down his throat. Tammi was daydreaming of trying this move on Leon when there was a stir and the congregation rose to open their hymnals. She felt her chest flush warm as she scrambled to her feet, groping for a hymnal. It was a good thing no one could read her thoughts.

After just one stanza the Reverend Goodlow held up his palms to silence them. "I've been led by the Spirit to change my message tonight." He looked out solemnly.

"Yes, beloved, I've been given a vision. A vision for this flock. For without a vision the people perish."

The Reverend Goodlow waited for several phlegmy coughs to subside and unbuttoned his cuffs, carefully folding them upward. He swung his arms like he was preparing to bale hay. "The things of this world cannot satisfy. We long for more. We crave more."

Several nods and "amens."

"But the people of this world live for today! 'I want it now!' they shout. As children of God, our vision must be wider in scope than the here and now. We must set our sights on eternity! The hope of heaven must be the backdrop of our lives on this earth.

"Are you listening?" He rose on tiptoe. An uncomfortable shifting of the congregation filled the sanctuary. A waft of mentholated lozenges floated around Tammi.

"Many of us are still sitting at the world's banquet table, glutting ourselves with earthly pleasures. Satiating ourselves with things of temporal value. Leaving little room, little thought and preparation, for the glories of heavenly, eternal things.

"We see, we touch, we taste, and we experience *now*, but we cannot begin to know, to fathom the glories that will be revealed in heaven. These sensual pleasures are fleeting, people, and they will damn the soul!"

The congregation fell deathly quiet as the Reverend Goodlow paced from the pulpit to the baptismal font to the altar rail. He shook his head, closed his eyes briefly, then looked up again with a smile. "Lust for worldly, sensual things will tarnish your soul."

Tammi tasted the metal of fear. The hairs on the back of her neck stood up. Was this the pure light of God shining on her? She had a mental picture of herself standing before the X-ray vision of the Almighty.

"When we enjoy the passing pleasures of worldly, sensual things to the exclusion of heavenly matters, we are losing our vision. Our vision of eternity!" The Reverend Goodlow's voice shook the rafters. "The things which are seen are temporal, but the things which are not seen are eternal."

This brought several amens from the congregation.

"Well, how are we to live, then?" The Reverend Goodlow's eyebrows flew up to ask the question. "We're not to entangle ourselves in the desire for sensual things. We're to seek those things above, where our eternal home is."

The Reverend Goodlow shifted from one foot to the other, searching the sea of faces. Tammi watched anxiously as he picked up a worn black Bible. "Let's turn in our Bibles to Ezekiel 6, verse 9."

Pages rustled around Tammi. Ezekiel, Ezekiel. Where in the world was Ezekiel?

The Reverend Goodlow began reading long before she'd found it.

". . . I am broken with their whorish heart, which hath departed from me, and with their eyes, which go a whoring after their idols."

The Reverend Goodlow cupped his ear. "Do you hear God's pain in these words?"

Tammi stared at the reverend. She had to admit that she'd never figured on God feeling pain. Why didn't He just zap things the way He wanted them? Save Himself the sorrows?

Walking down the aisle between the pews, his eyes scanning the congregation, the reverend continued. "We must change our ways, people of Rigby," his voice rang out clearly. "We must view this drought as our wake-up call. Our livestock are perishing. Our spirits are withered as we worry about our endangered crops. God wants to jolt us out of our complacency.

"Search your hearts. See if you are right with God. See if you are not worshipping the sensual things of this world. Pray. If your heart is deceitful, you have the option of good old-fashioned repentance."

After the benediction, a hushed congregation lingered in their pews. Out of the corner of her eye, Tammi spied Pepaw kneeling at the altar rail, his head bent in earnest prayer. A chill went through her, and with it, the image of his downtrodden face as he listened to the weatherman on the radio.

Tammi wandered out of Promiseland and sank down into the cold backseat of the Cadillac, a small, dull ache of disappointment pulsing in her chest.

When they reached home, she slipped into her nightgown and lay in bed. She did not muse on *Texas Toast* or on Leon. She intended to search her heart, but she was fearful of what she might find there. It wasn't fair! Here she'd been, happily standing at the gate of earthly, sensual pleasures, ready to lose herself in the smoldering passion of the romance novels until this cold, sobering blanket from the Reverend Goodlow dropped on top of her.

But then again, she could not bear the thought of her errant ways causing Pepaw to lose his cattle. *Was* she frolicking in earthly, sensual pleasures? Did she have a lust for worldly things that would tarnish her soul? The romance novels writhed in her mind like a pit of vipers.

CHAPTER 8

As 1975 dawned, Tammi still had a vague guilty feeling, but a conscious act of her will could wipe even that out. The more she ignored the concerned voice of the county agent blaring out over the radio, and the beseeching voice of the Reverend Goodlow in her head, the easier it was to live in the present and enjoy the sensual side of life. Her conscience thus numbed, she threw herself back into the steamy world of *Texas Toast*. It was certainly the "haunting and provocative page-turner" the back cover promised.

If only she'd known how hard it would be to stop at the club's predetermined chapter and then, worse, to have to pass the book along to Minna with shreds of the plot left dangling. She was exhausted with waiting for her turn to read, hanging on till book club time by a fraying thread. *Hurry up four o'clock.* She fussed as she slipped into her warmest frock and a pair of heavy boots to step outside through the nippy morning to feed the chickens. An egg-yolk sun held down one edge of a pearly gray sky, and the specter of a half-moon held down the other. She drifted into the corner of the barn to a bag of chicken mash, and scooped up a canful, turned quickly on her heel, and ran smack dab into Pepaw. He was carrying his coffee cup along with the egg basket.

"You forgot something," he said, looking at her concernedly.

"Sir?" she asked.

"You forgot the egg basket."

"Thanks." Tammi hung the basket on her left wrist, blushing from her mistake.

Pepaw shifted from foot to foot, watching her. "You doing all right, gal?" he asked.

Tammi shrugged. "Just sleepy, I guess. Chickens are calling . . ." She moved past Pepaw.

"Well, you seem sort of, I don't know, upset over something or 'nother," he called after her.

"This drought sure has me worried," Tammi mumbled, the lie slipping out easily. Well, it wasn't a total lie. Occasionally, a small snippet of concern about the drought did wedge itself between thoughts of Leon or Clemmie and Bart. But she always managed to thrust it down deep inside before it could interfere with her ravenous appetite for the romance novels.

"Ain't no need to worry," called Pepaw. "The Lord's got us in His palm. I turned it over to Him in prayer, and ain't no use worrying no more. It's a sin to worry if you've prayed over something. Matter of fact, giving up worrying is my New Year's resolution." A barn owl's soft hoot coated the morning fog.

Tammi willed a smile, little beads of perspiration popping out on her forehead. Pepaw's concerned visage stayed imprinted on her brain until she was back at the big house, in the kitchen with Granny, who was bent over watching the glass knob on the percolator to see how strong the second pot of coffee was going to be.

"Happy New Year, Granny," Tammi said, handing her the basket of eggs.

"Happy New Year to you too child." Granny placed the eggs into the Frigidaire.

"You make any resolutions?" Tammi asked. "Pepaw says he's not going to worry about the drought anymore."

"It's not resolutions we need," Granny declared. "It's repentance."

Tammi flinched. "Um, yeah, sure. You're right," she said as she flung herself out the back door into the light and warmth of the sun. She stayed outside until Priscilla came and engaged her in a game of "throw the stick," until she finally felt at ease in her soul again.

"Do you think Bart will get away from those mean cattle rustlers?" Orr asked that afternoon, picking his way along behind Tammi as she walked down Minna's driveway on her way to the book club meeting.

"Yeah. Sure. He's strong and he's smart."

Orr twisted his hands together. "But the sheriff says they're *lawless*. He told Clemmie it'd be a miracle if they didn't hang Bart."

"Hmm?" Tammi was distracted now, waving to Parks and LaDonna as the Trans Am came to a stop beneath Minna's pecan tree.

"Will they hang him?" Orr skipped ahead of Tammi and turned to face her, walking backward.

"Of course not! If they did, there'd be no more book to read, and we're only a quarter of the way through." They were on Minna's front steps now, and Tammi stopped at the door, turning to wait for Parks and LaDonna. *Texas Toast* was tucked underneath Parks's arm, and LaDonna held a plate covered in plastic wrap with a red bow on top.

"Howdy!" Parks called. "Happy 1975!" She was wearing shiny black knee-high boots, her expansive thighs jutting up from them in faded jeans she'd scribbled peace signs all over with a ballpoint pen. A plunging pink sweater hugged her generous curves. By comparison, LaDonna looked like a peahen in her loafers, dun-colored corduroys, and brown sweater.

"Happy New Year to you," Tammi said, holding the front door open wide. Just inside was a card table laden with a brick of Claxton fruitcake, chalky peppermint sticks, chocolate crème drops arranged on a platter, Fritos, creamy onion dip, and a carafe of something hot that smelled of cinnamon. Elvis singing "White Christmas" blared from the 8-track.

"Got us a party going on, don't we, Mr. Vice President," said Parks, punching Orr's arm playfully.

"Yep," Orr said. "And it's not even Christmas anymore."

"Where's Minna?" LaDonna asked as she set her platter down on a corner of the card table.

"Coming!" called Minna's breathless voice. "Make yourselves at home."

Tammi was pouring five steaming cups of what turned out to be spiced cider when finally she heard the clip-clopping of heels as Minna entered the room. Minna held both hands aloft, fingers splayed out. "Sorry. Had to finish painting my nails. Now, I'm counting on y'all to eat this stuff up. I'll bet I've gained twenty pounds this holiday season. Can you tell?" She spun around. Her red knit dress was strained to the bursting point at her curves.

The girls all made soothing noncommittal noises.

"You look like a water balloon," Orr said, popping a Frito crowned with onion dip into his mouth.

"Oh, Orrville," Minna said fondly. "Ever the honest one. Good thing I found myself an old blind boyfriend. Now, who brought these delicious-looking morsels?" She lifted the plastic wrap from LaDonna's platter. "Ooh whee, fudge!"

"I did," said LaDonna, perched primly on the ottoman.

"My absolute favorite," Minna said. "Worth every blessed calorie in it. Thank you, darlin'. You're mighty sweet."

"I could do the snacks for every meeting. I mean, there doesn't seem to be much need for a secretary in the Romance Readers' Book Club." LaDonna's voice was tentative and sounded somehow contrite. Tammi figured she was repentant over her behavior at the last meeting.

"Aren't you a doll!" Minna gushed, ladling up a sizable mound of onion dip and stacking three squares of fudge beside it.

"You have a blind boyfriend, Minna?" Orr asked, as the bright afternoon sun washed in through the window behind him and made his sparse hair light up.

Minna guffawed so hard tears sparkled just slightly above her false eyelashes. "Orrville," she said, once she'd collected herself, "when you get my age, a blind boyfriend is the best kind to have." She patted his back. "Freddie's his name." Minna paused to wink at Tammi. "He brings me tasty things to eat all the time. He's the one brung me that Claxton fruitcake yonder. Freddie doesn't care how big I get because he can't *see* me."

"Poor blind Freddie," Orr murmured.

For a moment, Tammi almost believed in Freddie, too, though he lived only in Minna's imagination. He was her running joke, and whenever she wanted to eat lots of food, let her roots grow out, or not clean her house, she would declare that Freddie was back with her. Sadly, it was hard for Orr to understand offbeat humor such as this. Tammi would try to explain about Freddie to him later.

Minna clip-clopped over to turn the stereo off. "Time for getting down to business," she said, settling herself on the couch and looking expectantly at Tammi.

Tammi was sitting very upright, sipping her cider. "Okay. Chemistry. Love at first sight," she said. "Who wants to start us off on our discussion topic?"

LaDonna shook back her hair. "I'm still going to have to say that I don't believe in love at first sight. Lust, yes. But not love." She lifted her chin and raised her eyebrows, inspecting each face. "I mean, look at Clemmie. She did have a spontaneous reaction when she first spied Bart, but really, all it was was physical. She had heart palpitations and trembling sensations in her . . . well, her female region. She knew nothing about his character—if he was kind, or smart, or witty. She didn't even know if the guy was married or not! You can't tell me she loved him!"

"It wouldn't have mattered to her if he was married or not," Parks said.

"That's terrible, if it's true," LaDonna said. "That would make Clemmie a slut."

"Look, babe . . ." Parks paused to light a cigarette. "All's fair in love and war. Bart is Clemmie's perfect man. That's what she said, 'He's my perfect man.' Said she knew it the instant she laid eyes on him."

"Perfect man to *look* at, maybe," LaDonna said. "But not to marry." She sighed in exasperation.

"Who said anything about marrying?" Parks drained her cider and burped softly. "She's just looking for the perfect *lay*."

"Exactly." LaDonna said in a trembling voice. "That just proves my point. *Love* would mean marriage. 'Till death do us part' is *love*. Love does not equal wanton sex."

Apprehension rose in the pit of Tammi's stomach. She looked frantically at Orr, hoping this was all over his head. He seemed oblivious, playing with a tiny rubber baby Jesus from Minna's Nativity set. But you never could really tell with Orr. Things soaked into him even when you thought he wasn't paying attention.

Minna slid her reading glasses off and rested the tip of one earpiece against her glossy red lips. "If I had to describe my perfect man . . . ," she mused, "*physically*," she added, looking at LaDonna, "I would have to say he couldn't be too good-looking. Tall, dark . . . definitely tall. It's a proven fact that women like their men to be tall."

"Is Freddie tall?" Orr piped up. So he had been paying attention! Tammi noted the chocolate ring around his lips.

"Yes, darlin'," Minna said with a mischievous smile. "My old blind boyfriend is tall. Rich and smart and witty, too. Even got all his own teeth."

"Good," Orr whispered.

"Minna, I think you're right about not hooking up with a man that's too pretty." Parks mashed her smoldering cigarette butt into the ashtray. "Anyway, for me, it's not the face, it's the *body*. Give me hard six-pack abs and some muscley biceps and steely thighs . . . mmmm, don't forget a nice, firm butt."

LaDonna groaned.

"Well, what's *your* perfect man look like? Forget all that 'my perfect man must be loyal and smart and kind to animals' stuff." Parks said the last part in a mocking voice. "Get real, babe. What gets you hot?"

LaDonna blinked. "If you mean, who do I think I have chemistry with—chemistry being defined as a spontaneous interaction, or aroused interest, then . . ." Her narrow face was lost in thought. She glanced up at the ceiling, down at the shag carpeting, until at last a knowing look came into her eyes. "I could not be attracted to an arrogant man," she said simply.

"What in tarnation do you mean by that?" Parks muttered.

"Arrogant," LaDonna repeated. "You know. Thinks a lot of himself. And don't tell me that's not a physical characteristic, because I can spot an arrogant man a mile away. In the way he struts, holds his head."

"Am I arrogant?" Orr piped up.

"No, Orry." Tammi closed her eyes, sighing as she leaned over to whisper in his ear. "I believe I heard Priscilla scratching at the back door to get in."

"I'll go let her in," Orr whispered back. "Must be mighty cold out there. Even though she does have on a fur coat."

". . . and I guess I do prefer them on the tall side, like Minna," LaDonna was saying when Tammi reconnected with the conversation. LaDonna's cheeks were scarlet, and she held one slim hand to her mouth like what she was saying was taboo. "I've never liked blond-headed men, now that I think about it."

"Then what gets you hot is the proverbial tall, dark, and handsome man, dear." Minna chuckled.

"I didn't say he had to be handsome. He could be handsome or not. But he can't be vain." LaDonna pulled her shoulders up, looking very pleased with herself.

"Okay. He can't be vain if he wants to catch LaDonna's eye." Minna glanced at Tammi. "Now, it's your turn to describe your perfect man. What turns you on, hon?"

Tammi sank farther into the couch, Leon's image swimming in her brain. He definitely belonged in the tall, dark, and handsome category. And she definitely believed in lust at first sight. "Well," she said at last, not ready to cast Leon's name out yet, "I think tall, dark, and handsome is good . . . about the love-at-first-sight thing, I think Clemmie's the type of woman, hot-blooded, who's immediately attracted to a man without knowing a thing about him. And not caring, really. She lets her emotions, or hormones, I guess, rule. But I do know that some people are the cautious type." She looked pointedly at LaDonna. "Preferring to look before they leap. We're all just wired different, I guess."

Minna's eyes widened. "Hot-blooded! That's very wise, Tammi. Yes, some of us are definitely hot-blooded."

"I believe I'm one of those hot-blooded types," Parks crowed. "I grabbed on to this feller at Crystal Ward's Christmas party when he passed under the mistletoe, and I laid a big, juicy one on him."

"You didn't know him?" LaDonna gave Parks a disgusted look.

"Nah. Didn't even know his name."

"What did he do?"

"Well, I reckon he was hot-blooded, too. Because he grabbed me and pushed me down onto Crystal's couch, made my knees go weak."

Tammi squeezed her Styrofoam cup so hard it split down one side. She lifted it mindlessly to drain the dregs, coughing on the sediment of spices at the bottom. This was some racy talk! Thankfully Orr was still off with Priscilla.

"Reckon it was Clemmie who inspired me." Parks's eyes were dreamy as she stubbed out her cigarette. "I'd just finished that scene where she was rolling around with Bart underneath the chuck wagon. Got my blood so hot I 'bout burnt slap up!"

"Yes," Minna mused. "That was a goody, all right. Too bad Clemmie's father caught them and fired Bart."

"He also threatened to write Clemmie out of his will," Parks said. "Mean old sumbitch. If I was Clemmie, I'da spit in his face and run off with Bart. Screw the inheritance!"

"But he's her *dad*!" LaDonna cried. "He loves his daughter, and he's only trying to do what's best for her."

"If he really loved her, he wouldn't have hired those men to extinguish Bart." Parks was clenching the armrests of the wing chair.

"Well, just think about how sweet it'll be when those two hook back up," Minna said, swatting playfully at Parks as if to say "lighten up." "Yessum. Going to be some hot-blooded goings-on when *they* get back together."

A slow grin spread across Parks's face. "I can't wait," she said. "Wish I wasn't the last person in the club to get a crack at the book. Hey! Let's reverse the reading order this go-round." She cast a plaintive look at Tammi.

Caught off guard, Tammi was speechless. It was inconceivable that she might have to wait through Parks, LaDonna, and then Minna's reading of the next chapters in *Texas Toast*. But, on the other hand, wasn't it her job as president to see that things ran harmoniously? That the members were fulfilled? It was tough, but a heady feeling, too, to wield such power. "All right," she said grudgingly.

Parks let out a loud "Whoowee!" that brought Orr scurrying back into the den.

"What is it?" he asked. "What'd I miss?"

"Nothing," Tammi said. "I bet Minna'll let you take the rest of that Claxton home with you."

"Yes, Orrville," Minna agreed. "But do leave that scrumptious fudge."

Tammi turned back to the group. "There are still two things we need to talk about," she said. "We'll be reading chapters twenty-one through thirty for our next meeting. And does anyone have a discussion topic they'd like to propose?"

"What about 'How to Be Hot-Blooded'?" Parks teased, with a poke at her cousin's elbow.

"'How to Be a Tramp' is what you meant to say," LaDonna retorted. "I can't believe you kissed some guy whose name you didn't even know! You must've been drunk off your butt."

"Knock it off, you two!" Minna frowned. "How about we discuss 'How to Flirt'? Does that suit everyone?"

They all nodded.

"All rise for our pledge." Tammi stood, beckoning the others until everyone was in a circle. "All for fun and fun for all," they chanted, turning to gather coats and gloves and call their good-byes.

Outside the sun had changed into a fierce orange ball, low enough in the sky now to make Tammi's eyes water when she glanced toward the big house.

"We get to read now." Orr raised his eyebrows at Tammi. "We get to find out about the bad guys." He galloped off ahead of Tammi, holding the brick of Claxton fruitcake like a wise man presenting a gift to the Christ child.

"It'll be a while yet," she called.

Orr pivoted on his heel and stared at her. "Why, Tammi?" He spoke so low she could hardly hear him.

"Well, that's why Parks was so happy. It's her turn to read first. Then LaDonna's. Then Minna's, and last of all yours and mine."

"No," he mewled, plopping down on the dirt as if he had had the wind knocked out of him.

Tammi squatted beside him. "Won't be but an extra three weeks or so. It'll fly by, Orry." Even saying this, she wasn't so sure herself. She glanced over her shoulder and saw Priscilla tearing along to join them. When she reached Orr she nosed the tinfoil off the fruitcake he held and swallowed some cake whole without chewing. Orr didn't even notice till Priscilla was rooting around in the foil for more.

"Oh no!" Orr cried. "Freddie brought that cake to Minna! Poor Freddie. He's blind."

"Freddie's not real," Tammi said softly. "He's a pretend boyfriend."

"Pretend?" Orr's eyes searched hers in puzzlement.

"You know," Tammi said, trying for a forceful tone. "Like the characters in our books."

Orr shook his head, looking all of five. Vulnerable and confused.

The weeks seemed to crawl by until it was Tammi's turn to read again. She felt both desperate and relieved when she at last held *Texas Toast*. Late that night she sat in bed, angling her bedside lamp's beam to read the assigned chapters while keeping an ear out for Granny. When she came to the end of chapter thirty, she kept rereading the last paragraph until it was burned into her brain. That next afternoon she read the selection to Orr, trying her best to smooth over the turbulent patches of the story.

On the third Sunday of each month there was a fried chicken dinner for the extended family at the big house. This was practically the only time Tammi saw her uncle Carson and aunt Onzelle, whose two children were off at boarding school.

Tammi forked a bite of rice, listening as Granny started talking about some new sinful activity called streaking.

"It's just a harmless fad, Mother," Minna sighed. "Why do you always have to turn everything into a sin?"

Granny didn't blink. "Why, it's plain as the nose on your face that it's a sin to go running around naked."

"God made the human body, and it's beautiful," Minna declared. "We're the ones so uptight. If He'd meant us to wear clothes, we wouldn't be born naked."

Granny's mouth opened and closed, and then she pounded the table. "The road to hell is wide, Minna Lee."

Minna yawned. "Tell me which of the Ten Commandments says 'Thou shalt not be naked.' "

Tammi wished she could be as bold and free as Minna. If Granny had told her that running naked through public was a sin, she'd have said, "Yes, ma'am, you're right."

But then maybe it *was* wrong to parade your privates around. Maybe it *was* just another step in America's moral decline.

Carson grunted dismissively. " 'Sposed to be a clear day in the 60s tomorrow," he announced, "and I'm gonna play me nine holes down at the club."

"That's good, son," Pepaw said in a grateful tone. "You haven't had much time to do your golfing. Least the dry, warm weather's good for *something*."

Carson chuckled and shook his head. "Damned if we do and damned if we don't."

"Carson Pledger Elco!" Granny warned. "There'll be no cursing at my table!"

"Sorry, Mother. All I meant is we really *need* us some cold weather."

"I thought we needed rain, Papa." Orr's round face was lost in wonder.

"Yep, we do, son. But we also need us some chill hours—before February's gone. We've had too mild a winter. Peach trees need cold weather to set the fruit buds, to make a good crop."

"It's a wonder the Reverend Goodlow's not been holding prayer meetings for snow, too." Minna said, grabbing a chicken wing.

"Ought to be," Pepaw said. "Us peach growers are going to be hurting *really* bad if we don't get us some cold weather directly."

A knot pulled in Tammi's stomach, and with it, sudden thoughts of the Romance Readers' Book Club. The weight of this lay coiled inside her chest as she pushed the remnants of her dinner around on her plate.

Pepaw rattled his ice to signal need of a refill, and Granny rose for the kitchen. This move allowed Tammi a clear view of Orr. He was asleep! His head flopped forward with his mouth open, snoring. Granny returned with the sweating, silver tea pitcher. She filled Pepaw's glass, then made her way clockwise around the table. When she passed Orr, he began to talk in his sleep.

"Poor Clemmie!" he garbled, clenching the linen tablecloth. "The bandits are carrying Bart off to Galveston! Her wanton heart is all tore up with memories of his tremulous kisses!" Orr began to move his arms the way Priscilla's legs jerked when she dreamed of chasing rabbits.

Tammi's insides shriveled. She became vaguely conscious of a momentary stillness at the adult table before Granny finally shrieked, "Orrville's having a seizure!"

"No!" Tammi said, jumping up to fly to his side. "Orry, wake up," she whispered into his ear, shaking his shoulders, her eyes on Granny.

Orr jerked, his eyelids fluttering open a moment before closing again. "He'll come back to you, Clemmie," he murmured.

"Hey, Orry, it's me!" Tammi whispered, rubbing his cheeks with her fingers. "You're having a bad dream!" There was an uneasy silence as Tammi shook Orr again, this time with such force she was able to rouse him. Orr blinked, squinting and looking curiously around the table.

"Where's Clemmie?" Orr's face was confused.

"It's just a nightmare, Orry." Tammi aimed a biscuit into his mouth. "He's weak from hunger. That's all."

"I'll tell you something," Granny said in a serious tone. "He's been having a lot of spells like this lately. These new imaginary friends with the strangest names. Nodding off at all hours and having trouble sleeping at night. I'm going to call Dr. Emmerson."

Dr. Emmerson was a thorough doctor, and his thoroughness made Tammi nervous. His visits included lots of questions along with a physical examination. There were causes for physical problems that were not necessarily evident, causes he tried to get at the root of, searched for with questions. Once his interrogation had informed Granny that the pain in Tammi's side wasn't appendicitis, but anxiety about a Spanish test.

Tammi slumped in her chair miserably, listening to Granny asking who wanted banana pudding. If Dr. Emmerson came and rooted out the true cause of Orrville's discomfort, Tammi was going to be the one needing medical attention.

CHAPTER 9

The next day after school, Tammi rushed through chores, then zipped upstairs to grab *Texas Toast*. Orr's front door was standing open, his front hall strewn with pine straw.

"Orry," she said, out of breath, nudging him with her knee when she found him napping on his couch, "get up. You scared me to death. We've got to talk. Now."

Orr got creakily to his feet, rubbing his eyes as he pulled on a jacket to follow Tammi. When they reached Viking Creek he hunkered down on the same flat rock he always chose, folding his hands in his lap, looking eagerly at Tammi.

Tammi remained quiet for a moment, then she removed a matchbook she'd taken from the fireplace in Granny's living room, flipped it open, and stared at it pointedly. "You ever think about how it would be if you got sent to hell? About all the fire and stuff down there?" Tammi fingered the pink tip of a match. " 'Course hellfire's a lot hotter than our fires."

He frowned.

"You think Rigby's dry, there's not a single drop of water in the bad place. It's an eternal drought."

Orr closed his eyes. "I know I do bad stuff," he confided. "Sometimes I don't say grace before I eat."

"Aww, *that's* not bad. I'm talking about killing, lying, stealing, and stuff. And sensual pleasures."

"Huh?"

"Remember what the Reverend Goodlow's been talking about?" Orr shook his head.

Tammi stepped over the creek and lowered herself beside him. She touched his cheek gently. "I know it's confusing. He said children of God are supposed to deny their fleshly desires. There's stuff we can't see or taste or smell or hear or feel that we're supposed to value above everything."

"Oh," he said finally. "We can't smell God."

"Well, that's not exactly what he meant."

Orr thought a minute. "We can't see God?"

"Look," she said, "I guess what I'm trying to say is that we need to burn this." She held up *Texas Toast*. "The rest of our books, too. Repent and pray for cold weather."

"But it's our week to read!" He shook his head.

"If your right eye offends you, Orr, you should pluck it out."

"Huh?" He rubbed his eyes.

"The Romance Readers' Book Club is causing us to stumble off the path. We've got to be strong and deny our sinful cravings. Pepaw needs cold weather." She reached for his hand, but instead of squeezing hers in return, Orr's hung heavy and limp.

"Listen, Orry, we've got to get back on the straight and narrow path. Walk blamelessly before the Lord. Don't you want Pepaw's peach trees to do good?"

"Yes," he mumbled.

"Sure enough, you'll be glad later." She released his hand to tug a match loose. She nodded her head while running the match along a red strip on the matchbook. Nothing happened. "Well," she said, glancing at Orr, who was staring vacantly into the woods. "We'll try another one." Again, nothing.

"Maybe God's trying to tell us something," she mused. "Maybe we aren't supposed to burn the books."

In a sort of prayer, Tammi whispered that she'd try just one more match. "If this one doesn't light," she said, "it's a sure sign from God that the Romance Readers' Book Club should continue."

She stared at the third match. A bird warbled in the sweet gum tree overhead, and she looked up beyond its branches to the chalky sky. "God will answer with this match."

Stroking the cool cover of *Texas Toast*, Tammi hoped it wouldn't light. Then she'd know that the club was okay, that reading these novels was only an innocent pastime. It didn't mean she didn't care for heavenly things. It was just a *story*, after all. Surely no harm in that.

Taking a deep breath, Tammi set *Texas Toast* on the rock between them. "Watch out, Orr."

He shrank away. "Tammi, we could read the last page first. So we'll know if Clemmie's okay . . ." Orr's voice was squeaky. "Just to see! And then we can repent. I've been waiting to see if Clemmie marries Bart and is happy ever after. Pretty please with sugar on top?"

"We've got to try this match!" Tammi snapped. "We have to think of Pepaw. Think of the flames down there in the bad place."

"I'll think of the bad place," Orr said softly, steepling his finger-tips into a church shape, bowing his head.

"That's good. We have to do this. For Pepaw and for our eternal destiny, we've got to come clean."

Orr unlocked his fingers and looked down at his hands.

"*Inside* we've got to come clean." She smiled weakly. "You don't want to have a deceitful heart, now do you?"

Orr didn't answer. Sometimes things were just beyond him, and nothing she could say or do would make him understand. "No, sir, we do not," she said, shaking her head vigorously to illustrate her point.

Taking a deep breath, Tammi scratched the match across the strip. It ignited instantly. She watched the yellow flame dance and flicker like it was laughing at the two of them. "This is nothing like the flames in hell," she said, touching it to the corner of *Texas Toast*. "In hell, they're so huge they make folks cry and gnash their teeth."

Orr nodded.

The tiny flame licked a thin trail halfway across the glossy cover, then suddenly sped up, literally engulfing the book in orange petals that made Tammi's eyes water. Staring into the fire, her heart pounding, she wondered how she had strayed off the narrow path so badly.

Orr was quiet, a dazed smile on his face by the time *Texas Toast* was reduced to a fuzzy white skeleton. A kind of holiness hung in the air as Tammi reached for Orr's hand.

Cleansed, her brain cried, *cleansed!*

"Time to pray now," she said. "We're going to ask for snow. We know that would have to come from God. We never get snow."

Orr nodded, and she bowed her head to enumerate her sins silently, for Orr was an innocent bystander in the Romance Readers' Book Club. The more she confessed to God about the trick-or-treating, the secrecy, the fleshly novels, her leading Orr and LaDonna and Parks astray, the stronger and cleaner she felt. Pure, and outraged at herself for jeopardizing Pepaw's peach crop.

Confession and repentance girded Tammi with the knowledge that now God would listen. "Oh merciful God," she whispered upward, "we beseech you for some snow. We need it right quick for the peach trees to get their buds. Amen."

Tammi bent and cupped a shallow palmful of water to fling at Orr. "There." She laughed. "Don't you feel better now?"

His face registered nothing.

Tammi stood, swiping her hands together in an I'm-done-with-that gesture. "Race you back!" Her smile shone through the wooded shadows. "Last one there's a rotten egg!"

Tammi couldn't believe her eyes when she woke up to a world in the grips of a winter storm. Rigby looked like a sheet cake covered with a luscious layer of vanilla frosting. Looking out her window, she saw that the side pasture was a smooth unblemished expanse.

Certain school would be canceled, she slipped into three pairs of socks to keep Pepaw's old work boots on her feet and headed outdoors. Every lungful of air and every step on the path to Orr's house was pure pleasure.

He was still in pajamas, standing in his open doorway.

"Hi," he said when she prodded his ribs.

"Hi, yourself. Looks like He listened to us. I bet Pepaw's rejoicing. Get on some warm clothes and we'll go see Pepaw and have us a look around." Tammi walked into Orr's kitchen, plugged in the percolator, and measured coffee for a strong pot. While the coffee gurgled and sputtered, she rested her elbows on the table, settling her chin on her fists. Somehow it all felt like a dream. This snow. This answer to prayer! She couldn't think the clearest thoughts yet. Maybe coffee would help.

Instead, when she held a cup of steaming coffee, the nutty, rich aroma enveloped her, reminded her of a campfire in the Wild West, of Clemmie and Bart and their passion. She stomped a boot on the wooden floor. She'd kill at the moment to read one of the romances. *I can resist temptation*, she thought as she tried to cast these urges out of her mind with a scalding gulp of coffee. *I can walk the straight and narrow. This is the way to happiness for Pepaw. I'll see God's favor rest on Rigby.*

"Hurry up, Orry," she called. It was hard enough trying to keep her mind on heavenly things, but waiting to see Pepaw's face was pure torture. Tammi was on her third cup of coffee by the time Orr finally appeared, dressed in several flannel shirts and a quilted goose-down jacket so plump his arms stood out a ways from his sides.

"Snow!" he said.

"Yep," she said, gulping the last of her coffee. "God chose to answer the prayers of our repentant hearts." She grabbed Orr's shoulders. "Now, He answered us and we're happy, but there's one thing you have to promise."

"What?"

"Do not go talking about our prayer. You hear? Not to anybody. 'Specially not to Granny. Not even to Pepaw. Let him think it was his own praying that did it."

"All right," Orr said, twisting away from her grip.

She held tighter. "Promise me, Orrville." She shook him a little.

"I promise," he said. "Now can we go?"

Stepping outside onto the front porch, they stood a minute, blowing white breaths and pretending to smoke. Orr poked his hands into his pockets and hunched his shoulders up to his ears, his eyes on the icy camellia bushes beyond the railing.

"My camellias are froze." He cupped a wilted brown bloom.

"Don't worry about it. More'll bloom," she said. "You always have *tons* of blooms."

She watched him grasp the stair rail and half slip-slide down and around to face the bush. "They were so pretty." He shook his head, moving from flower to flower.

"The Reverend Goodlow says we're called to sacrifice." Tammi pulled Orr away. "Jesus sacrificed for us." She closed her shaking hands into fists. Was it the caffeine or the anticipation of seeing Pepaw's face? Perhaps it was the excitement of being so in tune with God.

One by one, they passed familiar shapes coated in ice: the well house, the old Sinclair gas pump, the privet hedge. Tree limbs drooped and sparkled so that they reminded Tammi of the chandelier in the dining room. The ground was slippery so she linked her arm through Orr's.

"My face is froze," he said, wrinkling and unwrinkling his nose while picking up each leg and carefully placing it on the crunchy surface.

"Next we'll pray for rain," Tammi whispered as they pushed the rickety barn door open. It was dark inside, and they crept along the cement floor toward the back corner, where a slim line of light shone from underneath Pepaw's office door. Tammi's heart was racing as she turned the knob and shoved the door open.

In the next split second, as she stood searching the tiny office for Pepaw's face, there was a sharp crack, a sound like a rifle shot. The room went black.

"What?!" Tammi cried out as Orr's hand grabbed her arm.

"Gunfight!" Orr declared. "It's Wyatt. He wants Clemmie, but she loves Bart! They have the real passion!"

"Ain't no gunfight." Pepaw's voice floated toward them. "Sounds like a limb snapped to me. Sap in our poor pines is freezing."

"It's Wyatt, shooting his rifle," Orr protested. "He's always after Clemmie's tail."

"Silly!" Tammi laughed a loud "ha, ha." "Cowboys here! What an imagination. What a crazy thing to say in a place like Rigby." She paused to get her breath. "So, Pepaw, what do you think of this beautiful snow?"

"Well," Pepaw said, "ain't exactly snow. What we got here is an old-fashioned ice storm."

"But it's good for peach trees, right?" Tammi said, Orr still clinging to her arm.

"I reckon it's good to get these chill hours," Pepaw said, "but I'm worried about the roof up at the big house."

"The roof?" Tammi heard the shrill note of her own voice.

"Yep. Lots of pine limbs above the house. Above your house, too, Orrville. And Minna's." He clucked his tongue.

"Tammi and me are happy it snowed," Orr said. "Aren't we Tammi? We prayed real hard and we burned the—"

Tammi's neck drew up. She squeezed Orr's forearm. "Don't you ever listen? It's *not* snow. We've had us an ice storm. It's what's making the sap in the pines freeze."

"Is there sap in peach trees?" Orr asked.

"Of course not!" Tammi snapped, startling him when she grabbed his arm and dragged him back through the door into the main barn. "I imagine we ought to let Pepaw get back to work," she yelled over her shoulder, striding quickly outside.

"Dern it, Orr," she hissed when they were far enough away. "Are you deaf?! I believe we discussed not mentioning the books, not the burning, or the praying . . ." She released him, walking as fast as she could on the slippery ice. Orr began to jog to catch up with her, pumping his arms and calling her name.

As Tammi neared Orr's house, she heard a big *whomp!* and Orr's voice crying out sharply. She turned to see him flopped down on the ice, spraddle-legged.

"Owwww." Wincing, Orr rubbed his elbow. "I'm hurt bad," he whined.

Tammi picked her way back to him and squatted down. "Quit fussing."

"I might have broke something," Orr said pleadingly.

Tammi considered. "You're okay. Now, get on up. Let's go to your house and light a candle." She pulled his arm.

Orr's round face contorted; tears dribbled down his cheeks and hung on his jaw. If there was anything Tammi hated, it was to see him cry. Orr could be the most dramatic person in the entire world. He was the only Elco she knew who could talk himself into an actual state of pain. This was his way of getting what he wanted—but the thing about it was that he didn't realize what he was doing. To him, the pain was real.

"Only thing broke is your feelings," she said softly, patting his cold cheek. "But I forgive you. Next time, please remember to keep your mouth shut."

By February first, book club day, the ice storm was only a memory. In the end no damage was done by the ice, and only time would tell if the peach trees had benefited from the cold. Tammi's stomach churned every time she contemplated telling Parks, LaDonna, and Minna that the club was finished.

"Hi darlin'," Minna said that afternoon, opening the door, a sweet rose-petal fragrance from her curling around Tammi's head like a garden. "You look pale. Come sit down." She led Tammi to the sofa. "It's not your monthly, is it?"

Tammi shook her head, rolled to her stomach, and pressed her face into the pillow. It was a grave responsibility to be holy, to have had such a prayer answered. She'd bitten her nails down to nubbins at school today, thinking of ways to explain to the club why it was ending. She pictured herself as a martyr, sacrificing herself for the good of Rigby, praying fervently that her brain could ignore the tempting call of the romance novels.

"Well, you just rest," Minna said, covering Tammi with an afghan.

"Howdy ho!" Parks sang out in a loud voice, flinging the door open so hard it banged the wall. "I believe it's party time!"

"Wha—?" Tammi struggled to her elbows, the afghan sliding to her waist.

LaDonna was right behind Parks, carrying a pitcher in one hand and a tray in the other. It was a long moment before Tammi answered softly, "Hey y'all."

"Hey, Tammi," LaDonna said. "Pretty day, isn't it?"

"Any day we have book club is a great day!" Parks said. "Listen, mind if we reverse the order of reading again? Please. I'm itching to find out if Bart really is doing the dirty deed with that Vonita slut from Miss Delia's. If he is, and I was Clemmie, I'd cut the man's balls off!" Parks made scissors with her fingers, snipping the air.

Tammi felt the heart-stopping, strangulating feeling that had kept her up all night. She tried to brush it away with a smile. "What did you make?" she asked LaDonna.

"I baked heart-shaped sugar cookies," LaDonna said. "Made pink lemonade. In honor of Valentine's month." She settled the tray on Minna's coffee table and peeled back the plastic wrap. Red sugar sprinkles decorated the cookies.

"Pretty," Tammi murmured, heading to the front door to intercept Orr. She had never for an instant imagined that he could keep his lips sealed today, especially if he weren't reminded at frequent intervals. Tammi knew there was a proper time and tone to end the Romance Readers' Book Club.

Promptly at five o'clock Priscilla gave one staccato bark, racing from underneath the porch to greet Orr's plodding figure. Tammi watched from behind the screen door, her eyes on him steadily, trying to discern his disposition. She had to get a feel for his intentions. *If he was going to spill the beans right away*, she thought bleakly, *I might as well get prepared mentally.*

"I miss anything?" Orr asked, his voice echoing through the foyer as he climbed the steps. He scuttled forward into the den, bending down to inspect the cookies.

"You didn't miss a blessed thing, darlin'!" Minna chirped.

Orr's Old Spice cologne hovered like an invisible cloud around him, and Tammi noted how nattily dressed he was: skin fresh and pink, hair in wet furrows, and she knew he'd just climbed out of the bathtub. He was prepared for what was an important occasion in his mind.

"You look mighty snazzy, Mr. Vice President." Parks punched Orr playfully on his arm. "Got a hot date tonight?"

Tammi winced. She sat down on the edge of the sofa, hands folded in her lap, ankles crossed. She held her breath, but Orr only smiled in response.

"Y'all help yourselves," LaDonna said, nodding down at her cookies. She poured pink lemonade into five cups.

"I already ate six of them valentines on the way over." Parks patted her belly as she reclined on the chaise, propping her feet up. She lit a cigarette. "And you know," she continued, "speaking of valentines, I wonder if there'll be any count to that sweetheart's dance down at the VFW hall. You going, Minna?"

"Maybe." Minna flashed a flirty little smile. "May find me a sweetheart."

"But what about Freddie?" Orr shot up onto his feet, looking hard at Minna.

"Don't you worry about old Freddie," Minna said. "He got to playing around on me. I caught him kissing Amy Carmichael, and I told him I wouldn't stand for no two-timing man. Wouldn't stand for a cheater!"

"That puts me in mind of our book," LaDonna said, "I think Bart might be cheating on Clemmie. Guess we'll find out soon enough."

Orr looked hard at LaDonna. He cocked his head, held up one finger as if he were going to make a comment.

The tender, crisp cookie in Tammi's mouth turned into a gummy ball that made her gag. *Here goes*, she thought. *I'm still not ready in the least for my confession.*

"Clemmie got too complacent is what I think," Minna broke in. "Took poor Bart for granted." She shook her head slowly. "Hot-blooded is all fine and good to begin with, but you've got to work at keeping that spark going."

"Well, ain't like she could run to the nearest beauty parlor out there on the wild Texas prairie." Parks thumped her cigarette into the ashtray. "Right, Tammi?"

Tammi felt the muscles in her stomach tighten. "You're right. The best she can do is wash her hair in the creek and pinch her cheeks to get some color." Tammi's voice was quavering, and she finished the rest of her thought in her head: *And we're never going to find out if Bart is actually two-timing Clemmie, and if she'll transfer her love to Wyatt.*

"Oh, that's not what I meant at all," Minna said triumphantly, her eyes racing around the room as if she'd just been baiting them with her comment.

"What did you mean?" LaDonna sipped lemonade.

Minna cleared her throat. "What y'all need to realize is that there ain't nothing like *complimenting* a man to make him feel good. *That's* the key to make him feel studly and smart and witty, and to *keep* making him feel that way. Then he'll crave to stay with you. And you can do that whether you've been to the beauty parlor or not. If you'll recall, at first Clemmie was flattering Bart up one side and down the other. Remember? Saying stuff like, 'Ooo, you're so strong, so sexy!' 'You get me hot and I crave your touch,' and 'I never imagined I could feel like this!' But then she stopped. Guess she thought she'd roped and tied the man." Minna paused for a bite of cookie. "When Clemmie stopped doing all that is when Bart backed off." Minna's frosted hair shimmied as she nodded her head. "That brings me to this week's topic. I happen to know that there's an art to flirting. Never assume anything. You've got to work it. Maybe Clemmie is going to wise up. Who knows? I can't wait to find out."

Tammi forced a bright smile, wondering when her cue would come. Tentatively she studied Orr. He rested his chin in the palms of his hands, his elbows on his knees, his eyes squinty as if he were giving Minna a careful examination.

There was a long silence. Parks leaned back, lit a cigarette, and grinned mischievously at Minna. "Got a question for you."

"Okay, shoot." Minna laced her fingers together in her lap.

"The key is to make him feel good, right?"

Minna nodded.

"Well, there's this man I've been seeing. Works at the Sears in Macon. Tire Center, tools. You know, car parts stuff. Well, he's cute as he can be, but he's got one little flaw. That man goes on and on about car engines and car axles and car this and that. Blah blah blah, like he thinks I think it's the most fascinating subject. I reckon I must be tuning him out, because every now and then he'll say something like, 'So, what do you think? You even listening to me?' " Parks shook her head slowly. "What should I do? I don't want to lose him. He's got the hottest buns I ever saw."

Minna smiled down into her cup. "Hon, it's our job to listen raptly to our men. But that said, I know it's not easy listening to an endless stream of car talk. All my Franklin ever wanted to talk about with me was baseball! It was home-run this and third-inning that. My own personal trick was to pick out a key word here and there while he was yammering away, something he said, a player's name, or a score, and repeat it to him in this knowledgeable, excited tone.

He never knew I wasn't hanging on every word he said. And most of the time, I could have me a whole other thought while he was talking and I was supposedly 'listening' to him."

Parks let out a long whistle. "Fabulous! Probably make him happier than my new red silk thong does."

LaDonna winced. "I thought our topic for today was 'How to Flirt.'"

"Yes it is," Minna said. "And believe me, all this is part of making your man feel great . . . listening raptly. But I bet you're wanting to discuss the nuts and bolts of flirting? Walking sexy, wriggling those hips, catching his eye while you run your tongue seductively across your lips?"

"Sure," LaDonna mumbled, gazing down at her thighs.

"Well, alrighty," Minna said, cocking her head. "Let's begin with walking sexy. Shall I demonstrate?" Without waiting for an answer, she leaped up, balancing expertly on her three-inch heels, thrusting her hip out to one side. "Now, Orr, this won't work too good for you because women want something entirely different in a man's walk." She giggled. "But this drives a man *wild*." Minna proceeded to walk toward the door with her arms held out a ways from her hips and this satisfied expression on her face as she moved like a feral cat, propelling each leg forward, her buttocks swinging, *va-va-va-voom*. She sashayed around the room several times, and something about Minna drew the eye, an electricity that seemed to give off sparks.

There was awed silence, then Minna stepped forward to stand in their midst with her hands on her hips. "Okay. Now we're all going to try it. Orr, you can be the judge."

Parks hopped up, mashed out her cigarette, and twirled in a graceful pirouette. "Come on," she commanded, pulling a blushing LaDonna up by her wrist. "You too, Tammi. Move those little behinds. Shake your moneymakers!"

LaDonna was behind Parks now, her hands on Parks's hips as Parks singsonged under her breath, "Shake, shake, shake. Shake, shake, shake. Shake your bootie!" She wriggled her big fanny rhythmically with each word. Tammi was startled as LaDonna actually thrust one narrow hip out, looking happy, radiant even. Minna was laughing and clapping, jutting her hips in a come-hither motion as she walked over to nudge Tammi, raising her eyebrows in a come-join-in motion.

A great bubbling blackness, like tar, filled Tammi's heart and mind. The color drained from her face. "I don't want to," she said in a small voice. "I'm seeking those things above."

Parks stopped where she was and turned to look hard at Tammi. There was a long moment of silence, then Parks's strained voice. "What'd you say?" followed by Minna's soft, "Oh, Tammi, hon." LaDonna merely stared.

"She isn't feeling well," Minna said to Parks in an indulgent tone. "And I don't believe she's thinking straight." Minna sank down next to Tammi. "Want me to go fix you a Co-cola on ice, hon?" She stroked Tammi's upturned wrist.

Tammi shook her head. "I *am* feeling well," she said carefully, gazing down at her bulky gray corduroy skirt, tugging the hemline till it met the tops of her brown loafers. Minna was following each of Tammi's gestures with her eyes, until suddenly her face seemed to cloud over, followed by a look of sharp recognition, as if she were becoming aware of some terrible crime. Her forehead wrinkled, and she pushed out her bottom lip.

"Oh, you poor, pitiful child," Minna crooned, shaking her head.

"What?" Tammi asked.

Minna looked Tammi full in the face. "I'm so sorry, love," she said. "I simply cannot believe I didn't see this till now. Forgive me, I beg you."

Stunned, Tammi let herself meet Minna's eyes. "For what?" She felt Orr move to her other side, snaking his arm around her shoulder to squeeze.

"Why, the very fact that I let her *dress* you like this," Minna responded in a tone heavy with fury. "Like some nun! I guess I've been blind. No wonder you don't want to get up and parade yourself around. Even LaDonna gets to wear blue jeans . . ." Minna shook her head like the world was coming to an end. "Hon, I vow to you, I'm gonna go talk to Mama this very day! I cannot believe it. Her making you hide your light under a bushel like this. Mmm mmm mmm. You'll never be able to walk sexy dressed this way. Much less land yourself a boyfriend!"

Tammi felt nothing but a gray emptiness where her brain ought to be. "I burned up *Texas Toast*," she stated flatly. "We have to end the club because we cannot glut ourselves with earthly pleasures. Sensual pleasures are fleeting, and they'll damn the soul. Lust for worldly, sensual things is a sin." She waited for the massacre. Seconds ticked by as she examined the peace in her heart, heard the distant sound of a heavenly choir strumming their lyres as an encore, saw in her mind's eye God nodding and a kind of holy light emanating from around His throne.

Several minutes passed and Tammi watched as Parks slowly came out of her trance, closing her mouth as fury flamed in her eyes. "You *burned Texas Toast*?!" she screamed so loud that Orr winced.

Tammi nodded. "Me and Orr burned it up. We didn't even finish the book before we burned it up."

"Then how the hell are we s'posed to find out what happened to Clemmie? Are you *insane*?!" Parks was stomping so hard her thighs shimmied up and down. "Whatever happened to 'Fun for all and all for fun'? Don't you dare go getting all holy on us now, girl!"

Orr raised his chin to challenge, "You can't see God. It's hot in the bad place."

Eyes narrowed to angry slits, Parks studied Orr for a moment, her eyes raking his face. "*Two* morons," she said at last, yanking LaDonna to her startled feet and hauling her out the door.

Orr remained solidly at Tammi's side while Minna fixed a Coca-Cola and brought it to Tammi, shaking her head almost imperceptibly as she fingered the hem of the offensive skirt, her eyes seeming to say, "You see how unfortunate this all is? We cannot hold this girl responsible."

CHAPTER 10

Georgia peach growers breathed a sigh of relief in early March when they looked out over an expanse of purplish pink blooms. At first, just seeing Pepaw's face was reward enough for Tammi. She enjoyed nurturing the secret pleasure of her sacrifice. But when April arrived and still the fat paperbacks held out enticing arms, she grew sick to death of denying herself. She longed for the feel of the glossy covers between her fingers, the words that satisfied her hunger. She longed for the camaraderie of the club meetings.

She tried to keep her mind on holy things, but there was something inside her that would not be quieted. She didn't know how to break this stronghold, and the inner struggle became a lot to shoulder. She reckoned that this fight between sensual pleasures and eternal treasures was her cross to bear till she reached Glory.

She managed to avoid LaDonna at school, and she became an expert at detecting signs of Orr's withdrawal. "I sure wish we could know what happened to Clemmie and Burt," he often whispered too loudly. Tammi read old Archie comic books and a farming magazine of Pepaw's to him. But these did not satisfy. All she could figure was that he could tell her heart wasn't in it. Finally Granny set her chin, said she was tired of turning a blind eye to Orr's affliction, and called Dr. Emmerson.

Ironically, it was on Good Friday that Dr. Emmerson was scheduled to see Orr. Tammi hadn't been allowing herself to even think about the examination, but after she'd cleaned the kitchen from lunch she walked outside along the path to the rose garden. Traipsing through grass bristling like straw, she settled herself onto a wrought-iron bench. The sun was directly overhead, way too warm for April. She noted with a wistful sigh that the dogwoods bordering the garden were not leafed out as they should be.

Her thoughts wandered to past-springs, fleeting images of seasons wet and lush and fragrant. She cast an eye at the wizened vines near her feet and realized that there would be no white rosebud for her to wear on Mother's Day Sunday at Promiseland (those with live mothers wore red). She felt a wistfulness so debilitating she couldn't hold back the tears.

Sniffling, she looked toward Orr's house. Oh well. Dr. Emmerson was fixing to blow the whole lid off, anyway.

Her biggest mistake was that she hadn't burned the remainder of their romance library. She kept intending to haul them out to a barrel behind the barn, douse them with gasoline, and fling a match in. She told Orr they would do this when both Granny and Pepaw were away from home for long enough. But as it turned out, an opportune time never arose, and now she knew that if she didn't talk to Orr before Dr. Emmerson did, he would spill the beans. She jumped up to run to Orr's.

He sat on the sofa, petting one of Pepaw's striped barn cats. "Hi, Tammi," he said.

"Hi." She sank down beside him, taking a long exaggerated breath, trying to think of how to mention the books without getting him all worked up. She ran her hand along the cat's silky back, and the animal began to purr.

"His motor's running," Orr said.

"It's a girl," Tammi said. "Don't you remember she had kittens last spring? In fact, looks like she's going to have some more. See how bulgy she is?"

"I'd love a kitten!" Orr cocked his head, considering. "But Mama'll give them all away again. Maybe we should hide her! *Hide* the babies when they come out."

"Hide them?"

"Yes."

"There are some things we need to hide from your mama, aren't there?"

Orr bit his bottom lip.

Tammi grabbed his hand. "It's not like we're lying when we hide things," she said. "There's something else we've got to hide from her. And especially from Dr. Emmerson."

"What?"

"It's very important," she said. "More even than the kitties."

Orr's mouth fell open.

"I'm serious as a heart attack," she said, nodding thoughtfully as her mind raced across a plan. "You know how wonderful our Romance Readers' Book Club was. Don't you, Orry? How much fun we had reading together and going on adventures? Well, now I want us to start a brand-new book! Your choice. Just you and me. Forget about the one we burned. I don't know what got into me. I'm talking about you picking a real exciting one. One with cowboys again, maybe. But, Orr, there's one thing." She stopped speaking and looked pointedly at him.

"What?"

"You have to *swear* this," she said. "You absolutely *cannot* tell Dr. Emmerson or Granny about the club. Remember how it was a secret before?"

He nodded.

"Well, it's even more secret now. Okay? Because, Orry, if you tell Dr. Emmerson today when he comes about the Romance Readers' Book Club, then he'll tell Granny and we can't start it up again."

Tammi left Orr's, the voices in her head going back and forth like a heated trial in a small courtroom. An insistent little voice cried out a bit louder than the rest, her own aching for a blameless life—telling her to burn the remainder of the novels, continue walking the righteous path. What in heaven's name had she just done?! Surely a bolt of lightning would knock her down. She was tempting the fires of hell. Plus, on some deeper level, reinstating the club meant betraying Pepaw. Her prayers for rain would surely be ignored.

Tammi dragged herself up the front steps of the big house and into the kitchen for a glass of water. Granny was seated at the table, her old Singer sewing machine zipping along, her slim hands running a length of navy fabric under the needle. She turned to look at Tammi and lifted her foot from the pedal on the floor. "Tammi Lynn, what on earth is the matter with you?!"

Tammi shrugged.

"Well, I imagine you're worried about Orrville, too."

Tammi let out a long breath. "Yessum. I just went over to visit him."

"Well, that was a very Christian thing to do." Granny's face softened. "I appreciate the fact that you give so much of your time and attention to Orrville. He's dependent on the goodwill and patience of others. I worry about what will happen when Melvin and I are gone . . ."

"I know," Tammi answered in a gentle voice.

The room grew quiet and the light overhead caught the shimmering of a tear in Granny's eye. "Listen at me! Melvin would be furious if he heard that! He hates it when I worry. But I guess Good Friday is a hard day for all of us to get through, hm?" She closed her eyes and tossed her head in a little shaking-off gesture.

"Yes." Tammi found it hard to breathe for a moment.

It seemed hours later before Granny piped up in a clear, bright voice. "Well! I do have something happy to focus on!"

"Celebrating Jesus' resurrection on Easter Sunday?" Tammi ventured.

"No. I mean, yes, that will be just wonderful. But what I was going to say was Leon's arrival! I'm sewing these curtains for his bedroom."

Tammi felt a sudden flash of elation. Leon would be living right here on the farm soon! She pictured his finely chiseled behind, and here came that pure and succulent sensation of tingling hunger in her middle. She shivered, involuntarily, desperately, all the way down to her toes.

"They're not bringing a stick of furniture with them," Granny said. "Good thing I own an antique shop, hm?"

"Sure," Tammi answered absentmindedly.

"I've offered Nanette to work behind the counter. I told her, I said, 'Nanette, you'd be a natural at Elco Antiques. All the folks around here know you, and you grew up around antiques.' And you know what she said, Tammi Lynn? She said, 'Oh, Mother, I think I'll just look for another secretarial position when I get there.' " There was pain in Granny's eyes as she looked at Tammi.

"That's too bad."

"Yes, it is. That child has always been contrary. It was like pulling hen's teeth getting her to Promiseland when she was a girl. I'm going to lay down the law when she's living under my roof this time, however. I'm going to say that she *must* attend services. Don't you think that's within my right?"

"Uh, sure," Tammi said.

"Well, in any case," Granny said, "I'm positive she'll come to repentance, salvation, when she's older. Lots of people do." She looked hard at Tammi. "You plant the seed when they're young, and, like Melvin says, you pray and you just don't worry. Let me tell you, there are plenty of folks at Promiseland who didn't start walking with Jesus till they were well up there! Eunice Thigpen didn't accept Jesus till she was eighty-nine!"

"Is that a fact?" Tammi said, jumping up and taking the stairs two at a time to her room, where she flung herself across the bed.

Now she allowed herself to be possessed by the fierce, wild passion she'd been holding at bay. She conjured up a succulent scene from *Texas Toast*, trembling lips and loins, so that she fell into a dreamy trance, felt the rough hands of a Texas ranch hand on her thigh. "Hot-blooded," she murmured into her pillow, her ears stopped up to that insistent little voice crying out for righteousness.

At supper Granny said the blessing, thanking God for Dr. Emmerson's insightful exam of Orr. Then she put her hands on her hips, shook her head, and said to Pepaw, "Poor boy. Doesn't seem fair, does it? Orr tetched the way he is and a bad case of allergies to boot. Dr. Emmerson said the pink rims around his eyes, his sleeplessness, indicate allergies to pollen."

Tammi's conscience felt a tiny twinge, but the thirst, the gnawing hunger for passion, was greater, and it had hold of her like a rip current, dragging her far out into turbulent waters.

CHAPTER 11

"**T**ammi girl! I knew you'd see the light." Parks bounded up the steps with a cigarette in one hand and a can of Mountain Dew in the other. "Just a matter of time, what I said to myself when you pitched that holy fit."

Tammi was waiting in the shadows on Minna's front porch, watching the late-afternoon sun of May first as it kissed the top of distant fields turning yellow in the dying light. Across her knees lay *Savage Moon*, a pulpy romance swollen even fatter by eager fingers. On the cover a bare-chested Indian brave with heavy-lidded eyes and flowing ebony hair laced with feathers seemed to be creeping up behind a beautiful maiden with a face strikingly similar to LaDonna's. The unsuspecting maiden was down on her knees cupping water to drink from a river, her hugely swollen breasts grazing the surface. Tammi goggled at the mesmerizing mix of dangerous feralness and unadulterated lust. Perhaps this would be the romance novel that would satisfy the trembling and insistent feeling deep inside her. She'd had half a good mind to greedily read the whole thing right away, not tell a soul, but then she'd decided having accomplices would somehow make her feel better in that part of her that the Reverend Goodlow's words still haunted.

She knew this theory to be the literal truth when she saw LaDonna slowly emerging from Parks's Trans Am, carrying a box of Moon Pies and a six-pack of Mountain Dew with one can missing.

"Look," Tammi said, rising to give LaDonna an awkward hug. "You're on the cover of our new book."

LaDonna peered hard at *Savage Moon*. "Get real," she said. "I'd need a boob job to look like her." She laughed, shaking her head like the joke was on her.

"I meant in the face," Tammi said. "She's beautiful."

"Thanks," LaDonna said. "Thanks for starting up the club again, too. Parks drove ninety miles an hour getting us here." LaDonna's sandals slapped the stone floor of the foyer just as the Carpenters began singing "I Know I Need to Be in Love" over Minna's 8-track. With a deep breath, Tammi stepped along right behind her.

"Hello! Come right on in here and make yourselves at home." Minna gestured with an armful of silver bracelets. Today she wore a purple miniskirt with a matching tube top, and platform Candie's three inches tall. She bustled over to the credenza, reached down inside for a tray, and shook five Moon Pies from their cellophane wrappers. "Time for refreshments," she sang out. "Oh, wait. We've got to wait for Mr. Vice President."

"Orr's not coming," Tammi said.

"What?!" Parks looked shocked.

"It was too hard on him," Tammi explained. "Got him so wrought up he wasn't sleeping good. Granny was having conniptions over his health, and I was afraid he'd let the cat out of the bag. Anyway, I started up another little mini-club. Just him and me. He's content." She paused for a breath. "But I don't want him to feel left out, so y'all be sure you don't breathe a word about this!"

"What Mother don't know won't hurt her!" Minna laughed.

Tammi laughed guardedly. She often had the sensation that she was falling into a great abyss of sin, as if the pure was gradually, inexorably draining out of her. She glanced at Minna, in awe of her tough nonchalance. "Sometimes," Tammi began slowly, "I cannot believe you sprang from Granny's loins! I mean, I'm utterly amazed . . ."

Minna raised a cryptic eyebrow. "Well, maybe wildness, being a free spirit, whatever you want to call it, maybe it skips a generation. Just think if I'd been raised by someone who *encouraged* wildness!" She popped the top off a Mountain Dew.

Tammi felt a tremble of intrigue at Minna's words, but she could tell by Minna's tone and posture that the subject was closed. She rose to get a Moon Pie and Mountain Dew. When she returned to her spot on the couch, Parks had scooped up *Savage Moon*, examining the cover with her mouth hanging open.

"Would you look at this guy's chest!" Parks gushed, holding the book to her lips as she pressed a myriad of noisy kisses all over it. "Can I be first to read again this time? Since I never got to find out what happened in *Texas Toast?*"

Tammi swallowed. It hadn't occurred to her that she'd have to win back the club's trust, and this was a small sacrifice. She nodded. "Let me read us a juicy excerpt," she said, waggling her fingers at Parks for *Savage Moon*.

"Hold your horses, child." Minna rested her half-eaten Moon Pie on the chair arm and got up to get a paper bag from the hearth. Emblazoned across the bag's front was FANCY PANTS. Fancy Pants was a trendy boutique in downtown Macon where all the popular girls at Rigby High bought their clothes. Minna set the bag in Tammi's lap. "Open it up, doll." Minna kissed Tammi lightly on the crown of her head. For one moment Tammi sat transfixed, her heart fluttering crazily. Then she reached into the sack and pulled out a pair of milky-blue bell-bottom jeans. Soft as silk. With a peace symbol patch on one knee and fashionably frayed hemlines. She looked at Minna.

"Something else is in there." Minna was grinning.

Tammi reached in to curl her fingers around a whisper of fabric. "Wow," she murmured in awe as she held up a pink cotton scoop-neck T-shirt with BABE in silver glitter across the breast. "Thank you, Minna. I love them. Guess I can wear them at your house, whenever we have our meetings . . ."

Minna gave Tammi a mock scowl. "Now, did you honestly think for one minute that I intended to let you keep wearing those old-lady frocks?"

Tammi began piecing things together in her mind. "Granny?"

"I talked to the old gal. Several times I marched up there, trying to reason with her. Begging her to let you wear slacks. 'Mother,' I said, 'poor Tammi's an *outcast* at school.' That didn't do a bit of good. She'd say, 'Minna Lee. As God's children, we're called to be aliens in this world.' " Minna bit a half-moon into her Moon Pie. After a long and thoughtful chewing spell, she swallowed. "At first I was struck plumb speechless, and I figured I'd never be able to convince her. But, late one evening, I was picking ticks off Priscilla, and an idea came to me that I call the 'sacred solution.' It *had* to be divinely inspired, I promise." Now she paused for a swig of Mountain Dew. Everyone held their breath, waiting.

"Like I said," Minna continued after a moment, "I was yanking one of those nasty fat gray ticks off Prissy's ear, and it came to me. I went running back up the hill, to the big house, and Mother was already in bed. I flipped on her lamp and I said, 'Mother! Get up!

You've got to listen at this!' She was all stiff, squinty-eyed, but she rolled over and perched up on one elbow. I said, "If you make Tammi dress that way, you might as well say to all those kids at Rigby High that if you're a follower of Jesus Christ, prepare to have no friends! That's no way to spread the Good News, Mother,' I said. 'It should be clear to you that wearing slacks like they do, T-shirts, and whatnot, too, would allow Tammi to *witness*! They'd *listen* to somebody who looks like them! Remember how it says Jesus had to be tempted in all points like we are? Hm? Jesus was God jumping into a man's body, for God's sake! God figured folks would *listen* to somebody who looked like them. So, think how easy it'll be for Tammi to tell others about Jesus if she's wearing slacks and T-shirts.' " Minna took a deep breath. "It was like a dern miracle."

Tammi's emotions were tender and twisted, and a tear squeezed out of her eye. LaDonna pulled a tissue from her purse. "Thanks, LaDonna," she sniffled. "And thanks, Minna. I guess I'm just so happy I'm crying.".

"Go put them on," Minna urged.

Perching on the edge of Minna's canopy bed, Tammi slid out of her jumper and into something like a big, soft hug as she pulled on the blue jeans and skimmed into the T-shirt. Feeling unreal and lighter than air, she crossed the room to stand before a mirror, smiling tentatively. The clothes transformed her, hugging her womanly curves like nothing she'd ever worn before. It wasn't just her body that was different. Her entire face was lit up. She put her hands on her hips and twirled sideways. For the first time in her life, Tammi felt like she might fit in. She looked like the popular girls at Rigby High.

Wearing a silly grin, she emerged barefoot from the bedroom. "How do I look?" She twirled breathlessly.

"What did you do with Tammi Elco?" Parks breathed.

LaDonna nodded. "You could be a teen model at Rich's. You look fabulous."

"Thanks." Tammi settled down next to LaDonna, clasping her hands together to chase away the unreal feeling flooding her.

"What a transformation!" Minna spoke in high gear. "We'll have to buy you some platform shoes—some of these Candie's. You'll definitely be turning heads. There's nothing in the world beats tight when it comes to catching a man's eye. 'Skimpy, sexy, tight, and lacy.' That's my motto when it gets down to dressing to lure a man. We'll also get you one of those halter tops the girls are wearing. Hip-huggers and hot pants, too. School will be out soon and I'll carry you to the mall."

"But Granny'll—"

"Gradually, dear," Minna said. "We'll have to wear her down, break her in gradually. Just remember to keep reminding her, you're *witnessing*."

"Witnessing," Tammi repeated.

"Skimpy, sexy, tight, and lacy." Parks grinned as she lit another cigarette. "That's catchy."

"Catch you a man that way." Minna laughed.

LaDonna grimaced. "Not all guys like the trampy look. I think what Tammi has on now is great. Honestly, but I just don't think we have to wear revealing clothes to lure a man. What happened to leaving something for the imagination?"

Parks shook her head in disgust, but Minna threw up a hand. "That's a good point," Minna said. "In our cleavage discussion, I believe we did talk about showing just enough, but not too much. I imagine we could apply that same principle to our 'skimpy, sexy, tight, and lacy.' Only sometimes, I myself have been in these situations, where you've got to do what they call in sales, 'Ask for the order.' "

"I think modesty is beautiful." LaDonna held the chair arms tightly, in a vulnerable way that made something inside Tammi pause and question the 'skimpy, sexy, tight, and lacy' mind-set.

"Time to read!" Tammi said, forcing more buoyancy into her voice than she had known she possessed:

Running Bear emerged from the Atawah River, his biceps bulging and glistening beneath his lovely red skin. Nekoosa, crouched behind a pine, was keeping her eyes on the small indents at his waist. They begged for the caress of her lips. She would never forget his scent— elusive, musky, laced with traces of the river. Nor could she forget their wild, abandoned love in the shadowed forest. Without a sound, she crept out, her soft mound aching as she remembered all too well how he'd brought her to the point of ecstasy many times.

She approached him, her tightened nipples pointing the way, desire so strong it was as if she'd lived only for the moment when they would be united in the flesh again, until his hardness pressed against her with a savagery all its own.

Parks lit a cigarette with a faraway look in her eyes. "Reckon them Indians ever got married back then?"

"Goodness no." Minna laughed. "They were like the wolves and the bears. Wild things—doing whatever, with whoever, whenever they took a notion."

LaDonna let out a big huff of exasperation. "That's not true! Indians are virtuous, beautiful people! *My* people."

"Sorry," Minna said in a placating voice, patting LaDonna's thigh. "All I meant is that they had what our romance books call 'unfettered, smoldering passion.' "

Tammi blinked. A tingle brushed her heart, and she had to bite her lip to quell the tangled mass of thoughts and hormones raging inside. What Minna said sounded like it could be true. Suddenly Tammi was so wound up she felt like she could just go *snap!* and explode right then and there.

"Gimmee!" Parks waggled her fingers for *Savage Moon*. "What's our new assignment?"

"The first fifteen chapters," Tammi said, and everyone nodded. "Okay, let's all rise for the pledge." Tammi rocked forward to stand, but Minna grabbed her by the elbow and pulled her back down.

"Wait a sec," Minna said. "We have to decide on our next discussion topic."

"How about 'How to Kiss'?" Parks said.

LaDonna cocked her head, looking as if she smelled something bad. "All right," she said finally, "but next time *I* get to pick."

Now Tammi stood, sweeping her arms out until the other women formed a circle. "All for fun and fun for all," they chanted, indulging in a quick group hug before Parks scooped up *Savage Moon* and dashed outside with LaDonna close on her heels.

Tammi turned to face her aunt. "Minna, I can't thank you enough for talking to Granny about my clothes. And for buying these. You don't know what this means . . ."

"I should have done it a long time ago. You without your mother and all."

Tammi felt tears of grief and self-pity well into her eyes. She could barely get a breath. What made things unbearable was that at times she fancied she still heard accusation in Granny's voice whenever she talked of the tragic wreck. Presently, Minna saw the look on Tammi's face and said, "I've got something else I've been saving for you, hon." She hurried to a stack of magazines and picked out a tattered issue of *Glamour*. "There's a fabulous article in here called 'Enhancing Your Natural Beauty.' "

Tammi had glanced through women's magazines in the drugstore downtown, but Granny never let her buy them. She was constantly tantalized by their glossy covers peeking out from other girls'
lockers at Rigby High, and she clutched this one to her chest and
looked at Minna wordlessly. She could hardly believe this day. Her
heart felt too big for her chest as she stammered a "Thank you,
Minna," and hurried out of the house.

CHAPTER 12

O n the first day of summer vacation Tammi was out of bed before daylight, stumbling down the dark hallway to the bathroom to splash cold water on her face. Perching on the cool rim of the commode, she spied the outline of the moon through the sheers at the window. *Savage moon*, she thought, wondering what the day would hold, how long her chores would take, and when she could sneak away to read. LaDonna had passed the romance novel off to Tammi on the last day of school, and she had spent the bus trip home devouring the words. The back cover claimed that it was irresistible, which was true. The plot involved a tribe of Indians who were one with the land. They were one with the river, the trees, and the sky; a people so natural and unashamed of sensual pleasures, they swam in the river nude, water gliding over their tawny limbs.

Tammi pulled a hairbrush though her hair, fastening it at the nape of her neck with a rubber band. Her hair was a long, silky mane, like Nekoosa's, the heroine of *Savage Moon*. Nekoosa's lips constantly swelled with passion, and they resembled the centers of orchids after she kissed Running Bear, a brave with thighs firm as the trunk of a chestnut tree.

Savage Moon left Tammi burning hot, and she thought of Leon, wondering what it would be like to swim naked with him in the river, to feel the primitive pulse of his body against hers as she kissed him underneath the stars.

Kisses led to other things, she knew, and figuring out what the "promised peak of glory" was remained somewhat of a mystery. *Savage Moon* spoke of two lovers engaged in a raw, primitive rhythm that led to waves of climactic release. She'd read enough to know that sparks didn't always fly when a man and woman got together. Sometimes they felt like they were kissing rubber tires. Sometimes sparks flew in only one of the people. But sometimes, and this was the goal, they were both thrust into the giddy whirlpool of desire, dancing on the knife edge of anticipation.

This was a feeling so potent it held the raw power that drove the man to pull the woman into the cradle of his thighs, where she felt the full power of his arousal. Tammi wondered at this as well, and sometimes she felt like she was turning a little crazy. Practicing kisses on the mirror, her pillow, and in her imagination were only frustrating her more. The big house buzzed steadily in a flurry of preparation for the family reunion. This was no surprise. Every summer Granny went spinning into a tizzy for days as she coordinated things, spending hours on the phone telling relatives what to bring so that they wouldn't end up with ten coconut cakes and a dozen Pyrex bowls full of baked beans. When she wasn't fretting over who was and who wasn't coming and what they were bringing, she spent her time arranging things in the newly furnished bedrooms waiting for Nanette and Leon.

The morning of the reunion, Tammi's job was to fetch four flat stones from the creek, one for each of the corners of the big daisy-print sheet Granny had shaken out and floated down onto the rusty old flatbed farm wagon.

Only Granny would spread out reunion victuals on the back of a flatbed. Practical. When the sun shifted, all she had to do was get Pepaw to drive over to some new shade. Not too bad, considering the chopping, peeling, stewing, and baking that had been going on in the kitchen for two whole days.

Tammi tiptoed barefoot down the hallway. She'd been trying to stay out of sight since she'd changed into the tight shorts she and Minna had purchased in a secret shopping trip several weeks back. Granny's ears were like antennae. "Tammi Lynn?"

"Ma'am?" Tammi halted.

"I imagine you need something to keep you busy."

Resigned and wary, Tammi said, "Yes, ma'am," staring at the old ramrod back standing in front of the stove, willing Granny's eyes to remain on the tea bags boiling.

"Run put out the Chinets and Dixie cups," Granny said.

Tammi hurried into the pantry off the screened porch and pulled the screaky old door to. She stood in the musty grayness, gulping in relief as she gathered plates and cups to carry out to the flatbed.

She was hopeful to escape Granny's scrutiny today, encouraged by the way Granny'd been more than lenient since she'd begun dressing differently. Once, a Wednesday afternoon, Tammi stood anxiously on the landing, wearing a pair of snug white painter's pants and a flesh-colored clingy top, wobbling on a pair of platform sandals. "Woo hoo," Granny had called. "Time for Promiseland. What are you doing standing up there?"

Tammi had been waiting for Granny to squawk in horror and demand that she change, but Granny said, "You look lovely, now come along."

With a smile on her face at this recollection, Tammi slipped outside with her arms full of plates and cups. She carried them over and set them on the flatbed, then hurried across the yard away from Granny's scrutiny. Already over 100 degrees, the air was downright sweltering, laced with the smell of the hog pen and the chickens. Little beads of sweat glistened on her collarbone as she headed to Viking Creek. Wading out into the trickle of tepid water until she was between thick honeysuckle vines, she tensed her muscles and ran her hands down her thighs. Lean as a little filly, she thought, recalling a line from *Texas Toast*. Thoughts of Leon's imminent arrival sent a shivery pleasure through her as she heard a car door slam, and then another and another, high voices of greeting carrying through the pines.

Heart beating in anticipation, Tammi made her way back. Folks were arriving fast, and soon the yard was full and the flatbed was groaning under all the food. Tammi was wondering why Granny wasn't out directing everyone when she heard a surprised gasp from the driveway, and the crowds of relatives began to push in that direction. Picking her way up to the edge of the grass, she saw a low-slung black car with dark windows pulling up the drive. It circled the mailbox and came to a stop beside the birdbath.

Tammi heard one of the real hick cousins say, "Shee-ut. Would you look at that? It's one of them Jaguars. Foreign." The way he said "foreign," it sounded like "fern." She stretched her neck with everybody else and waited while the car hood gently shimmied and then was still. A long gleaming door swung open and out stepped Granny into the blinding sunlight.

Was this a dream? Tammi saw Granny fiddling in her giant handbag for something. She pulled out a red foil bow that Tammi recognized as being left over from the mailbox at Christmas. She stuck it on the windshield. Then her old wavery voice began belting out "Happy birthday to you. Happy birthday to you. Happy birthday, dear Leon, happy birthday to you."

Somebody pushed a blushing, modest Leon out of the throng up toward Granny, who embraced his stiff figure, burying her head in his chest.

Tammi's mouth hung open as she watched Granny usher Leon into the driver's seat. Finally Minna squealed and galloped over to the car. "Eighteen years old!" she gushed, bending over into the car to hug Leon. He looked down at his lap and mumbled something.

"Come on out of there, Minna Lee." Granny yanked Minna's sleeve. "Let Leon take it for a drive."

Tammi watched several of the menfolk close in, stroking the car's fenders, talking in low tones among themselves. She didn't move until the tail end of the Jaguar disappeared behind the big house, then she crept out from the trees and crossed the yard to the flatbed for some iced tea. In a daze she watched the little kids snatching potato chips and pickles, chasing each other. Flies were settling on the desserts, and several of the women waved them away, draping the platters with opened-up paper napkins.

The ice was melting in Tammi's cup as she stood there listening to the *chink, chink* of a horseshoe game and dreaming of riding in that sexy black car with Leon. There was some ulterior purpose in Leon's moving into the big house, there had to be. Like the Reverend Goodlow said, he didn't believe in luck. He never let himself say "good luck" to folks because luck had nothing to do with it. The Lord God in heaven orchestrated each facet of life, down to the minutest detail.

Aunt Onzelle tapped Tammi's shoulder and said, "Better get some of that good Jell-O salad down there. It won't last long out here in this heat." Tammi only glanced at the quivering red dome with sliced bananas like eyeballs marching around its perimeter. She paused briefly near the great-aunts to listen in on a conversation about broken hips and pound cakes, then returned to station herself against a pine in the makeshift parking lot.

At last the Jaguar crept back up the drive, and Tammi fixed her eyes on the driver's door. When Leon emerged she moved toward him, walking like Tatiana in *Island Pulse,* undulating her hips provocatively. "Hello, Leon," she purred. "How're you?"

"Fine," he answered. "Yourself?"

She giggled at his properness. "Fine. Bet that's a fast car."

"I don't know," Leon said, looking off into the distance.

"You want something to eat? Let's go get our plates." Tammi led him along to the flatbed like the lady of the manor. They were quiet for a spell as they stood in line, and then Tammi said, "I really can't believe she gave you that car."

Leon appeared to stop breathing.

"You've seen her ancient Cadillac!" Tammi said quickly, seeing his crestfallen face. "Bet she'll have you driving her all over the place in your Jaguar."

"Fine." Leon rubbed his chin.

"Want some barbecue?" Tammi playfully held a spoon of stringy pork aloft. Leon didn't resist, so she heaped it onto his plate, ladling red-hot sauce onto it. She also filled one of the Chinet's compartments with the runny Jell-O salad, the other with green beans that had bits of salt pork floating on top.

"Let's sit in the shade," she said.

Leon followed her to a bedspread with pinkish white splotches of bleach stain on it. He waited till she was seated, then settled himself, tucking his napkin into the neck of his shirt.

Tammi nibbled an ear of sweet corn, watching Leon from the corner of her eye. After a bit she noticed that he had a red-brown smudge of barbecue sauce on his right cheek, near his gorgeous lips. A blot of imperfection that mesmerized her. She dipped a finger into her iced tea, leaned forward, and rubbed the spot.

He flinched as their skin met.

Tammi gasped in the awkward moment. She certainly was no brazen hussy like Clemmie in *Texas Toast*. Clemmie would have licked it off him. She looked down at her finger. It pulsed with the memory of Leon. She put the finger into her mouth, tasting vinegar from the barbecue sauce.

"You had some sauce on you," she said.

"I did?" His hands were trembling, and she decided he'd felt it, too. He went on with his meal, carefully swiping his napkin across his mouth after each bite.

Orr came loping toward them, waving two plastic spoons. "Leon!" he said, sweat running down his grimy temples. "Wanna make tunnels at the creek with me?"

Leon stood and yanked the napkin from his neck, dropping it onto his plate. He wasn't through with his food, and Tammi looked up to find his eyes, but he kept them trained on Orr as he answered. "Yeah, sure. Let's go, buddy."

When they were out of sight Tammi picked up Leon's tea and put her lips on the rim, her heart racing like Nekoosa's in *Savage Moon* so that she lost interest in her food. After a moment she stood up and surveyed the reunion. Everyone was hunkered down over their plates like there wasn't a thing in this world more important than how much they could consume. Tammi sighed, walked over to the flatbed, and rested her elbows on it near the desserts. A whole swarm of yellow jackets had settled onto a coconut cake.

They ate fiercely, twitching their tiny wings, shuddering in delight. *This is their heaven,* Tammi thought. *They'll never be any happier than they are right this moment. These creatures are pure pleasure seekers, drowning in ecstasy. They know what they want out of life, and they go headlong after it!*

Tammi didn't realize she was heading down the path beyond the big house until Priscilla bounded up to nudge her hand.

At the sandbank on the part of the creek closest to Orr's house, she spotted the shiny dome of Orr's head and ran blindly through poison ivy. He looked up from his squatting position next to Leon. "Hi, Tammi." His eyes were bright.

"Having fun?" she asked.

Orr nodded emphatically. "You can play, too." He scooted over while squatting, like a big crab, handing Tammi a stick. "Dig."

Tammi scratched in the dry sand awhile, drinking in Leon's shape from the corner of her eye. She gathered a half-dozen little twigs for a tiny fence. "Want some dessert, Orry?" she asked, her heart hammering in her throat.

He shook his head and kept digging.

"Pepaw's making your favorite," she urged. "He's making peach ice cream, and it was almost ready when I ran down here."

Orr grunted as his spoon struck a root.

"Won't you be a sweetheart and go get us some of that cold peach ice cream, Orry? Please? I'll let you have one of my Archie comics."

Now Orr looked up at her and cocked his head slightly. He smoothed a mound of dirt at his knee.

"It's that Veronica one you love," Tammi sang, patting his damp forearm. "Pretty please? I'm so hot."

Leon spurted upward into what looked like a sprinter's starting position, saying, "I'll go."

For a moment Tammi was shocked into motionlessness. What would Nekoosa do? Nekoosa was bold, and she didn't pussyfoot around. Tammi felt the power of knowledge oozing out of her brain, seeping down into her tongue as she ordered, "No! You stay here, Leon! I want Orry to go because he wants the Archie."

Orr took off then, and Leon sank back down on his heels, staring into the woods, his face closed and still. Tammi shuffled on her knees through the sand so that she was face-to-face with him. She lifted her chin and smiled brazenly. "Well," she said, her pulse beating fiercely in her neck, her wrists, and between her breasts, "I guess we'll be seeing a lot of each other with you living here and all." She gathered her hair up off her shoulders and held it high in a ponytail that she hoped was alluring.

He raised his eyebrows. "Guess so."

"Mind if I kiss you?" she said in one breath, and it was just like she *was* Nekoosa as she rocked forward onto her knees, covering his mouth with her pulsing lips. After a split second he pulled away, his mouth hanging open in an unbecoming fashion.

"That was my first kiss ever!" she breathed, squinching her eyes shut and hugging herself. "Did it make your loins ache?"

Leon wouldn't say a word. The men in the romance novels admitted undying passion after something like that. He really did like it, though. She knew because she'd heard a moan in his throat as they kissed. Tammi pondered this, and in the next moment a feeling came over her that she could only name from reading about it: all-consuming. She sprang forward again, like a jungle cat, this time to flicker her tongue in a glistening patch of sweat at the hollow of Leon's throat, squeezing his shoulders with her trembling fingertips.

Leon remained loose and rubbery until her mouth traveled up his neck, across his cheek, and she took the fleshy lobe of his ear between her teeth, biting gently. She began to flick the tip of her tongue in and out of his ear, and this was when his breathing quickened and he pulled back to meet her eyes for one brief moment before greedily pressing his lips on hers and flinging her backward onto the hot creek bank. She felt herself beginning to melt, turning to fire! To hot liquid fire that burned in that deepest part of her. Was this what Nekoosa had meant by wild, abandoned passion?

Now Leon was going crazy, making grunting sounds and drawing her lower lip between his teeth as he struggled to get even closer to her. "I want you sooo bad," she whimpered up through the canopy of sweet gum limbs. Still clumsily groping and pulsing, Leon managed somehow to remove his shirt and was fumbling with her blouse when there was a rustle and they jerked apart to watch Orr loping toward them, balancing three Styrofoam cups on his palms. In one motion Leon yanked his hand away from Tammi, grabbed his shirt, and held it over his chest. Tammi pushed a damp strand of hair off her face. "Hi, Orry," she said through her swollen lips.

"Hi," Orr said, setting down three cups of melted slush. "You two have the urgent ache of desire like Clemmie and Bart."

All the color was gone from Leon's face, his dark eyes staring vacantly in Orr's direction.

"Eat your ice cream, Orry," Tammi said finally. "You won't tell a soul, will you?"

Orr didn't answer. He slowly meandered out into the dry gully of Viking Creek, slurping peach ice cream. Tammi tiptoed after him. "Please don't tell a soul," she pled.

When she turned around, Leon was gone.

Orr followed Tammi back up to the big house while she relived the kiss over and over. She was tickly inside, and it felt like her feet weren't connecting to the earth. That kiss had just set her free from the dull, passionless first fifteen years of her life, and it was like a silvery thread that connected her to the novels.

CHAPTER 13

Each time she relived the kiss, Tammi felt that dull pulsing ache she couldn't quite put into words. She made her way over to Minna's house after the reunion feast had been cleaned up.

"You look absolutely radiant, darlin'!" Minna exclaimed, opening the door and throwing up her plump white arms.

Tammi grinned. "I'm glad Leon's here."

"He surely is gorgeous," mused Minna. "Looks like one of them Greek gods. He could easily be a movie star. Want a Fresca?"

"Sure," Tammi said. "Wasn't it nice of Granny to buy him the car?"

"Mama's so excited she's about to bust into pieces." Minna popped open two cans, handed one to Tammi, and sank down on the sofa beside her. "She thinks Leon hung the moon."

Tammi's heart did a little flip-flop in her chest. A long minute passed and she looked up at the white marble mantel, to a picture of Minna and Franklin, their arms around each other, standing in front of Niagara Falls on their honeymoon. Minna was skinny then, and you could tell she was happy by the way she was smiling.

"When you kissed Franklin, did your very core leap up like a burning flame?" Tammi asked tentatively.

"Ha!" Minna began to laugh. She hugged herself and her chins shook while she really let it all out. "Ha ha ha!"

Tammi narrowed her eyes, looking hard at Minna. "What's so funny?"

Minna drew a calming breath and patted Tammi's cheek. "I'm sorry, hon. Your choice of words just got me tickled."

Tammi wanted to tell Minna about the kiss with Leon, and the way she felt inside whenever she thought about it, but first she had to make some sense out of it all. "Well, that's what they say in the romance novels, and I just wondered," she said, "if that's how it was with Franklin. His kisses and all."

"Not really. Franklin adored me, and I think I just wanted to get married and play house." Minna sighed. "Mainly get out from under Mama's finger. Anyhow, hon . . . " Minna's eyeballs went up and to the left to allow her to think. "One night when we'd been courting awhile, Franklin brought his guitar over and we set out under the moonlight, up on the hill overlooking the peach trees, and he sang, 'I can't help falling in love with you.' "

"Oh. So you fell in love then?"

"No. He sounded just like Elvis."

"That's why you married him?"

"One reason."

"But when y'all kissed," said Tammi, "weren't you tremulous? The furnace of passion consuming you both?"

Minna clamped a hand over her mouth as she began giggling again. "A flame leaping up! That kills me! Say that first thing you said again, hon."

Tammi did not reply. Angry with Minna, she rose to head outside. She wanted to erase this whole conversation.

"Come back, sugar," Minna called in an "I'm sorry" kind of tone Tammi couldn't ignore. She made her way back over to the sofa, and

Minna grabbed her wrist to pull her down beside her. "I don't remember any such flames of passion." She scowled seriously. "Franklin was good to me. God rest his soul."

Tammi nodded like she understood, rose, and walked out the sliding glass doors. Gazing at Minna's kidney-shaped pool, she noted clouds reflected in the water. She looked up and could tell from the undertint of purple in the sky that fall wasn't far off. Things were constantly changing. Maybe Minna'd changed so much, from the skinny bride living on the nectar of love to this plump person who took pills to keep herself happy, that she'd forgotten all about the fire in her loins.

Tammi got no more private moments with Leon that day as he was busy unpacking and settling in. She lay down to sleep that night, conjuring up an image from *Texas Toast:* Clemmie with every cell of her body alive, riding a sweaty horse, brambles catching on her silken gown as she struggled through the forest to wrap her body around the raw potent force of Bart, covering his mouth with hers. She knew how to live! Tammi sighed. These images were what had carried her through spring and the long summer. She couldn't wait for book club tomorrow. She would tell them about her kiss. She felt she'd burst if she kept it inside a second longer.

A new day dawned and slowly became one of those Deep South afternoons when the sun sank its fierce rays down to earth and scorched the few gardenias at the big house. The air was so heavy with heat that everyone had become a little bit cranky. Even Parks seemed dispirited, her shoulders slumped and her hair hanging lank in her eyes as she entered Minna's den for the book club meeting. "Howdy," she said in a voice as limp as her posture, frowning at the thick cushioned sofa in the den and making her way to a chair at the dinette in the kitchen.

Everyone followed her lead, and Minna twisted ice trays into a silver bucket for the Pepsi LaDonna set on the table. "I made Chex Mix," LaDonna said, popping the lid off a lettuce-green Tupperware bowl.

"Yum," Minna said. "I love Chex Mix."

"I loved our last reading selection," Parks said, scooping up a heaping palmful of Chex Mix. "My favorite part, I believe I read it six times, is when Nekoosa's sister falls helplessly in love with the paleface and puts the move on—"

"Wait a minute, Parks," Tammi said breathily. "I've got some news I want to share before we commence." She closed her eyes, sighing out the words "I'm in love."

They all stared at Tammi as her words spilled out all over themselves. ". . . and it's better than I imagined it could be," she finished. "I promise you, he's my one true love! My passionate flame, my Bart, my Running Bear. My everything."

At last LaDonna touched Tammi's wrist gently. "Who is it?"

"Minna knows him," Tammi said. "My cousin Leon."

Parks laughed, slapped her thigh.

"Not my *blood* cousin," Tammi added quickly. "My stepfather and his mother are brother and sister. *Were* brother and sister."

"Well, this is sure something," LaDonna said questioningly.

"We kissed at the reunion yesterday," Tammi added. "It was incredible."

They all grew silent for a while, sipping Pepsi, munching Chex Mix, until Minna said, "We shall see, I suppose, how this romance goes. Granny'll have herself a cow if she ever gets wind of things."

Fear flooded Tammi. "Don't tell!" she cried, on the verge of tears. "Don't say a word to anyone!"

"Maybe you should think things through some more," LaDonna said cautiously. "Give it some time."

"It's meant to be!" Tammi said in desperation. "Smoldering passion. You cannot know until you experience it for yourself."

"Just be careful, dear," Minna said. "I don't want you getting hurt. Things could get ugly with everyone under the same roof." She drew a breath before picking up the thread of conversation from Parks's earlier comment. "Yes, I found that a real exciting and spicy scene, but I thought Nekoosa's sister's betrayal with Smith was disturbing. Even though she *claims* it's the real, forever kind of love."

"Yeah," LaDonna said. "If she were my sister and the little bimbo was letting some silly crush get in the way of our inheritance, I believe I'd have to fling her in the river."

Tammi cocked her head and stared at LaDonna. Wasn't passion worth more than any stupid piece of land? *Face it,* she thought, *LaDonna has no concept whatsoever of passion. She really doesn't. She's the only one in the group who's never kissed a man.* Maybe Tammi could convince LaDonna of the importance of passion. "Let's go ahead and talk about how to kiss," Tammi said hopefully. "I found that actually experiencing a kiss in real life is *tons* better than reading about one! For me, it was just incredible, the exquisite waves of longing sweeping through my body!" She glanced at LaDonna, who only wrinkled her forehead. "There's not even words in the English language to describe it," Tammi continued, her voice crescendoing. "Let's see . . . I was riding the sweet roller coaster of desire, possessed by a wantonness so deep it threatened to overwhelm me."

"Sounds like a fabulous first kiss, darlin'." Minna smiled indulgently as she nibbled a Wheat Chex. "My first kiss was terrible. Billy Campbell. He had these blubbery lips and bad breath, and he smashed his smelly mouth onto mine, poking his tongue in and out of my mouth, so . . . industrially, I guess you'd say. I was in seventh grade, and it totally grossed me out." Minna shook her head. "Thank goodness my second kiss was better. It was with Jackson Goodard, eighth grade. Now, he was good! Had his lips all soft and pliant, yet firm. Wet them just right, tilted his head, and made soft, moaning sounds. He was tender, yet greedy, if you get my drift . . . "

There was a long silence as Tammi mused on her encounter with Leon. The memory of their kiss had taken on a life of its own, become idyllic, almost like a glossy movie scene where she'd edited out all that was not perfect. She chose not to remember their noses smashing into each other or the jarring scent of barbecue on Leon's breath, or the way his fumbling fingers had groped her own. She wouldn't trade that kiss for anything.

Parks lit up a cigarette, slugged down the last dregs of her Pepsi, leaned back, and smiled. "My first kiss was in the backseat of Tucker Howington's dad's Buick," she said languidly. "It was on a dare when I was in sixth grade. I had to kiss three boys in the neighborhood to see who was the best kisser."

LaDonna gasped.

"Who won?" Tammi asked.

"Well, let's see . . . I believe I ranked them this a way: Jack Howington, Lloyd Wiggins, and Tucker Howington."

"You kissed Jack Howington?!" LaDonna cried. "He had to have been in college when you were in sixth grade!"

"Yeah, he was." Tammi could hear the smirk in Parks's voice. "That's why he won, I reckon. Practice makes perfect."

"He was nineteen and you were, what? Eleven!" LaDonna was scandalized. "That nasty boy!"

"Well, I better hush," Parks said, standing up. "I don't want to upset Miss Goody Two-Shoes here. Guess we got to be heading on home."

"Wait!" Tammi cried. "We've got to say our pledge. And then it's LaDonna's turn to choose next meeting's discussion topic." She jumped to her feet and lifted her Pepsi can. "All for fun and fun for all!" she heard herself say, Minna and Parks chanting along with her. But LaDonna looked away, her arms crossed over her flat chest.

"Read chapters 16 through 30," Tammi said, putting *Savage Moon* into Parks's hands, shooting LaDonna a desperate look.

"Okay, I'll choose us a topic," LaDonna said, crossing her arms. "'How to Tell If It's Love or Lust.' No, wait. 'How to Tell If He's Really the One.'" She looked pointedly at Tammi.

CHAPTER 14

Tammi ached for another moment alone with Leon. She'd seen him only at mealtimes since the reunion. Whenever she went hunting for him, he seemed to have disappeared. "It's just taking a bit for my boy to settle in," Aunt Nanette said after five days had passed and Tammi accosted her. "He's got to get his feel of the place, plus he's a very private person." That afternoon he went off somewhere in the Jaguar, then shut himself away in his new bedroom for hours on end. Tammi could not understand his reticence when it came to their smoldering passion, and late that evening she sat cross-legged on her bed, poring over the article on "Enhancing Your Natural Beauty" in *Glamour* magazine and determining to approach him the next morning, make plans with him before he had a chance to get away.

She was determined to be stunning and irresistible when Leon came downstairs for breakfast. Developing your full beauty potential took a good bit of work, especially when you had to do it in secret around somebody like Granny, who didn't believe in outside adornment, as she called it. To get a pouty and kissable mouth, you smeared a shiny coat of Vaseline all over your lips, then a touch of white undereye concealer (Tammi used Pepsodent) on the center of your lower lip. She wanted her succulent lips to draw Leon at first glance, wanted him to blindly reach for her, to feel the sweet slide of flesh against flesh, quivering loins . . .

"I've been living every moment till you got here," she would whisper as she leaned across the breakfast table, her words a throaty purr against his racing pulse. "Me too," he would say into the hollow place at her throat.

But Leon slept in, and by nine the Vaseline began to suffocate Tammi's lips. Wanly she slathered Pond's cold cream on her hands and slid them into rubber gloves to wash the breakfast dishes. "Enhancing Your Natural Beauty" said the hot water acted like a spa to make your hands supple while you scrubbed.

Just as she was washing the last fork, Leon entered the kitchen and, simultaneously, thunder rumbled like a sonic boom.

"I can't believe this, Leon!" Tammi murmured in awe. "Looks like you might have brought some rain with you. You can't possibly know what a miracle that would be." She turned to him and licked her lips seductively, tasting Pepsodent. "Want to go into town a little later with me and check out the new pizza place?"

"Sure." Leon's voice was husky and low like the ominous clouds hanging in the sky, and Tammi felt her breath catch in her throat at the euphoric tremor of anticipation rippling through her body.

The clouds were still only threatening that evening as Tammi listened to Granny's high excited voice in the front parlor. She'd been talking to Leon literally all day. Supper was over now, and she was saying, "We'll get us some Persian rugs, angel. They sell like anything."

It was after eight when Granny finally excused herself to head to her room at the back of the house. Tammi was waiting outside in the muggy twilight, watching the gray sky and willing the rain to come on down.

The clouds gave the evening an otherworldly feel as she and Leon slipped down the long drive in the noiseless Jaguar. They did not speak, and when they reached the Big Star shopping center, Tammi merely pointed out the red awning of the Mad Italian fluttering in a corner next to Rigby Drugs. Leon pulled into a parking space directly in front, cut the engine, and rolled the windows down, sighing as he drew in a deep breath of evening air mixed with the tantalizing aroma of warm bread. Tammi felt an intense, heart-stopping sensation that seemed to have its genesis in nothing at all but the musk of unconscious sensuality coming from Leon.

There were a few scattered cars in the lot, and Tammi wondered if anyone from Rigby High was eating pizza beyond the glass front of the Mad Italian. It was impossible not to smile when she thought of them looking at her sitting next to this gorgeous stranger in the low, shiny car.

"What was Granny going on about so long today?" she said at last, looking sideways at Leon.

"An antique auction."

"Why's she talking to you about *that*?"

He shrugged and Tammi frowned. Elco Antiques was more or less a mystery to her, a crumbling brick building in the middle of downtown, between RadioShack and Merle's Beauty Nook, crammed full of dark furniture and mountains of china.

A light sprinkle began to fall. Inspired, Tammi opened her door and flung herself out into the parking lot. The blacktop was hissing from the rain, and she was like a person who didn't quite know what to think or do. She turned her face heavenward, opening her mouth to taste the rain, spinning around and laughing.

Leon eased out of the car and came toward her. Did she look alluring out here, all wet in her clingy shirt, with rain drenched lips? *Here it is, the moment I've been living for*, she thought, grabbing his slim-fingered hands and pulling him off the parking lot, up on the walkway of the Mad Italian.

Desire made Tammi tremble. "I've been living for this moment, Leon," she breathed. "I couldn't wait for you to get here."

Leon pushed a black wing of hair out of his eyes. Tammi had the feeling he was stalling for time, choosing his words carefully. "Wholesome," he said finally. "All the fresh air and the plowing and gathering eggs. Eating from the garden." He looked so vulnerable, like a little kid waiting for a doctor.

"Well . . ." she said, thrown off-kilter for a moment as she realized he was gushing about Rigby. "It's really not as wonderful as you make it sound. For one thing, it's boring. Chores running out your ears and the nearest neighbor a mile away. And to get to town! Didn't you realize it took us fifteen minutes to get here?"

"I don't mind a little peace and quiet in the country."

"Well, when I get my diploma I'm getting the heck out of Dodge."

Tammi saw Leon trying to hide a smile. "Where are you going to go?"

"I want to live in a big city! With lots of shops, restaurants, and people all around."

"I lived in a city in Nevada," he said. "It wasn't that great."

Tammi was surprised at how sad he sounded. "I'd love it! Were there lots of places open late, with lights and neon signs?"

"Lots of nightclubs and adult bookstores, if that's what you mean." He shook his head. "We haven't seen Daddy for three months."

Leon was visibly upset now, and this put an uneasy feeling in Tammi's stomach. What she would have to do was relax him. "Hey!" she said quickly. "Let's get ice cream!"

Leon looked surprised. "You don't want pizza?"

"Nah. I want something *sweet*," she said in a teasing voice as they climbed back into the Jaguar. Her head snapped forward and back again as Leon shifted gears and sped down Shapiro Avenue. She stared at the muscles in his forearm, flexed and tense beneath honey-brown skin as he turned on the radio, listening to a serious announcer talk about the FBI finding Patty Hearst in California.

"Here we are," she said when they were in sight of the Tastee Freez, the only other place in Rigby open at this late hour. The lot was empty except for what Tammi knew to be the manager's Pinto in the rear. A nice private opportunity. "Let's eat out here in the car," she said pleadingly. "I'll be real careful. Cross my heart." She drew an *X* across her chest, thinking of the way Clemmie would run her tongue across her lips when she wanted to seduce Bart.

Now desire felt like a greedy, self-propelled hunger, insisting on being satisfied. There was that warm buzz in Tammi's brain and tiny electric impulses going *ping!* throughout her body. She was desperate to kiss Leon again, but she wasn't sure how to lead into their next passionate encounter. Shouldn't she wait for the right moment? When was the right moment?

Leon turned off the engine. "What kind of ice cream do you want?" he asked.

She knew what she wanted, but to keep his attention, she stalled, tilting her head coquettishly, saying, "Let me see . . ." through pouty lips, purring out finally, "a butterscotch-dipped cone, please."

Tammi watched Leon's loose-kneed, sexy walk take him to the counter, then she freshened her lip gloss, bending forward to volumize her hair. She wished she could talk to Tatiana or Clemmie or Nekoosa, ask them for advice on getting what she wanted from this man.

The smell of greasy fries wafted into the car with Leon. He presented a cone to Tammi, and she looked deep into his eyes as she bent forward to lick the thin butterscotch shell with the faintest hope that he'd just forget the ice cream, fling her over backward, and have his way with her.

She couldn't believe how easy her novels made this passion thing seem, at least after that first kiss when the sparks flew. You could count on the man to have this huge appetite and crave the woman so badly that whenever the opportunity arose, they were at it again. And here was the perfect opportunity! An empty parking lot, two hungry, beating hearts.

She wished he'd say something. "I sure wish this rain would come on and let go," she ventured at last. "All those clouds and only that little bitty sprinkle. Bet Pepaw's out on the porch right now, praying it'll just go on and pour down. He's thought about irrigation, you know. But Granny won't let him spend the money. Uncle Carson said it would pay for itself in only two seasons. It's like investing money, he said. He couldn't believe she sprang for this car, seeing as how tight she is. It cost way more than irrigation. I heard them fighting over it, but Granny said *somebody's* got to . . ." Tammi saw Leon's stricken face and caught herself just in time. She bent down to lick ice cream drips oozing out from underneath the butterscotch cap.

Leon stopped licking his cone and jerked his head up to look out the windshield at a myriad of twinkling stars in the clear sky above the roof of the Tastee Freez. At last he sighed, turned to Tammi, and said brusquely, "You done?" as he tossed the rest of his ice cream out the window onto the steaming asphalt and cranked the Jaguar.

"Not really," Tammi whispered, her glistening shell of happiness bursting. She sat numbly, holding her soggy cone until they reached home. It hurt even to breathe.

CHAPTER 15

The next evening, Tammi heard voices coming from the walk-up attic. She climbed to the top of the narrow staircase to hover soundlessly in the shadows. Leon sat on the end of a tall shipping crate, his dark head drooping as he looked at something laid across his lap. Granny's shadow was long and razor-sharp in the light of a 40-watt bulb hanging from the rafter. She was yanking things out of a trunk, talking a mile a minute.

"Take these crocheted placemats, Leon," she said. "I made them way back when your mother was in grade school. Made them for her hope chest." Granny breezed past Leon to drape the ivory colored rectangle on top of a hamper. "Guess all hope is lost now, hm?" She snorted loudly and Tammi saw Leon draw in a little. "Her running off, eloping with that devil, Finch, I'll tell you what, I *still* haven't forgiven her for that. But, you know, now I can see that she's always been what Minna likes to call 'carefree.' So I reckon I ought not to be too surprised that y'all took off for Rigby without packing up your school supplies." She put a hand on Leon's shoulder. "But don't worry. There's bound to be something up here that'll do as a book bag for you when school commences. Maybe one of Carson's old army backpacks."

"Great," Leon said, still looking down at his lap.

There was a long, deep silence, then Granny started in again. "Why, I knew way back then that your daddy wouldn't ever amount to anything. Lazy. Mmm mmm mmm." She shook her head vigorously. "What I hope is that when the judgment comes, we all get to listen in on everybody else's, because I'd love more than anything to be there when the good Lord judges Finch Dupree!" Granny crossed her arms. "Mark my words, Finch is going to get his just reward."

For the longest time Tammi stood watching while Leon sat there like a squashed bug. At last she slunk back downstairs and outside to crouch underneath the magnolia, where insects sang loudly in the nearby thicket. She wondered why Leon wasn't standing up for his father. Did he agree with Granny? Surely not. That was his very own flesh and blood she was running through the mud. But then, where was Leon's gumption if he didn't? Fury sprang into Tammi's heart. Was Granny even listening when the Reverend Goodlow preached on the idea of "Judge not and ye shall not be judged"? Probably she figured she was above falling. But wasn't that what being a hypocrite was? Pepaw, on the other hand, never judged folks. He even made allowances for Granny, raising his eyebrows slightly and saying things like, "Well, you just never can know what a particular person's been through in their life that's made them what they are, gal. There's this thing called grace that the good Lord uses when He looks down here at us. Without grace every last one of us would fry."

The minutes stretched into an hour, and soon gray dusk was falling, with long Orange Crush–colored rays of sun tickling the horizon. Tammi's feet, wedged beneath her knees as she sat cross-legged, had fallen asleep, but she didn't switch positions for fear of breaking her concentration. Later—much later it seemed—she saw Leon coming out the back door and down the steps, dragging his feet slowly, his hands shoved deep in his trouser pockets. He walked across the stone patio in a straight line, out to the shed, where he climbed into his Jaguar and sat behind the wheel with the door open.

Tammi held on to the magnolia's trunk and pulled herself up. She stamped her feet to wake them and strode out to the shed. "Leon?" she called, bending down and knocking on the passenger window. "Can I get in?"

"I guess so."

She climbed in, crossing her legs and turning her body so that she faced Leon in the murky darkness.

"Did you want something?" he asked after a spell.

There seemed to be no words to lead with, without revealing that she'd been spying. She looked up, felt him waiting for her to go on. "Do you ever think about the fact that if you feel good about not feeling proud, then you're proud?" she said finally.

"What?"

"Just something I've been thinking about. Got my brain all in a twist, if you know what I mean."

"Yeah." He frowned and picked at a thread on his shirtsleeve.

"Well, I've been going round and round with it, wondering." She cocked her head and looked at him seriously. "I guess that would constitute being a hypocrite, huh? Some people are hypocrites . . . you know, they may *say* something negative about somebody, but they're not perfect themselves?"

"Beg your pardon?" he said.

"What I mean is, no one's perfect."

"Right." Leon ran his hands aimlessly around the steering wheel.

What now? Tammi thought that if she could get a bead on Leon's feelings about his father, she could ease into what she actually wanted him to acknowledge, which was what a hypocrite Granny was. She took a breath and sat up straighter. "So, what's going on with Uncle Finch?"

"Um . . ." Leon was hesitant. "I don't know. I guess I must be tired or something. Hard to think—" He twisted his hands between his knees.

"Take your time." Tammi made her voice pleasant. "I've got all night." She folded her hands in her lap.

Leon focused his eyes on some imaginary point in the dark recesses of the shed, and the silence between them spun out. "The summer I turned nine," he said at last, "I remember Daddy saying we needed a fallout shelter. It used to worry him to pieces that somebody might go and drop the A-bomb on us, and he said a shelter was the only thing that would save our lives. If we had a hole in the ground with a stash of canned food, jugs of water, a generator, and a radio . . . you know, he said we'd survive. Oh, and a gun. He said folks would fight you for your shelter if the A-Bomb got dropped. Survival instincts and all, you know?"

She nodded.

"I wanted him to be proud of me, so I decided I was going to dig this hole in the ground. Big enough for three people to hide in. So, while all the other kids were hanging out at the city pool and the Putt-Putt, I was out there in the backyard digging beside our clothes-line. I mean, I would literally dig, with this big stainless-steel serving spoon, from sunup to sundown. I hardly wanted to stop and eat a sandwich whenever Mama called me in." He paused to smile. "It really wasn't so odd to make a shelter, you understand. Some folks converted their basements, but we didn't have a basement.

"So I convinced myself I'd dig this cavern, and when the air sirens went off, I'd save our lives, and my father would shake my hand and say something like, 'Well done, son. You saved our lives. I love you.'

"I wanted him to love me so bad, and I thought if I saved his life he would *have* to love me. And it never crossed my mind that that was a sad way for a little kid to spend his summer. I didn't have any friends to speak of, anyway. I rarely invited anybody out to the house. It was too crazy around there. I always wished that he would act more like a dad, you know? That when he was at home he'd mow the grass, or throw the ball with me. Stuff regular dads did."

Leon tipped his head back against the headrest. "But he couldn't, Tammi, he just couldn't. When he was home, it was like part of him was still off somewhere else. He put the stereo on loud and mixed cocktails. He got up on the coffee table, in his boxer shorts sometimes, and sang along. He wanted his life to be like one gigantic party, lights and booze and music flowing. Should've been a movie star—he always had to be the center of attention. Adored.

"Anyway, when I told Daddy I was digging this fallout shelter, he got all happy. He said, 'That's a damn good thing to do, boy,' and he even put his arm around my shoulder. Squeezed me. I can still feel it where he squeezed me . . ." Leon's voice trailed off.

"What happened with your bomb shelter?" Tammi asked softly after a spell.

He turned to look at her. "Along about July, we got us a rainy spell. Rained for two solid weeks, but still I'd go outside and dig the shelter. Lightning didn't stop me. Thunder, either. Well, eventually, the thing sprang a couple of leaks, and water started pouring in. I'd scoop it out, trying my darndest to patch up the leaks with mud." Leon shrugged, sighed, let his head flop back against the headrest, and grew quiet.

"I bet that was hard on you," Tammi urged after a bit. But he would not continue. She listened to the even rhythm of his breathing in the darkness, and her heart hurt for him, but somehow this became eclipsed by a longing to mash herself against his body, and this led to a hot rush of shame, followed by fear that he would think her insensitive or sex-crazed! Tammi had such a mix of intense, flooding feelings that she clamped a hand to her mouth, but not before a strangled sob escaped.

Leon turned to her with a smile. "You've got a big heart, don't you?"

"Yep." Tammi breathed, barely able to look at his face.

The next morning, Saturday, Tammi stood beside Pepaw as he rested against the hay barn. He pulled a hankie from his pocket, shook it out, and wiped his forehead. "Shoo-wee," he said, "couldn't get any hotter, could it, gal?"

Tammi shook her head. "You don't know where Leon is, do you?"

"Your granny sent him into town," Pepaw said, frowning out across the dry pasture.

"What for?"

"Antique shop, I believe."

Tammi squinted through bright sunlight to the sound of the back door of the big house opening. Granny emerged with a basket of wet laundry. Tammi watched as she set the basket down, slapped a towel against her thigh, then clipped it to the line.

"She say when he'd be back?"

"Don't rightly know," Pepaw said. "Believe it was something to do with one of them fancy end tables. Yonder your granny is, why don't you ask her? She told me she was going to put Leon to work in the fine antiques business, that he has a good eye for it. Told me she wasn't going to let him get dirt under his nails."

"You wanted him to farm?"

"Yessiree." Pepaw nodded solemnly. "Was going to teach him a trade."

"You mean she's taking him over when *you* need him?" Tammi squeaked.

Pepaw closed his eyes and shook his head. "Ain't no arguing with your granny, child. Reckon Leon'll be working at the antique shop."

Leon under Granny's wing? Tammi felt the ground beneath her tremble a bit before it spun on. In her imagination she saw Leon and Granny bent conspiratorially over some old piece of furniture, Leon with a forelock of his jet-black hair hanging in his gorgeous face, an unsuspecting pupil of that practical and unpassionate woman!

It was unimaginable. He would never kiss Tammi again if he started being Granny's shadow. "I'm going to go talk to her," she said in a shaky voice. She sailed around the hog pen toward Granny thinking, *I've spent most of my life out here at the farm, with nothing but my imagination. I've never asked for much, never refused to do my chores, and now that I've got something to look forward to, you're taking it away!*

Tammi stopped and stood a distance from the clothesline, the purposefulness in her heart increasing until she could feel its shape. "Granny," she said, "I was wondering . . ."

"What, child?" The flesh on the backs of Granny's arms hung like withered flaps as she clipped up an apron. She spun around to look at Tammi.

"I want to know . . ." Tammi faltered. "What I wanted to know was . . . are you . . ."

"Spit it on out, child." Granny flipped a bony wrist in impatience. "I've got to finish up here and tend to the garden in time for my siesta."

Mention of the siesta irritated Tammi, and now she summoned up the words and met Granny's gaze a little defiantly and a lot fearfully. "I want to know," she said, willing the words out, "just what you mean by sending Leon off to your antique shop . . . and Pepaw needing all the extra hands on the farm he can get!"

Tammi's heart hung in her throat. She watched Granny frown as she shook the wrinkles from a wet apron. "Tammi Lynn," she said at last, "is it too much to ask to see a little *gratitude* around here? I work hard to keep this farm afloat!" She shook her head. "And for your information, Leon shows an interest in, and an aptitude for, antiques. Remember that *I* make the rules around here, and it's none of your business what I do or who I send where! You should be glad I house and feed and clothe you!"

Tammi stood mute, desperately at a loss for even any contradictory *thoughts*. Turning on her heel she ran down the dirt path to Viking Creek, slid out of her flip-flops, and plopped down onto the bank to flutter her toes in the trickle of water. She rested her chin in her palms and let the tears collect. She would collect her thoughts, too. She knew that Leon was very vulnerable right now and that Granny wasn't wasting a minute of it.

At the supper table, Leon was stationed between Granny and Pepaw. "Sprinkle didn't do us a bit of good, far as I could tell," Pepaw was saying. "We're hurting worse than ever. Now, if we had us one of those irrigation setups, we could handle this drought like kings."

Granny grimaced.

"I can tote water, Pepaw," Leon volunteered.

"Take a lot more'n folks toting water to help our corn, son."

Leon cleared his throat. "Look, I don't need the Jaguar. It's real nice, but I've got my bike."

"That car's an investment!" Granny called out suddenly. "We're dressed for success! Leon went out in the Jaguar today and got a candlestand worth a thousand for seventy-five! Old Worley doesn't like to part with his things. Not for that cheap! Did you tell him you were my grandson?"

Leon shook his head.

"We make a great team. I find them and send Leon out in the Jaguar to fetch them." Granny reached up to smooth Leon's collar with her fingertips.

Pepaw chuckled. "Seems to me you could've got it for *five* dollars if he'd shown up on my old mule."

"Melvin!" Granny hissed. "You're not up on the current psychology—takes money to make money."

"You're exactly right, Constance." Pepaw said. "That's my thought on the irrigation."

"Whose antique shop brings in the money when you go in the hole?" Granny raised stiff eyebrows almost to her hairline.

"Um." Leon squirmed and spoke to his plate. "If Daddy passes, Mama says we get fifty thousand dollars of insurance money. We can use it to pay for irrigation."

Everyone blinked, and Pepaw laid a hand on Leon's forearm. "Son," he said gently, "Lord willing, your daddy's going to be fine."

"I hope not!" Leon hollered out, yanking his arm away and slapping the table. "Look what he's done to us! To Mama! Anyway, he's in intensive care now. Pickled his liver."

The whole table was silent for a good two minutes. Then Granny pulled herself up even straighter, if that was possible. "Is this true, Nanette? Is Finch in intensive care?"

Nanette nodded.

"Well, I'm not surprised. Way that man drinks. But why didn't you tell us?"

"Maybe Nanette wants to bear her own burdens. Maybe it's all private," Minna said, folding her arms. "And, anyway, I imagine Finch'll rebound. He always does."

Leon sank back in his chair and closed his eyes, sighing. "Never learns a thing," he murmured. "Anyway, it isn't his drinking that put him in intensive care."

"What?!" Granny demanded.

Nanette's barely audible words were sobering. "Shot, too."

"Shot him in his crotch," Leon said, his somber words spoken more to himself than anyone else.

Granny turned her head rapidly from Leon to Nanette.

"His girlfriend shot him," Leon said. "For cheating on her."

"Is this true?" came Granny's shrill voice.

Nanette nodded, tears in her eyes.

"That rotten son of a bitch!" Minna shouted. "Have them slice his balls off while they got him in there!"

"Minna Lee Elco!" Pepaw said through clenched teeth, his face a bright pink.

Tammi searched Leon's face as he methodically cut his pork chop, rubbing a bite in a puddle of gravy. When his eyes finally caught hers, she smiled tenderly, felt tears, hot and salty, gathering behind her eyelids. *It's okay*, she mouthed, but he looked away quickly.

Chapter 16

"I don't want to talk about it," Leon said. "It's nobody's business what Mama's gone through, what I've gone through. I didn't mean that I wanted him to die. I just said 'if,' *if* he died. Anyway, *I* certainly didn't shoot him." His voice was way too high, cracking on every other word or so like he was going through puberty. "I mean, it'd be a natural consequence, if he died. Chasing all those women, staying drunk . . . like the Bible says, we'll reap what we sow."

Leon and Tammi were on the front steps. She'd come out to sit beside him after finishing in the kitchen, but he'd more or less been ignoring her until these comments. He was pale and drawn in the moonlight. She scooted over closer until their shoulders were touching. Here came that pulsing ache again. She was confused. Shouldn't she be in a more nurturing mode? Try to help him deal with all this pain, instead of just wanting to kiss him? "Things'll be okay," she murmured.

"He . . . he did it with my algebra teacher," Leon said. "And with Wanda Macabee, who runs the dance studio, and also with Merlene. She's the one that shot him."

They sat quietly in the dark shadows, listening to low rumbles of heat lightning.

"But if it damaged his thing," Tammi said at last, "he'll have to be more faithful."

Leon slunk down even farther, and she moved into him. "Kiss me, Leon," she whispered, telling herself that two hearts pounding and two pair of lips consuming would help him rise above the ugly parts of life.

She felt his trembling lips even before they touched hers, and a rapturous joy filled her heart. This was what she was made for! Their lips had just barely grazed each other when he jerked back. "I will not be like *him!*" he said through his teeth, in a tone laced with disgust. "I want you, Tammi. Truly I do, but I cannot be like my father!"

"What we have is nothing like your father's flings," she whispered over the knot in her throat. "Trust me." Leon's beautiful sad eyes were the last image she had before the door from the house swung open and a sliver of light fell across the steps. They wrenched apart and looked up into tiny sparkles of light refracting off the rhinestones on Granny's glasses.

"What's going on out here?"

"Nothing," Tammi whispered.

Granny turned on the porch light and clip-clopped out to stand at the top of the steps. She craned forward, sniffing the air above them. "Tammi Lynn, get yourself back into the house this instant."

Tammi pulled herself away, the flush of passion fading from her cheeks as she took the steps to her room. She lay stunned and immobile on her bed for the longest time, listening to Granny's agitated voice in the kitchen, talking to Pepaw and Nanette. Much later she heard Leon trudge upstairs to his room, his door slamming shut, and it was then that she felt a fierce longing for the comfort and distraction of her romance novels. She willed to mind the wild, woodland setting for *Savage Moon*. It appeared and she placed herself there, wrapped in

Leon's arms, his dark eyes smoldering as their bodies lay entwined on the banks of the Atawah River, moonlight dancing on the water like melting butter on a hot griddle. He began to untie her lacy gown, and she gasped as his sweet lips found the hollow of her throat, the sulky air of dusk like feathers on her skin as she fell off the edge into sleep.

Tammi sprinted to the Romance Readers' Book Club the next afternoon. She was going to insist that her turn to read *Savage Moon* be first this go-round. Parks would argue, but Tammi was ready to plead emergency.

There was a pie on the credenza, and Tammi smelled coffee percolating. She'd recently transferred the remainder of the romance library from Orr's hidey-hole to Minna's house, and when she peered into the den, she saw Parks, LaDonna, and Minna bent forward looking at the books spread out across the coffee table. Tammi smiled when Minna lifted one entitled *Seducing a Stranger* and said, "This one's got my vote!" The cover was a smoky black-and-white land-scape, a bloodred rose lying provocatively on the ground.

LaDonna shook her head. "I don't think *Seducing a Stranger* sounds very nice," she said. "How about we pick *Knights of Desire* or *Winter Bride?*"

"I want to read *Hot-Blooded* next," Tammi announced.

"Hey, girl!" Parks looked up. "I didn't hear you come in. You're voting for *Hot-Blooded?*"

"As the president," Tammi said, "I'm saying we'll read *Hot-Blooded* for our next selection."

"Hot damn," Parks said reverently, "you are one in-control female today!"

Tammi felt a twinge of guilt over being so bossy, and she cut her eyes at Minna and LaDonna to see how they received her directive. They were smiling.

"Hello, darlin'," Minna oozed. "Now that you're here, we can serve this delicious pie."

"Hey, Tammi," LaDonna said. "How are you?"

"Fine, I guess." Tammi shrugged. "How are you?" There was really too much on her mind for small talk, and she plopped down on the sofa and settled *Savage Moon* on her knees. "This meeting of the Romance Readers' Book Club will now come to order," she said. "Before I forget it, our assignment for next meeting is to finish *Savage Moon*." It was a heady feeling to see everyone nod. "Now we'll have pie." Deftly, Tammi sliced the pie, placing four wedges on china saucers.

"I love lemon meringue," she said, licking a finger.

"Thanks." LaDonna dipped her head modestly.

"Did you girls know," Minna said teasingly, "that lemon pie is reputed to be an aphrodisiac? Women feed their men lemon pie to get them into the mood."

"No kidding!" Tammi said, thinking that she might volunteer to make dessert for supper.

"Perfect for jump-starting a sluggish motor." Minna grinned.

"Beer's what works for me," Parks drawled. "Nothing like a six-pack of old Pabst Blue Ribbon for hitting the 'on' switch." She smiled through smoke drifting from her cigarette.

"God knows there are plenty of aphrodisiacs out there that promise to stimulate and enhance your sensual encounter!" Minna said in obvious delight.

"Do they work?" Tammi asked.

"Well, I haven't tried them all," Minna said. "Some folks swear by them, and some think it's just . . . what's that word I'm looking for? Snake oil!" Minna shrugged. "I don't know, sometimes I think they're fabulous, and sometimes I think the night magic's all in the mind. But I do have a few favorites."

Tammi regarded her thoughtfully. "Like what?"

"Oh, those good old-fashioned strategies of love and courtship, such as . . . candles, romantic music, writing love poems, whispering sweet nothings into his ear."

There was a long silence in which all that could be heard was the scrape of forks on china and the occasional sip of coffee. After they'd finished, Parks released a deep lungful of smoke, narrowing her eyes at Tammi. "So, girl, how goes your romance?"

"Slowly," Tammi mumbled.

"Old Granny on to y'all yet?"

"Not much for her to be 'on to.' "

"Gosh, Tammi," LaDonna said, eyes wide, "whatever happened to love at first kiss?"

"Well, I guess guys take it slower than us gals," Tammi began tentatively. "He's holding back some, I can tell. There's definitely all-consuming passion between us, pure chemistry, because I felt it at the reunion. And last night, I asked him to kiss me, and he did. It was powerful like you wouldn't believe, until Granny interrupted us."

"Ooh whee!" Parks hooted. "Did she *see* y'all?"

"No, almost. She might suspect something now. But Leon freaked out."

"Maybe it's the whole cousin deal," LaDonna said, patting her lips prissily with a napkin.

"No!" Tammi was on her feet in a second. She put her hands on her hips. "I told you we're not blood cousins!"

"I guess I meant there's always the chance that he still feels like y'all are cousins," LaDonna said gently. "Since that's how you were brought up to regard each other."

"Kissing cousins," Parks said playfully. Then she put a hand on Tammi's wrist and squeezed. "Just teasing with you, girl."

"That's not it," Tammi said, feeling her indignant anger lift. "His holding back, I mean. It's like he won't let himself go totally, so he can *feel* what's right there between us. What I think it is is that he's scared. Uncle Finch has a bunch of girlfriends, and I think Leon's terrified he'll be like him. I tried to tell him, y'all, that it's not that way with us. With me and Leon. We're the true thing. Each other's one and only. I know it in my heart." Tammi placed a palm on her chest and smiled tremulously.

Minna set her coffee down and looked at Tammi. "Darlin'," she drawled, "don't try to hurry love. Just let it happen naturally, gradually. Let it flow. Force it and it'll backfire. I know it must feel to you like there'll never be enough time, but if it's true love, I can assure you, there's always going to be enough time."

"Yeah, don't pressure him." Tammi heard LaDonna's impassioned voice. "Remember how Running Bear got all jittery when Nekoosa was coming on too strong to him? He freaked out! You should read that scene again, Tammi. In fact, I'll read it aloud right now." She grabbed *Savage Moon* from Tammi, flipped through the pages till she jabbed her finger on a page with an excited little "Aha!" and began:

Running Bear stood tall and bronzed in the light of the full moon, an overwhelming picture of godlike masculinity. Nekoosa's eyes were full of desire, her body eager to taste him as she stole through the trees, not able to stifle her rich, delighted laughter as she crept up behind him and grasped his chiseled buttocks with the wild abandon of a primitive savage. "I must have you now," she said between moans and kisses on his hard shoulders.

Running Bear shook his head, uttering small animal-like sounds of torment as he turned and pushed Nekoosa away, his eyes filled with disgust. "Go! You do not know me. You cannot put an acorn into the soil and expect an oak to grow immediately! It must grow naturally, like love. Like passion between two people."

Tammi listened raptly, sitting transfixed until Parks broke the spell by snorting in disgust and slapping her thigh. "I'm sorry," Parks said. "If it was *me* and I was out walking in the woods and saw Running Bear looking that studly, I'd have to hog-tie him and get me some!" Parks nodded thoughtfully now. "I'm sure you've heard that old saying, Tammi—'If you love someone, let 'em go. If it's meant to be, they'll come back to you, and if they don't, hunt 'em down and kill 'em!' " She gave a half-laugh and looked hard at Tammi. "Seriously, sounds like you just need to go have some *fun* with the boy. Somewhere away from Granny's old eagle eye. See what develops."

"But where could we go? There's nowhere to go in this dinky town!" Tammi wailed.

The discussion turned to various romantic spots the two could get away to. Minna favored empty barns, Parks the deserted dirt roads of rural Rigby, and LaDonna suggested the Fall Festival coming up in two weeks. It was all music to Tammi's ears, and she vowed to herself that, one way or another, she'd get Leon alone.

The afternoon was edging on toward dusk when Tammi glanced at the mantel clock. "Ohmigosh!" The words flew out of her mouth: "Quick— all rise for the pledge. Listen, I'm sorry we didn't even get to discuss our latest chapters today, but let's go ahead and finish *Savage Moon*. Next time we'll talk about 'How to Tell If He's Really the One.'"

When Tammi woke on the day of the Fall Festival the big house was noisy, full of men in coveralls hanging around in the upstairs bathroom to locate a leaky pipe that had burst in the night. During breakfast Granny and Pepaw left their plates to go and talk with the plumbers about something they'd discovered. Nanette was sleeping in, so Tammi and Leon sat alone, eating biscuits with muscadine jelly. How could an opportunity this perfect have dropped in her lap? Tammi smiled at Leon from under her lashes. Leon had been working long hours at Elco Antiques, and it had been ages since they'd had a moment without other people around. "I was just thinking," Tammi said, "that today's the Fall Festival and we ought to go."

Leon looked up at her, awkwardly gripping a butter knife.

"All the downtown shops are closed, you know. So that means you've got the day off from the antique store."

"Um, yeah, I guess you're right," Leon said faintly. He went back to spreading his jelly.

"It's a real cultural experience," Tammi said teasingly. "I'll buy you a bag of boiled peanuts and a cone of cotton candy."

He smiled, a small smile, but a smile nonetheless.

A clear blue sky hung over downtown, where streamers dangled from storefront awnings, and the air was laced with the greasy-sweet smell of funnel cakes. Cars and trucks jammed the side roads leading to the square, as pretty much everyone in Rigby and the surrounding counties gathered each year to watch the kickoff parade.

Tammi and Leon stood leaning against the warm marble of the Confederate war memorial as a fire truck led the parade slowly down Main Street. First in line were the Brownie Scouts, followed by Shriners wearing tall black fezzes and driving their tiny cars in figure-eight patterns. The mayor sat waving from a perch atop the backseat of his prized vintage convertible, periodically scattering cellophane-wrapped candies to children dancing on the curb as the high school marching band lit into a jazzy rendition of "Bad, Bad Leroy Brown."

Leon seemed to be entranced by a fleet of antique tractors rolling by, while Tammi snuck sideways glances at the crowd, feeling proud to be with Leon and hoping some of the snooty girls from school would see her.

"Check this out. It's hilarious," Leon said, elbowing Tammi out of her thoughts. She looked up to see a gigantic toilet perched atop Sidwell's Septic Tank rig. The words A ROYAL FLUSH BEATS A FULL HOUSE were emblazoned across the side, and Dusty Sidwell flung Tootsie Rolls to the crowd from the window. Tammi smiled, then let her gaze wander to the next entry in the parade. Rigby High's chief majorette, a tall busty blonde named Corina Steeples, twirled her silver baton and tossed it way up in the air, gracefully pirouetting several times before catching it flawlessly behind her back. Corina bowed, drinking in the crowd's applause.

Leon clapped enthusiastically, and a knot rose in Tammi's chest. Next in the parade lineup was Miss Peach Blossom, Mandy Wilmot, Rigby's equivalent of Miss America, enthroned in a powder-blue Mustang convertible. When Mandy passed by, everyone stopped whatever they were doing, even breathing, it seemed, to watch her wave her little white-gloved hand, waterfalls of honey-colored hair rippling beneath a glittering tiara.

When she was directly in front of Tammi and Leon they could make out each dazzling white tooth and the swell of her breasts ensconced in the bodice of her peach chiffon gown. Leon grunted, almost involuntarily. "Who was *that*?" he breathed.

"Mandy Wilmot," Tammi said between gritted teeth. She tucked a sweaty strand of hair behind her ear, folded her arms across her chest, listening to the booming cadence of a drummer as the ROTC marched by. Various floats and dignitaries followed but she wasn't much interested, even as the band came to an uproarious conclusion and a black patrol car glided along at the tail end of the parade. The crowd began to slip away toward carnival rides dotting a ten-acre field behind some tents.

"Can't believe they call this a *fall* festival," Leon said. "It's a hundred degrees in the shade."

"Yeah," she said, bracing herself for a barrage of questions about Mandy Wilmot, thinking that the end of anything she dreamed they might have together was certainly here.

"Want to ride the Ferris wheel?" Leon asked.

"Okay," she said, hiding her surprise with the most offhanded voice she could summon.

They walked along, past booths of civic, church, and school organizations. When they passed the watermelon seed–spitting contest a sudden flash of wistfulness tugged at Tammi's heart. "Orr entered this last year," she said. "He loves the Fall Festival almost as much as he loves Christmas. You should have seen his face this morning when Granny told him he had to stay home."

"Why didn't she let him come?"

"It was actually on account of this contest. Last year some old codger teased Orr. Told him that if he'd swallowed any watermelon seeds by accident, they'd grow inside him. That he'd sprout vines out his ears. He takes everything literally." Tammi sighed. "So, anyway, Orr put on some weight over Thanksgiving and he was positive it was a watermelon growing in his belly. It must've taken Granny an entire month and two visits to Dr. Emmerson to convince him it wasn't. She said she doesn't have time for that kind of nonsense this year." Tammi managed a smile as they walked across the Big Star grocery's parking lot toward the Ferris wheel stretching above the treetops.

By two o'clock they'd ridden the Ferris wheel twice, cruised every booth, and grown ravenously hungry. Tammi paused at the Kiwanis

Club's booth, where a lady sold her a bag of boiled peanuts and popped the cap off a bottle of Coca-Cola.

"Let's go sit down in that shady spot over there," Leon suggested, leading Tammi to a cooler patch of ground beneath a gnarled old tree. They sat down side by side, knees almost touching. After they'd eaten, Tammi stretched flat on her back, the dead honey-colored grass tickling her neck and earlobes, her pulse thudding hard in her ears as she contemplated Leon's nearness. She pushed her sweaty hair off her forehead. "Leon?"

"Hm?" He lay back, too, turning his face in her direction.

"I was just wondering . . ." she said hesitantly. "What did you think of your first week at Rigby High?"

"Um . . ." he said, "it was okay. Being the new guy's always tough, I suppose."

"I should've warned you," Tammi said, "there are lots of cliques in Rigby High. For instance, there are the *popular* girls, and then there are the unpopular." She sighed.

"I bet you're everybody's favorite," Leon said.

Tammi couldn't suppress a giggle. "Oh, please!" She rolled her eyes dramatically, as if she understood him to be joking. She looked at him—he appeared to be serious. What mattered more than his mistake was the beauty of his error. She returned his gaze coyly, thinking she might as well let him continue in his ignorance. What would it hurt? To have him picture her as popular, the belle of the ball? No. Her cover could easily be blown if he asked any tenth grader. "They all think I'm a pathetic nerd."

Leon shook his head, opened his mouth to argue.

"They do! And I guess, to them, I am. It's Mandy Wilmot who's hot." There, she'd said it aloud.

"I didn't think she was all that hot," said Leon.

Something in Tammi's heart squeezed. "You didn't?"

Leon looked amused. "Nope. She's one of those girls who's all makeup and hair dye. The kind that peak when they're twenty. No real substance. You know, an airhead."

Tammi's smile widened in spite of herself. "Well, she is in remedial classes."

"See?" Leon said. "In ten years she'll be, they'll all be, those fluff-headed girls, jealous of you. You've got brains *and* you're beautiful. You're just a late bloomer is all."

Tammi's breath literally caught in her throat. She had a ridiculous urge to confess to Leon all the indignities she'd ever suffered at the hands of her classmates. But she couldn't even imagine where to start. Instead, she slowly reached out to close her thumb and forefinger around the stem of a yellow dandelion, pulling so hard it came out by the roots. She placed this on his chest, saying, "Want to walk through the Fun House to cool off before we head back home?"

They walked along in the afternoon sunshine, past the ring-toss game, where a hugely fat young woman threaded her way through the crowd, calling, "Step right up folks! Win your favorite high-quality plush character! Makes a great souvenir!"

"Orr would love one of those," Tammi said when she saw the colorful lineup of Fred Flintstones and Dinos.

"Good thing I'm feeling lucky today," Leon said, pushing through the crowd. It was like a miracle as Tammi watched him sink three rings in a row over the necks of some tall green glass bottles. The next thing she knew he was pointing to a knee-high George Jetson doll on the highest shelf. He presented it to Tammi.

"Orr'll love this." Tammi smiled over the furry doll's head. She didn't think she could be any happier herself. A hot breeze lifted the hair off the back of her neck as they passed through the nylon doors of the Fun House. Just inside sat a five-hundred-pound bearded lady, and beyond her was a muscular man covered in tattoos, wearing a skimpy leotard, and then, about ten yards down, in a darkened corner of the tent, Tammi could barely make out a crude handwritten sign: THIS IS A CAT-BOY THAT IS A FREAK OF NATURE. A dark felt hat lay upside down on the floor in front of a wooden stool, where a skinny white boy sat on his haunches. The hat was filled with crumpled dollar bills. The boy's hair was a pale shade of blond, cut in a bowl fashion, so fine his pointed feline ears poked through. His eyes were sea green and steeped in a sadness that looked ready to spill over. A gray-striped tail curled around in front of his dirty bare feet.

Tammi was mesmerized by the thick loneliness that surrounded him. She nudged Leon. "Isn't that the most pitiful thing you ever saw?" She dug into her pocket for some money.

"I imagine he cries all the way to the bank," Leon said, winking at Tammi as he plunged his hand down into his own pocket, drawing it up and unclasping it to show a buck knife. Before Tammi even knew what was happening, he'd sunk the blade into the cat-boy's tail. The cat-boy didn't flinch a bit. At first, Tammi was horrified, but then she was hooting with laughter as she realized it was all a fake.

A row of crazy, shape-distorting mirrors lined the exit of the Fun House. Tammi stood before the nearest one, laughing at the blimp with stubby legs and a pinhead reflected back at her. The next mirror stretched her out like a crazy stork. She didn't give a fig if Leon saw her this way because all he seemed to be looking at was her eyes. Her eyes were dancing and sparkling like they hadn't in ages.

The next afternoon, as Tammi was carrying tomato skins out to the compost pile, she decided she would find Leon and get him to carry her to the city pool. She smiled at a mental image of them rubbing Coppertone onto each other as she stood in front of the mirror stroking on Faded Denim eye shadow and shining her lips with pink gloss. Bending at the waist to finger-fluff her hair, she took in a deep breath before tiptoeing to Leon's door.

She could hear him inside, walking around, scraping back a chair, sighing. "Oh, *Le-on*," she called in a singsong voice. The noises coming from Leon's room ceased. She leaned her ear right up against the wood of the door. What was he doing in there? She knocked and called again.

Finally Leon was at the door, opening it a tiny crack. "Yes?" he said tentatively.

"Let's go to the pool," Tammi said, pushing gently against the door with her shoulder and stepping inside, waltzing across the floor. There was a small Oriental carpet beside his bed that Tammi recalled Granny paying over five hundred dollars for the year before. It had been kept up on the wall in the parlor till now. This realization caused her to survey the rest of Leon's furnishings: a quilt rack at the foot of a walnut sleigh bed, Granny's prized linen press against the far wall, a tall bureau, and a nightstand on either side of the bed.

"Looks like the antique shop in here," Tammi told Leon. He gazed at her with tired eyes as she ran her fingers across his spotless white chenille bedspread. "So, do you want to come swimming with me?" she asked. "The pool will be closing after Labor Day, you know." Tammi paused for a breath. "I'll go put on my suit while you change into yours." She grinned and flounced back out of Leon's room.

She waited in the hallway a long time, happily adjusting the straps of the swimsuit she wore beneath a T-shirt and shorts. At last Leon emerged wearing a tank top and cutoffs. Tammi drank in his luscious hamstrings. She smiled. "Guess you're planning to change at the—"

"I'm not going to the pool," he said. "But we do need to find somewhere private around here to talk."

Something in Leon's tone made Tammi feel ill. "I know a place," she heard herself say.

Leon followed her outside and deep into the woods, crossing a ravine, then ambling up a high knoll, pausing when Tammi pointed to a line of stones silhouetted against the sky, a collection of granite boulders she privately called Pickle Rock Park.

She liked to pretend that she was the only one who knew about Pickle Rock Park, that she had discovered it, but she knew Pepaw must know, though they never spoke of it. She'd come here hundreds of times over the years, keeping her visits a secret even from Orr.

The day was totally still, except for the rustle of dry leaves in the breeze and the cry of a blackbird echoing across the land. The cluster of boulders was an otherworldly shade of purple-gray in the sunlight.

"Betcha never knew these dinosaur eggs existed, huh?" she asked Leon at last.

He blew out a whoosh of air, his eyes drinking the boulders in. "This is fabulous," he said at last. "Do you climb them?"

"Yep," she said. "All the time."

He left her side and began to wander between the huge stones, leaping onto some of the lower ones, gazing up in awe at the tops of others higher than his head.

"I call that humongous one there in the middle Pickle Rock," Tammi said.

He laughed. "It does kind of look like a big dill pickle. Can you climb it?"

"Yeah. On that far side."

"Let's go up," he said.

Tammi led him to the far corner of Pickle Rock, where she ran a palm over its warm side speckled with moss. "There's a few little indents for your fingers along here," she said, getting on her tiptoes to heft her body up.

Leon nimbly pulled himself up to join her. "Wow," he said. "Must be eight feet across up here. Beautiful view!"

"That's Taylor's Gap down that way," Tammi said, following his eyes to where the rocks plummeted to an endless valley of sycamores.

"I feel *good* up here," Leon said, his voice laced with wonder. "Like I can almost reach up and touch heaven."

"Yeah, it's my favorite place in all of Rigby."

There was a long silence as Leon spun in circles, gazing out at the land below, getting so close to Tammi that goose bumps popped up on her forearms. His tank top let her see the muscles moving beneath his golden skin, and suddenly Pickle Rock faded away. She grabbed Leon's shoulders, uttering words she'd learned from Nekoosa: "I've got this savage fire for you burning inside me, and no way to put it out!" Her sweaty hands grew slick on his skin, sliding down to his wrists, where she hung on, dancing delightedly on the razor-sharp edge of erotic anticipation.

Leon was a statue. "Tammi," he said, as cautiously as if he were explaining the death of someone dear to him, "there are some things I need to tell you."

Didn't he know there was no fact on God's green earth that mattered? Oh, she was pulsing, her heart beating like it would explode right through her chest. Throatily she whispered a line she recalled Clemmie saying in *Texas Toast*, "I'm baptized by the fire in your touch!" She leaned in to press throbbing lips to his neck.

He backed away, his hands thrown up so that he looked like a little boy caught with his hand in the cookie jar. "Tammi, I . . . I can't be with you like this."

"But we had so much fun at the fair together!"

He held up his hand and softly said, "You'll just have to trust me. I need to focus. You know about focus, don't you? Please respect this and allow me my space."

Oh, he was so serious, so restrained. What should she do? Her passion for him was magnificent. Nekoosa would know what to do! She would take possession of him with violent kisses.

But wait a minute! That would only drive Leon away. The Romance Readers' Book Club was right-on when it advised her to let it flow naturally. She slumped down onto warm granite, remembering *Let the acorn have time to sprout.* "Go," Tammi said, her voice trembling, as Leon slipped down from Pickle Rock and disappeared into the woods.

CHAPTER 17

Tammi scribbled Leon's name over and over on the Big Star grocery sacks covering her school books. His name was music to her ears as she whispered it breathlessly throughout September, praying for just a glimpse of him in the hallways of Rigby High.

She gave Leon his space as he'd requested, exchanging the usual pleasantries at mealtimes when he returned from his after-school position at Elco Antiques. But at night, when she crawled into bed, she conjured him into her arms in a kind of dreamlike amalgamation of the plot in *Savage Moon*. The book had begun to take on extra-special depth and meaning. Tammi *was* Nekoosa, and Leon *was* Running Bear.

She willed the days to pass more quickly, to hurry up so Leon would come to his senses and possess her. She was growing weary of waiting for the acorn to sprout. The romance novels were pushing her off the edge of her former ignorance into what felt like a bottomless abyss without Leon.

It couldn't hurt to give the acorn a little fertilizer, could it?

Tammi got to Minna's at four-thirty on Tuesday afternoon. Minna's hair was up in rollers, and she was in the kitchen painting her toenails. She winked, smiled, and called out, "Hey there, darlin'!

Come on in and take a load off!" It struck Tammi that the wrinkles at the corners of Minna's mouth and eyes were much smoother these days. Tammi liked to think it was the rejuvenating power of the Romance Readers' Book Club that had transformed her aunt.

"We start *Hot-Blooded* today, hm?" Minna asked, looking up from dabbing a bit of paint onto her pinkie toe.

"Yep," Tammi said, sinking down onto a stool. "Boy, do I need it bad!"

"Ought to be a good 'un," Minna trilled. "Shame on me, but I took the liberty of reading a steamy little scene in the middle. It's your fault, though. For hiding them here at my place!"

Parks came laughing through the door promptly at five. "Howdy, ladies!" she said, her voice lilting with pleasure. "Time to chat about Nekoosa."

But LaDonna's face was somber as she stepped inside, plunking a tray of powdered-sugar doughnuts and a half-gallon of sweet milk down on the credenza. "I was disappointed at the ending of *Savage Moon*," she said, settling into her customary spot in Minna's den.

"All's well that ends well." Parks shrugged. "I know it was pretty scary there at the close, but Running Bear ended up surviving just fine after that poison arrow. With a piece of tail to boot." She lit a cigarette, smiling broadly.

Tammi cleared her throat. "This meeting of the Romance Readers' Book Club will now come to order. First of all, I'd like to say that in the next-to-last chapter, when Nekoosa is running for the medicine man's hut, after Running Bear gets shot—"

"I think," LaDonna interrupted her sharply, "that the author let him get shot right near the end of the story like that simply because she needed to fill some more pages. It was redundant! I think the book could've, should've ended twenty pages earlier. When they're at the river. It was the perfect place."

"It ended fine." Parks scowled.

"I think they added more just for the extra sex scenes," LaDonna said. "Their whole objective is to titillate us. To make it addictive."

"Ooh, honey, it sho 'nuff is!" Minna giggled. "It's all I can do to keep my promise not to read more than we agree on! Gets me so hot under the collar I . . . oh, I better shut my mouth before I embarrass us all!"

LaDonna's neck turned pink, and Tammi felt herself flush warm as well. "But it's also like seeing the world," Tammi added quickly. "Traveling to Hawaii and Texas and all."

LaDonna scowled. "Don't push it. I wouldn't call them travelogues. Who knows if they're even factual or not?"

A little more than half an hour later, after scrutinizing and discussing every aspect of Nekoosa's role in *Savage Moon*, the group was still arguing over the same scene.

At last Parks let out a big sigh. "Relax, girl," she said to LaDonna. "We're just here to get our fix, okay? It's not brain surgery, and there's nothing wrong with us needing our fix. Men have their girlie magazines. We have our romance novels. I loved *Savage Moon*, and I would read it again in a heartbeat." She turned to Tammi and playfully poked her in the ribs. "Tell us, girl. What's happening in your romance?"

Tammi squirmed. She didn't want to disappoint the group, but she knew they could tell from her face that things were not all satin and lace. "Um," she said, "Leon's so busy, we don't really have much time together. But I'm certain things'll—"

"Don't forget that there's lots of other fishies in the sea!" Parks interrupted.

"I'm not looking for any other fish," Tammi said in her most affronted voice. "Leon's the only one for me. Just because we're not all hot and heavy at this exact moment doesn't mean we won't end up in each other's arms at the end of the story!" She pulled her shoulders up. "Look at Nekoosa . . . why, there's proof right there. This is only a temporary dry spell."

Minna nodded, a warm light of empathy in her eyes. "Bet he's busy at the antique shop, hm, darlin'?"

"Yeah." Tammi bit wearily into her powdered doughtnut. "Also with school."

Parks turned to search Tammi's face. "So," she said, "how're the new threads working out? You been witnessing better at Rigby High?" She threw back her head and laughed.

Tammi exhaled slowly, a long, guilt-burdened breath. "I'm much happier in my new clothes. Thanks."

"It's Leon who's making waves at Rigby High." LaDonna chuckled softly. "Every other girl in our class has a crush on him."

Tammi felt her pulse race. LaDonna could laugh about it because she simply had no idea how deep it cut into Tammi's soul to have to watch those bouncy girls vying for Leon's attention; the way they wriggled their hips and thrust their breasts out toward the one she loved. It was like being in the middle of a constant nightmare. Minna reached over to pat her wrist and with typical empathy changed the subject. "Alrighty, ladies," she said, brushing white powder from a doughnut off her shoulder, "our topic for today is 'How to Tell If He's Really the One.'"

LaDonna cleared her throat. "I chose this topic because I feel the club has focused too much on *lust*. On mere functions of the body . . . tingles, shudders, things becoming engorged by blood! This discussion will focus purely on *love*. No talk of shuddering loins."

Parks puckered her mouth. "Love," she muttered. "What is love? I *like* hearing about all those engorged organs."

"Girls," Minna said firmly, "let's stick to our topic. But may I please say one thing about organs before we move on to love?"

LaDonna nodded wearily.

"I believe, and remember, I've had literally worlds of experience at this man-woman thing"—Minna's voice was reflective and strong—"that the biggest, most powerful sex organ there is is the *brain*."

Tammi was quiet. She'd never really pondered the matter of the brain being a sex organ. She pressed her palms together and listened intently to Minna's next words.

"How I knew Franklin loved me . . ." Minna stroked her chin. "Well, Tammi and I were discussing this matter not long ago, and it caused me to really think about it. I reckon it was the day me and Franklin were walking up along Dicken's Ridge. I'd packed us a picnic. It was July, as I recall, and we were going to spread a quilt in that shady part along the creek. Sip some sweet tea . . . listen to the birds . . . hold hands. Well, I wanted to take a shortcut. Franklin, he agreed, and held up the barbed-wire fence for me to squeeze underneath, him toting the quilt and the basket, too. We were moseying along and suddenly there appeared this *huge* Angus bull, eyes mean as anything. He caught sight of me, and he was pawing at the ground, dipping his enormous head to charge! I was paralyzed. You gals know that feeling you get in dreams when you're so scared you can't move? Well, there I was frozen to stone. Sweet Franklin, God rest his soul, he got between me and that bull."

Tammi was on the edge of her seat. "Did he get hurt?"

Minna's voice was reverent, every syllable receiving careful enunciation. "Yes, dear, he got badly hurt. Keeping me safe, putting me first. I guess I knew then that he was the One."

Tammi gave her a long look. "I thought it was because he sounded just like Elvis."

Minna reached out and rested her hand on Tammi's. "That didn't hurt, either, darlin'."

"That's interesting," LaDonna said. "Franklin put you first—with no regard for himself. Sacrificial. Almost like a Christ figure." She looked pointedly at Parks. "How about you?"

There was a long moment of silence as the big girl lit a fresh cigarette.

"Tell us, Parks," LaDonna urged. "How to know if he's the One."

Parks settled deeper into her chair. "What is love?" she said in a reckless, cynical voice. "For me, I don't know . . . if we're talking sacrifice equals love, then I imagine it was when Randall Billings cosigned for my Trans Am."

"Isn't Randall mad that you don't go with him anymore?" LaDonna's voice had an incredulous tone.

"Heck yeah!" Parks exclaimed. "But what can I say? Now I got the hots for Tucker Howser."

LaDonna rolled her eyes. "And how do you know Tucker's the One?"

"You're making me *think*, girl!" Parks sighed as if the very question was heavy. "Tucker is the One because . . . because he's the type who'll do anything! A daredevil. Races dirt bikes. Ain't scared of a thing in this world."

"So that makes him the One?" LaDonna prodded. "I really can't see the connection here."

Parks was clearly struggling for words. "Tucker, he . . . gives *me* courage! That's it. I'm scared of heights, you know, and he got me on the Ferris wheel at the festival. I had me a blast! Rode that blessed thing three times! You cannot know how proud I felt of myself after that."

Tammi found it hard to conceive of Parks being scared of anything. She thought of all her own fears and wondered if Leon could deliver her from them. There were so many, it seemed! They ran the gamut from worrying that she was going to hell to temporal things like boredom and a passionless earthly life.

"So, okay, Tucker's the One because he gives you courage." LaDonna sat back in her chair, sipping sweet milk.

For the longest spell, the only sound was the faraway rhythm of Pepaw's tractor chugging away. Finally LaDonna turned her attention to Tammi. "You're the only one we haven't heard from on this. How do you know Leon's the One?"

Tammi jumped at the sound of Leon's name. Hadn't LaDonna forbidden mention of pulsing loins? After a bit she recalled how she'd laughed and enjoyed every minute of her day at the festival with him. "He makes me smile!" she blurted.

"He makes you smile." LaDonna shook her head, unconvinced.

"A smile is a valuable thing," Minna said. "I can remember times I'd have paid a million bucks for just a reason to smile."

There was no arguing over this, and relief flooded Tammi. "Minna has previewed *Hot-Blooded*," she said, changing the subject, "and declared it worthy. Right?"

"Ooh whee!" Minna fanned her face with rapid little waves of her fingertips. "Yes, indeed! It will be one delicious book."

"Let's read the first twelve chapters for our next meeting," Tammi directed.

LaDonna scowled. "Well, I hope they're at least *married* in this one."

"Yeah, they are, but not to each other!" Parks teased.

When the pledge was done, Minna looked at Tammi. "Next meeting's discussion topic! It's your turn."

"'How to Land a Reluctant Man,'" Tammi said. "That's what I need to talk about."

"Sounds good to me," Parks said, eyebrows raised playfully as she hooked arms with LaDonna and pulled her down the steps to the Trans Am.

CHAPTER 18

It was a hot afternoon in October, and Granny was out on the porch waiting on the Gospel Jubilee to begin, already settled in good for her siesta, a pot of coffee percolating on the butler's tray stationed in front of her wicker love seat. Ordinarily she had the door leading into the house shut firmly, scowling at any intrusions. Today it stood open, and Tammi, who was dusting the parlor, saw her rise to fiddle with the knob of the radio. Startled, Tammi heard Leon say, "Let me do that for you."

"You're a dear boy." Granny sipped her coffee. "Not a thing like your dad. In fact, I warned your mother. First time I laid eyes on Finch Dupree, I said to Nanette that I could *see* the devil in him. The way he held himself so proud, like he just knew he was something to look at. Thought he was God's gift to women, he surely did."

Silence. Then the radio coming in loud and clear. "Ahh, good," Granny said. "Now, Tammi Lynn's got a wild streak to her, too." She added this suddenly, like a lightning bolt of knowledge had ripped through her brain.

Tammi stopped dusting. She stood in a ray of sun and stared at a myriad of free-floating dust specks, straining to hear Leon's response.

"Hm?" He was thoughtful.

"I've got to stay on top of that girl. Keep her busy every minute. Idle hands being the devil's workshop. Ever since she was knee-high to a grasshopper—bad to daydream. Well, you know what I mean."

"Yes, ma'am."

Traitor! Tammi should have said it out loud. No, the word "traitor" was too mild; try "brownnoser" or "suck-up." That was more like it! She crept over nearer the porch door and leaned against the wall silently so that she had an unobstructed view.

Leon was sitting across from Granny in a white wicker rocker. His legs were crossed, and he had his hands resting in his lap. Prim. Almost prissy. Tammi was mesmerized. He even had a cup of that old rotgut coffee! And here it was 80 degrees out. Granny pushed aside a pile of needlework in progress from beside her on the love seat, patted the green vinyl cushion, and said, "Come on over here and sit beside me."

Tammi felt a sudden rush of fear. This woman was dangerous! It was her face that alarmed Tammi now—her narrowed eyes and pursed lips. She was on a big mission. A shaft of late-afternoon sun fell on the back of Granny's head, illuminating a halo of fine wiry hairs that had escaped her bun. "I asked you to come out here with me today for a reason, Leon," she said, looking at him over the top of her glasses.

Tammi watched Leon shuffle across and settle in beside Granny, placing his palms together and sliding his hands in the crease formed between his thighs. Tammi half expected to hear Granny's dry old bones creaking as she leaned over and reached out a hand to cup his knee. Leon kept his head bent, only moved his eyes modestly to look at her face, giving her a timid smile.

"I imagine you're full of questions, aren't you son?"

"Yes, ma'am."

"You'll understand by and by," Granny said, stirring some nondairy powdered creamer into her second cup of coffee. Tammi pressed her back harder against the wall to sink soundlessly to the floor. Part of her wanted to listen to this and part didn't. Leon's hair was immaculate, with tracks of a comb still in it. He wore a spotless white shirt and trousers sporting a neat crease.

Granny was unusually animated. "Hold your horses just a minute, darlin'." She leaned forward and raised the volume so that the thin chords of somber organ music preceding the Gospel Jubilee Hour rang out loudly. With a satisfied *smack!* she gulped coffee and closed her eyes.

Leon waited, the polite thin smile still on his face. Tammi wondered how he could stand to sit that close to Granny. She had what Tammi called dragon breath—a nasty mix of stale coffee and denture adhesive. "Leon," Granny said as the music waned, "ever since you and your mother came home, I've wanted to sit you down, alone, and talk to you. And today, the Reverend Cotton's topic is Sins of Our Fathers. He announces the upcoming topic at the end of his messages, and I reckoned this was God's way of saying, 'It's time, Constance. I'm opening a door for you.' So, my dear boy, the Reverend Cotton's going to talk about how to break the yoke of bondage a person might be under. If, for instance, his father is a low-down sinner."

Leon nodded.

"I look at you, and I *know* you're nothing like Finch! If I didn't know he was your father, I'd laugh if anybody told me he was. You can't tell me God would visit that man's heinous sins on you! When I heard what that man did to your mama, and to you, well, I was mad as a hornet. But I wasn't surprised a bit. I said to Minna, I said, 'It was just a matter of time. I've been waiting for this.' " She stopped to pat her chest. "I know, Leon, in my heart, that you're cut from a different cloth than Finch Dupree, and I want us to listen to the Reverend Cotton together. We'll purge out the evilness! Face it and attack the devil before he gains a foothold in your life. The good Lord won't hold you accountable. How could He visit the sins of your father on you?

"I just won't allow it," she said. "God can't make you suffer. You're not the one who has lusted after foreign women. You haven't taken to drink or gambled away all your money. The Reverend Cotton will tell us what we're facing, and I'll help you!"

Leon cleared his throat—a strangled high pitch that reminded Tammi of a rabbit caught in a trap. Granny dabbed at her cheeks with a hankie. Had Tammi ever seen her cry before? Well, maybe when they put Junior's coffin into the ground, but not before or since.

The Reverend Cotton came on and invited the listening audience to join him in an opening prayer. Granny put her hands together and touched the tips of her pointer fingers to her chin, watching Leon. He followed like he was her reflection, but closed his eyes. Granny kept her eyes open and on Leon during the entire prayer, closing them quickly when the Reverend Cotton said, "In Jesus' name we pray. Amen."

The Reverend Cotton started by reading four very similar Bible verses, two from Exodus and one each out of Numbers and Deuteronomy. Something about sins of the fathers. Tammi blew out a long silent stream of air as the Reverend Cotton tied the four verses together. He had such a country, nasal old-man's voice that Tammi pictured him as a stringy scarecrow in manure-splattered overalls. "Brethren," he said, "the iniquity of the fathers is visited upon the children! That's what it says right here in four separate places, which leads me to point out that Our Father God thinks it's mighty important!

"It's interesting to note," he continued, "that we have a saying, in secular society, that goes 'the acorn doesn't fall far from the tree.' "

Granny's eyebrows flew up, and she squeezed Leon's knee. Leon tilted his head toward her meekly. Tammi felt almost envious when she considered their intimacy.

"I honestly believe," said the Reverend Cotton, "that children *learn* what they *live*. Say 'amen,' brethren!" He paused for the studio audience, and Granny nodded her head vehemently. "But we can overcome through our Lord and Savior Jesus Christ. We can beat the devil at his own game. In Jesus' blood we have redemption from our earthly frailties."

Granny set her cup down and squeezed Leon's kneecap tighter. He sat up sharply and placed his hands on top of hers while the Reverend Cotton continued. "Yes, brethren, you can shuck off the yoke of bondage."

"Ah," Leon said, staring at the radio.

"Shh," Granny admonished.

"Brothers and sisters," the Reverend Cotton continued. "We must *deny* ungodliness! *Deny* worldly lusts! I'll illustrate with a true story."

Granny narrowed her eyes as he began. "There was a man. Spent his family's sustenance on liquor and harlots. Poor wife took in laundry, did mending . . . they had two sons to support. I warned this man, pled with him, to abstain from fleshly lusts that war against the soul. Did he repent?

"No, he died in the arms of one of his paramours when those sons of his were just beyond their teenage years. Down the road a bit, I went to the jailhouse to visit one of his sons, and I asked him, 'How come you do like your daddy, when you saw how he turned out?' That boy, he gripped the metal bars and said to me, 'Reverend, how could I help it?'

"Well, before long, the other son come to my office and said he was called to be a minister. I said, 'How do you figure you're not following in your father's footsteps?' He said, 'But I am. My *heavenly* Father's footsteps.' "

Accordion music came on. Granny said, "He'll come back on in a spell, with an application for the listeners."

"Ah," Leon said, his face puzzled. Or was it thoughtful? Whatever it was, it was gorgeous to Tammi, who could hardly keep her eyes off him.

"It's a miracle," Granny said, "the very timeliness of this message. I hope you don't have to go anywhere for a while."

"Um, no." Leon's voice tilted up at the end of his response so that it sounded like a question.

"Good. I want you to hear what the Reverend Cotton says at the end." Granny poured more coffee for herself just as the Reverend Cotton came back on. She took a long swig and held the stained pot out toward Leon. He shook his head, waving a hand over his cup, blinking as she refilled it, anyway.

"My friends!" The Reverend Cotton sounded like he was blasting spittle onto the microphone. "We've been redeemed! No longer enslaved to earthly passions and appetites! Yes, we have a choice. The sins of our fathers don't need to enslave us. We can break off those yokes of bondage. We do that by adhering to the straight and narrow way. But it is a *choice*, a conscious decision. And 'de-cision' means a cutting away. We must cut away the sins of the flesh."

The Reverend Cotton lowered his voice to a near whisper. "It's our responsibility to *deny* ungodliness and worldly lusts, as it says in the book of First Thessalonians. 'For this is the will of God, that you should be consecrated—separated and set apart for pure and holy living; that you should abstain and shrink from all sexual vice; that each one of you should know how to control his own body in purity, separated from things profane, and in consecration and honor, not to be used in the passion of lust, like the heathen who are ignorant of the true God.' Shout 'amen,' people!"

"Amen," Granny said.

Tammi had heard the Reverend Cotton's voice, but not his words, for years. She'd dismissed him because he was somebody Granny liked. He called the listeners his "friends out there" and said he prayed for them. Tammi scoffed at this. He didn't even know them! Surely Leon wasn't taken in by the stuff he had heard today.

Don't listen to this, she urged, searching his face. *Just tune it out and think about you and me together, Leon. How it feels when we touch each other.*

On a positive note, Leon did look a little uneasy at present, cupping his coffee between both hands like it was a small bird.

But Granny was in heaven. Eyes lit up, practically sitting in Leon's lap. Tammi decided it was because she had her two most favorite things in the whole wide world at one time, the Gospel Jubilee and Leon Dupree. Granny pushed her cat's-eye glasses higher on her nose and tilted her chin up so she could look through the bottom of the bifocals to study his face. "God is calling *you*, Leon. To be His earthen vessel."

Leon shook his head.

"What?" her voice was on the shrill side.

"I'm not worthy," he said solemnly, closing his eyes.

"Well, of course you are," Granny told him. "You have always been the sweetest thing. Why, I remember when you were just a little thing, insisting that you pray before you would eat your animal crackers at snack time."

"I did?"

"Yessum. You were always asking questions about God. Carried the little picture-book Bible I gave you everywhere."

That doesn't mean a thing, Tammi thought. When she was little, she prayed the same prayer each night. Folded her hands, knelt at her bedside like the tiny watercolor illustration in one of her picture books, and prayed. She certainly didn't remember young Leon as being any more spiritual than herself. Granny was picking and choosing isolated incidents to suit her purposes. She could just as easily have said that Tammi might be called of God. Ha ha!

Leon bent his head low now, and Granny pulled his hand over into her lap, twined her fingers in his, and held them against her bosom. "The Lord has you in His palm, dear boy. Been preparing you for the ministry with all these sorrows and hardships in your life. How could He use a vessel who'd experienced no hardship? Yessum. He's been preparing you. You'll be able to empathize with your flock's pain. You've stood in their shoes, walked through the valley. You will abstain from fleshly lusts that war against the soul, Leon. Because you've seen what fleshly lusts *do.* You know all about your daddy's dark soul."

It felt like somebody had ripped the earth out from under Tammi's feet. She rose and crept through the kitchen to the laundry room to return the dust rag. She couldn't believe all these things Granny was saying, and the fact that Leon was actually listening to that dried-up old Reverend Cotton. She sat on the stool beside the ironing board and laid her head down on it, sitting there in the dark and wondering to herself just what she was going to do. *What if Leon listened to Granny?*

A few minutes past five, Tammi heard the two come inside. They sat down at the kitchen table, where they continued to murmur together. Tammi waited a spell before she sauntered out to stand in front of the refrigerator, opening the door in what she hoped was a nonchalant manner. Things could still be in her favor. She felt her heart wishing for the happy ending of one of her romance novels. She was scared to look over at Leon's face.

She bent down and rummaged through the produce drawer. The cool felt nice after the stifling air of the laundry room, and she gathered a handful of cherry tomatoes, tumbling them around in her fingers.

"Shut that door, Tammi Lynn. I can't pay for you to cool the whole house." Granny's voice sliced through her.

Tammi swallowed and stood up slowly, and as she did she glanced in the direction of the table. One look at Leon's eyes and Tammi knew the answer. Her heart fell to the floor.

That night Tammi lay in bed, her jaws clenched so tight her teeth hurt. Granny was ruining a perfectly gorgeous hunk of love, and Tammi was more than a little mad about it.

Look at Leon! While the rest of the seniors were hanging out at the Tastee Freez after school, here he was going to work at a dusty antique shop. Being a preacher was a crazy thing for Leon, too. It was fine for plain old men with nothing better to do.

Tammi closed her eyes. She saw preachers marching in somber robes holding black Holy Bibles aloft. Grim faces, eyes slitted against all earthly pleasures, they walked an endless road of duty and denial. Her thoughts traveled to Missus Goodlow, the reverend's plain wife, her somber clothing, meek, unadorned eyes, and calloused hands. There was no way that Tammi could ever be a minister's wife!

CHAPTER 19

Leon was purposely avoiding Tammi. At home he spent even more hours alone in his room, and when she caught his eye at Rigby High, hunched over his lunch in the cafeteria or hurrying to the antique shop after the last bell, he always looked away from her. Tammi licked her wounds by reading the first twelve chapters of *Hot-Blooded*. Over and over. It was all she wanted to do, and she locked herself in her bedroom and read until the words, the delicious sensations, grew realer and realer and somehow eclipsed her shattered heart.

Her last day with *Hot-Blooded* fell on October thirtieth, a coolish Saturday, and Tammi hurried through chores, then flew upstairs to hollow out a little nest for herself in the bedclothes. Granny was off on an antique junket, and Pepaw's voice rose from the side yard and through Tammi's open window. "You load fifteen tons and what do you get? Another day older and deeper in debt," he sang with the timbre of a bullfrog, lilting up in a trembly alto before plunging down to a rumbly bass. It was the voice of a totally satisfied being.

Tammi listened closely to the next verse. "Saint Peter, don't you call me 'cause I cain't go. I owe my soul to the company sto'."

Tammi looked down and saw herself pinching the coverlet so hard her arms were shaking. Those words he sang about owing a soul! She never imagined you could owe your soul to something. Anyway, what was a soul? Granny talked to Leon that day about fleshly lusts that ruined a soul.

When Tammi thought of souls, she thought of wispy vapors rising up from bodies at the point of death. Or was that the spirit? Something in Tammi (was it her soul or spirit?) swelled with hope as she determined to pick the Reverend Goodlow's brain about this matter.

With her Sunday school dress ironed and her nails scrubbed, Tammi pushed open the big wooden door to the front of Promiseland. It was Saturday, a cloudy morning in early November that seemed like dusk and that discombobulated Tammi's sense of time. She smiled as she sat down in a frayed wing chair facing the Reverend Goodlow's desk.

"Hello, Tammi Lynn," the Reverend Goodlow said as he set a steaming cup of coffee down and rested his elbows on the desk. He looked pointedly at her, a serious half-smile on his face. "How are you? Nothing like a beautiful day such as this to make you want to praise the Lord!"

"Um, fine. Yes, praise the Lord," she said distractedly, trying to read titles of books behind his head.

"You said you had a spiritual question for me?" He widened his eyes, arranging a small calendar on his desk.

"Yes. It's just that I don't really know . . . um, maybe you have some book I can look at about spirits?"

The Reverend Goodlow nodded. "The *Holy* Spirit? Familiar spirits? The spirit of a man?"

"The spirit of a man!" Tammi said. "And the soul of a man. Specifically, I want to know how God tells somebody He wants them to be His earthen vessel."

"He wants *everyone* to be His earthen vessel." The reverend flung his arms wide in an expansive gesture. "We're all called to spread the Word."

"I know," she said. "I mean how He gets somebody to be a preacher."

"How He calls someone into the ministry?" The Reverend Goodlow wheeled his chair around to face the wall of books behind him. "How he contacts their spirit inside?"

"Yes! That's what I mean!" Tammi had goose bumps. She held her breath while his fingers tickled across a row of spines and settled on a thick burgundy volume. He pulled it out, opened it, and read:

> The body is the house of the soul and spirit, and according to Genesis 3:19, the body goes back to dust at death.
>
> The soul and the spirit of a person are immortal. They make up the inner part of a man. If they dwell in a righteous person, they go to heaven at the point of death.

Tammi cleared her throat. "So, God talks to the spirit or the soul of man to call him? Is the spirit the same as the soul?"

"I don't mean to sound evasive," he said, "but they're so closely related it's difficult to pinpoint the difference between them."

"Oh, well, take this Bible verse then," Tammi said, unfurling a piece of paper to read one of the verses the Reverend Cotton had used on the radio. "Dearly beloved, I beseech you as strangers and pilgrims, abstain from fleshly lusts which war against the soul. First Peter 2:11."

The Reverend Goodlow looked up at the ceiling to think. Or was he looking right through it up to God? "Okay," he said, "the soul of a man is what possesses the appetites. Emotions, passions, certain feelings, desires . . . the soul of a believer is at *war* with earthly lusts."

"Oh, sure, of course it would be, Reverend," she said. "At war. About the call to ministry . . . how did you know *you* were called? Was it your soul or your spirit?" She noted pinpricks of perspiration popping out on the Reverend Goodlow's temples.

"The call." He steepled long, pale fingers. "God calls the spirit, that invisible force in a man that comprises knowledge; the intellect, the mind. If you will."

"How did He talk to *your* spirit?"

"Well, that's a long story."

"I've got time," Tammi said. "I did my chores before daylight. Now let me get this straight, you're saying it's not the soul God tells? He tells a man's *spirit* if He's calling him?" She leaned forward to rest her elbows on her knees. "That means God wouldn't tell another person that He was calling somebody else to be a preacher, right?"

"Essentially, yes. Each one of us is an individual, and a free moral agent. In First Corinthians, chapter 2, we're told that God reveals things to each of us by His Spirit. It says, 'For what man knoweth the things of a man, save the spirit of man which is in him?' "

"So, God spoke directly to you?"

The Reverend Goodlow paused, coughing discreetly into his hankie. "Er . . . it's funny, you know," he said, shaking his head slowly.

In the silence that followed, Tammi's eyes met his and held them until he took in a sharp breath, leaned forward, and cried out, "I hated hog slaughtering!"

For a moment Tammi thought he was pulling her leg. She smiled and laughed a quick "ha, ha!"

"It made me feel so sick," the Reverend Goodlow explained.

She nodded, wearing her best compassionate face.

"When I was a boy, on the farm, we slaughtered a hog every February, and it was my job to, uh . . . wasn't but nine or ten." He squeezed his eyes shut tight, picked up a pencil from his desk, and fiddled with it, looking at the eraser, inspecting the tip, focusing on the black letters along its side. Slowly he began to tell Tammi how his stomach churned with nausea when he saw the stunned and glazed eyes of the hog, smelled the fresh blood. He recalled the death squeal as an ungodly pitch, sending him scurrying off into some trees beyond the barn. "I even remember trying to stuff cotton in my ears every winter, but it didn't help at all."

"That must have been terrible," she said sadly.

"You couldn't understand. I was a very, very sensitive child. Wouldn't even mash a spider . . ." His shoulders slumped forward. "But come one February, my daddy, he thought my squeamish stomach was funny. He said, 'Boy, this is the year you get to deliver the death blow.' " The reverend gave a weak laugh. "Well, I ran off into the woods. Daddy found me just a praying to the Lord to save me from the task at hand." The Reverend Goodlow paused and opened his desk drawer, rustled around, and came up with two butterscotch discs, offered one to Tammi, and popped the other into his mouth.

"So did you get out of it?" she asked, twisting the cellophane wrapper off her candy.

He looked at her a moment. "Nope. My father said I *had* to do it. Had to do the whole hog by myself that year. Said it would make me a tougher man." He stared out the window.

"Did you?"

"What?" He was looking at her like he'd just noticed that she was there.

"Did you have to do the whole hog?"

"Whole hog . . ." He stood up and walked to the window. "Did the whole thing, yes, I did. Crying like a baby, while my daddy laughed. He thought it was funny." He leaned on the sill then and forced a smile.

"God didn't deliver you?" She understood nothing from this story.

"He delivered me," the Reverend Goodlow answered.

"How? I don't see how . . . you still had to *do* it. You cried." She stared at him. "I think that was so sad!"

He nodded. "Oh, yeah. But when I was praying out there before that, I said to God that if he'd show me a way out of slaughtering hogs for good, I'd preach the Gospel."

Under the dim bulb his eyes seemed to sparkle. "So . . ." he said, swiping the end of his nose on the back of his hand and clearing his throat. "We carried some of the meat to our preacher. My daddy and me did. Back then everybody took part of their meat to the preacher. More than likely, a preacher in those days accumulated a lot more than one hog. Didn't even have to slaughter one. Didn't have to get his hands wet with blood.

"And when we carried the meat to our preacher that year, I realized he didn't even *own* any hogs." The reverend folded his hands as if in prayer, swallowing meaningfully. "And there was my answer." He looked directly into Tammi's eyes. "God spoke right to my spirit. That part of me that *knows* what I am supposed to do. He revealed it to my spirit by His spirit. Don't you see?"

"Sure." Tammi scratched her head. "But you didn't *hear* God saying 'be a preacher.' "

"Not in English, I didn't. Some preachers say God called them in an audible voice. But they're a minority, and that's not what the apostle Paul had in mind. The Holy Spirit, the Spirit of God, testifies to our *inner* man, our spirit."

"Well, sounds like God went directly to you," she said. "He didn't tell your *granny* He wanted you to be a shepherd of His flock."

CHAPTER 20

Tammi walked through the next two weeks brimming with confidence, almost anticipatory about telling Leon what she'd learned. Oh, yes, armed with this new knowledge from the Reverend Goodlow, she was counting on getting Leon to open up and let her in. She would tell him what she knew, release him from obligation to Granny, and he would be so grateful he would have to love her. Now she just had to find that perfect moment for her seduction.

The problem was that Leon was rarely around the big house. He dashed in only long enough to eat or shower before heading downtown to Elco Antiques or out to the barn to refinish furniture, stumbling back up the steps to his room in the wee hours of the morning, his fingers stained walnut or oak, dark circles underneath his eyes. He was holding his own as a senior at Rigby High, however. Granny constantly crowed over glowing comments from his teachers and his straight As.

As she waited, Tammi reflected often on the fiercely independent François from *Hot-Blooded*. She loved that scene where he finally yielded to Desirée and her animal passions. What did it say?

> . . . *François, miles away from reasoning, stunned by sheer, blinding passion, pressed his body to Desirée's mindlessly in primitive*

arousal. At last she could relax into her destiny of delicious tingles and shrieks of delight. Too long she'd lived under the agony of unrequited love. A helpless abysmal feeling.

This was a feeling Tammi understood all too well! It seemed an eternity since she and Leon had last kissed.

It was a few days later, during Thanksgiving holidays from Rigby High, when Tammi found the perfect opportunity. A brisk clear November day, her morning chores behind her, she glossed her lips and dabbed some musk oil on her neck.

"I've been thinking of us that time at the reunion," she said throatily, twining her body seductively around a post in the barn, where Leon was busily refinishing a walnut secretary.

There was a lengthy silence as Tammi stood like a statue, her eyes watering from the turpentine and lacquer thinner. At last Leon straightened up, looking at her quizzically. "You just don't get it, do you? I can't be like my father, and I can't keep holding you back. Anyway, there's something I should tell you."

She held her breath.

He shook a black wing of hair from his eyes. "I'm leaving for the Southwest Baptist Theological Seminary in Fort Worth, Texas, soon."

The blood in Tammi's veins froze. "What?!"

"In January. I'm graduating early."

"No!" Tammi whimpered, dropping to her knees, looking beseech-ingly at him. "You don't have to, Leon, because I know what she's do-ing. Anybody who's ever read the Bible knows God doesn't tell a person's grandmother he wants them to be a preacher. The Reverend Goodlow says, 'God speaks directly to a person's own spirit when He wants to use them!'" The frustration that had been eating at Tammi for weeks was causing her to tremble now. "I can't bear even one more moment like this. Don't you want me, too?" she whispered, her heart in her eyes.

Leon's face was grim. "I don't want to hurt you, Tammi," he said, planting his feet and throwing up a hand. "This is not Granny's doing. I've known since I was a child that God is calling me to be His mouthpiece in some form or another. It's my destiny, and you can't fight it. Neither can I."

This torrent of words scraped Tammi's ears. She tried to swallow, the color draining from her face so suddenly she felt faint. "What are you talking about? François submitted to his passion!"

"François?"

"He's an obstinate man, Leon. Extremely proud and stubborn, but not so foolish or blind that he'll suppress his passion for Desirée any longer!"

Leon looked confused. "I don't know these folks, do I?"

"Um—no," she said in a small voice, hesitating, then rushing blindly on. "They're in one of my romance novels."

Leon blinked. "*Romance* novels? Don't tell me you're filling your mind with that trash! No wonder. I knew something was fueling your fire."

"There's nothing wrong with reading romance novels! I think they're beautiful. They're about love."

Leon raised his eyebrows. "I think you need to go ask the Reverend Goodlow's opinion on romance novels."

Tammi stood mute. Her stomach lurched. She thought she was going to vomit up the eggs she'd eaten for breakfast. Was this what it had all come down to? Him telling her he was called of God, and in the next breath calling her romance novels trash? She felt her heart pounding in her ears so hard she was dizzy. She lifted her eyes wildly to Leon's, shaking her head in disbelief. "No, no, no!" she screamed, the words burning her throat.

Leon's tongue flickered across his upper lip. "Listen, Tammi," he said in a soothing voice, "I've always been interested in spiritual matters. I remember even as a child feeling this call on my life. I never felt like I fit in with the other boys. It's kind of hard for me to explain, but I need you to try and understand."

Tammi sank down onto the cold floor of the barn. She bent her head and closed her eyes, picturing a young Leon in her mind, small and distant and ethereal. She could not get her breath as she thought of God, sitting on His throne and pointing a finger at Leon. "Does Aunt Nanette know?" she said at last, tears in her voice. "That you're going to Texas?"

"Yeah," he mumbled. "Mama never has known what to make of it. My calling, I mean. For a while I think she thought I had mental troubles. I told her once that I could see angels, and she thought I was crazy. Still might, for that matter. Did you hear her yelling Tuesday night?"

Tammi shook her head.

"She pitched a fit when I told her I was leaving for seminary."

"She did?"

"Yeah. When I tell folks I have this call on my life, from God, it freaks them out. Even my own mother. She gets all uncomfortable." Leon sighed from the depths of his soul and sank down to his heels.

"It's hard, hm?" Tammi said softly.

"Yeah. But I can't, I won't, try to ignore it anymore. When I hear that voice saying, 'You're set apart for holy things,' I won't fight it." Leon clenched his jaw and crossed his arms, thrusting his hands in his armpits. "I will flee youthful lust."

Tammi could only shake her head. She began to feel a great ache in her center, despair that wrung her heart in exquisite pain, and after a moment she turned on her heel and flew out of the barn.

December first dawned, and at last the weather took a turn toward cool. Tammi wrapped up in a soft denim jacket that matched her bell-bottoms and trudged across the hardened ground to Minna's.

LaDonna and Parks were sitting outside in the Trans Am listening to the end of Roberta Flack singing "Killing Me Softly."

"Hey, girl," Parks said jovially, turning off the engine and stepping out. "What's shakin'?"

"Nothin' much," Tammi said as Minna's front door opened and Priscilla came bounding down the steps toward them, her front legs dancing happily, fluffy tail like a waterfall. She nudged LaDonna's hand affectionately, running circles around the girls.

In one hand LaDonna carried a can of Chase & Sanborn coffee, and in her other she held a platter, topped with a Bundt cake. Inside Minna's kitchen she proceeded to rumble around in the cabinets, plugging the percolator into the wall and making a big show of slicing the cake, which turned out to be some fancy thing called Tunnel-of-Fudge on account of having a chocolate pudding center.

Tammi felt grumpy sitting in the den waiting. She wanted to have a short talk about *Hot-Blooded* and then get on to assigning the next chapters. She didn't care to discuss ways to land a reluctant man. She especially didn't feel up to the usual barrage of questions about her and Leon. "All right," she said, shaking her head at the cake LaDonna placed at her elbow, "this meeting of the Romance Readers' Book Club will now come to order."

"What did y'all think?" Tammi asked, patting the cover of *Hot-Blooded*.

"It was excellent," Minna said. "Again, I had to literally force myself to stop at our designated place! Self-denial is not my strong suit, you know."

LaDonna clucked her tongue, but she was smiling. "I like it a lot better than *Savage Moon*. Every scene is believable, so far. I really like how the author gives us all these different points of view in the different chapters. I like knowing what's in François' mind."

"Hey, yeah, that's right!" Parks shook her head in wonder. "I hadn't even thought of that, but she does! I liked hearing Bettina's side of stuff. I mean, the poor girl has always felt like she's second fiddle to her beautiful sister, Desirée, and I can understand why she's making a play for old François. She's jealous, not to mention the fact that he's such an incredible stud muffin." She lit a cigarette and put it to her lips. A strong menthol aroma mingled with coffee as she cut her eyes at Tammi.

"Yeah," Tammi said. "I have to say I agree. It's nice getting into all their heads. Especially his. But I kept wondering how this woman author, Lacey Hammock, knows so much about the way a man thinks."

"True," Minna said. "The way she described François ' thoughts when he walked into that harem—it seemed exactly the way a man would think!" Minna waved a forkful of cake. "Sounded just like a kid in a candy shop!"

"Well, basically, that's about what men are," LaDonna said. "They're like children when it comes to big groups of half-naked women. Remember how it said he was standing there drooling? Men are so *easy*."

Parks laughed and Minna nodded.

Not all of them, Tammi thought grimly. She put down her coffee mug. "Well, tell me this. How did y'all feel when François accused Desirée of sleeping with his brother?"

LaDonna regarded Tammi thoughtfully. "I think," she said at last, "that he was just feeling guilty because he has the hots for Bettina. He was transferring his guilt onto Desirée. She's innocent. At least it seems like she is, from that last chapter written in her voice. Guess we won't actually know till we finish the book. Speaking of that," she looked pointedly at Parks, "let's make a deal. Please don't anybody tell anybody who hasn't yet read certain chapters what happens. *Some* people tend to get excited and tell other people, and that spoils the surprise."

"Sorry." Parks shrugged. "Guess I just get a little too excited. Listen to this, though. Wouldn't it be a trip if it turned out that both François *and* Desirée were both humping each other's siblings?" She roared with laughter.

LaDonna shuddered. "How can you be so coarse and so . . ."

"Look," Parks said, pointing her cigarette at LaDonna, "you need to get down off your Little Miss Goody Two-Shoes horse and chill!"

Tammi, who would have overlooked this argument any other time, looked fiercely at Parks and LaDonna. "Do y'all ever stop fussing?!" she yelled, jumping to her feet. "Here we are, trying to have some fun, and all you want to do is ruin it!" She stomped her foot. "I say we just agree to finish reading *Hot-Blooded* for our next meeting and get on out of here if this is the way y'all are going to act!"

The club grew silent.

At last LaDonna cleared her throat. "You feeling okay, Tammi?" she asked. "You seem so, I don't know . . ."

"Yeah, why the long face, darlin'?" Minna said.

Tammi shook her head mutely, turning to look out the window, studying the limb of a spindly dogwood until the silence seemed to balloon up to bursting.

"Tell us, darlin'," Minna whispered. "We can help. That's what we're here for."

Trembling, Tammi could not look at anyone as she spilled every last detail. When she finished Minna rose to rustle around in an arrangement of artificial flowers, removing a package of cigarettes. She shook one out, stuck it in her mouth, and lit it.

"Thought you quit," Parks said.

Minna took a deep pull before she said, "Well, I thought I did, too. But I swannee these things help me think better." She sat down, crossed her legs, and smoked that cigarette down to a little nubbin. "Seems to me, Tammi," she said, "you're putting all your eggs into one basket. Here you are, never had a boyfriend in your life. Such limited experience. So young. Never *kissed* anyone besides Leon either, have you?"

"No," said Tammi, and there was a smile in her voice as she recalled Leon's sweet lips on her own.

"So," Minna replied, "the fact of the matter is that you need more experience. What you think you have with Leon, this all-consuming, undying passion, as you call it, you might have with someone else. With *many* others, even. You don't know, and it's not fair to you, or him, either, if you don't at least see."

"Yeah," Parks broke in, "there's tons of men out there."

"I don't think you realize," Minna said, "living in this one-horse town. You owe it to yourself to get out there and sample a few more."

"Oh, I don't think so," Tammi said.

"Trust me on this one," Minna said. "On matters of the heart. I don't agree with all those folks who say there's just one person for each of us. As you know, I adored Franklin, but I also happen to love Elvis."

Tammi pulled a furry pillow into her lap and held it like a shield. She didn't understand how Minna could say these things. What Tammi possessed with Leon was once in a lifetime. Well, what they *had* possessed. Immediately she felt guilty for pooh-poohing something her aunt sounded so sure about. After all, Minna'd been around a long time before she married Franklin, and even now she kept company with a random assortment of fellows.

That late afternoon, Tammi, who had been willing to stake her life on the fact that Leon was her one and only, decided to do some investigating in the realm of love and passion.

CHAPTER 21

Tammi walked into biology class the next morning with a wildly thumping heart. She'd lain awake half the night pondering the male population at Rigby High. *I have no idea where to start,* she thought, letting her mind drift to Desirée in *Hot-Blooded.* She wished she could borrow Desirée's brain for just one day, her boundless capacity for passion, her unfettered spirit, and her totally intrinsic ability to lure men.

But Tammi could not afford wishes. This was her task alone, and today she would pick her first target. She would catch his eye, lure him in, use her feminine wiles.

Old Mr. Colbe stood at the front, unenthusiastically introducing the process of meiosis as Tammi's eyes skimmed the room. At last her eyes lit on Timber Nash, a feral sort of boy with shaggy blond hair and an irreverent nature. It was widely known that Timber's grades were barely enough to move up to a new grade each year and that he planned to drop out of school the instant he turned eighteen.

He ought to be easy enough, Tammi thought, her pulse taking off in a crazy flutter as she copied notes from the blackboard. Mr. Colbe wound down at long last and released them into a hallway swarming with students. Tammi spotted Timber slipping out a side door into the parking lot, and she followed at a distance to stand nonchalantly, watching him toss his book bag into the bed of a dusty pickup truck and lean back against the cab to light a cigarette. He flipped a hank of hair off his forehead and sucked in a deep drag, blowing out a string of smoke rings toward the sky.

Tammi unbuttoned the top three buttons on her blouse and let the warm sun lick her collarbone as she strode toward Timber. "Nice day, isn't it?"

Timber narrowed his eyes. "What say?"

"I said it's a nice day." She looked closer at him. He was dressed in a shabby T-shirt and slouching faded jeans, their frayed hems puddling on top of scuffed boots with worn heels. She relaxed enough to admire his rugged face. Blue eyes and a Roman nose and a bit of a snarl that was not unattractive.

He shrugged, sucking another deep pull of smoke, holding it in and closing his eyes.

"Old man Colbe's a real bore, isn't he?" she asked.

He nodded.

"Who'll ever need to know that stuff for real life, anyway?"

"What I think, too," he said. "Who *needs* any of this crap?" He nodded his head toward the school building.

She could think of only one thing to say next, and it was a bald-faced lie. "I'm going to drop out."

Timber perked up. "Me too," he said, smiling at her.

Here's your opening, Tammi, she thought. *You can do this.* "So, what you gonna do when you're out of here for good?" she managed in a casual, offhanded way, slipping closer to him.

"I dunno," he said, "work at my brother's carburetor shop maybe."

"That sounds interesting."

"Yeah." Timber yawned.

"Sleepy?"

He nodded.

"Want to take a little nap together?" Tammi said, just the thought of this making her pulse race. "I'm skipping next period."

Timber looked long and hard at her. "Ayyup," he said after a spell.

"This your truck?" Tammi sidled closer. He nodded, flinging his cigarette butt to the asphalt and grinding it out with his heel before they climbed into the cab in silence. The air inside was stifling, but Tammi realized she was shaking all over. "I am utterly exhausted," she said.

Timber smiled, letting his head flop against the backrest. "You're a pretty cool chick," he murmured thickly as he closed his eyes.

The moment hung palpably in Tammi's mind. It was time to make her move. This was not a time for the faint of heart. "You're cool, too," she murmured softly, her face hovering near his. He opened one eye and looked at her, his warm menthol breath on her face. She stared at his perpetually snarling lips, and her heart swelled with the promise of savage passion. Timber had that dangerous, bad-boy current running through every vein of his taut body. It wouldn't do to play a sweet young thing with him. She had to be brazen, worldly. She placed a firm hand on his knee and put on a sexy smile. "Timber," she breathed, "you're such a hunk. I've admired you forever."

His eyes widened as she moved in, wrestling herself between him and the steering wheel, straddling his thighs. He began to breathe heavily, pressing his pelvis upward into her so that she could barely breathe. "Oh, baby," he moaned.

Please let Timber's kiss be divine, she prayed, mashing her lips on his. *Let it wipe Leon from my longings.*

Instead, all she got was a sinking feeling in the pit of her stomach. There was definitely no spark. She reared back abruptly to search an astonished Timber's face. She saw no future in his eyes. At last she rolled from his lap, squinting through bright sunlight toward the orange bricks of Rigby High. She felt scalded. Her mind drifted back to that first kiss with Leon. To the white-hot clarity of that moment.

Timber turned to paw at her like a cat trying to revive a dead mouse until she flung herself out the passenger door.

After escaping Timber she cornered Marvin Beaton, the studious president of the Latin Club. Late in the day, she waited to catch him at his locker and crept up behind him, stealthy as a cat.

"Hi, Marvin," she said huskily over his left shoulder.

"Hello," he said, turning and giving her a salute like a soldier.

"I bet you're one of those silent rivers," she said, "teeming with passion under its placid surface."

He looked blankly at her, a hint of warm bologna emanating from his locker. "Kiss me now," she demanded. "Let me feel the elusive passion running so deep inside of you." Emboldened, she rose on tip-toe and pressed her lips onto his, stepping back quickly when he uttered a nasal "Stop" through clenched teeth. She glimpsed a flash of disgust in his cold green eyes, so searing it shriveled her to the bone.

By the end of that week Tammi had conquered three more boys—a football jock, the class clown, and a long-haired free spirit who liked to take photographs of strange objects—and she had washed her hands of any hope of passion at Rigby High. It didn't help that she was now a bit of a laughingstock, as word had gotten out that she was intent on finding "passion."

She rode the bus home, ran upstairs to her room, and threw herself across the bed, a feeling of such hopelessness washing over her that she cried and cried until she grew limp.

At last she struggled up to her elbows to stare out the window into the slate-gray afternoon sky. It made her think of heaven and God, and it occurred to her she hadn't prayed in weeks. She closed her eyes, waiting for the words to come, to feel that warm, divine connection.

No words came, and Tammi panicked. She could not feel God anymore!

The next day, a Saturday in mid-December, Tammi set out to see the Reverend Goodlow once again. It was cold, and she wore layers of sweaters and thick socks, trying to stay in the sunny patches along Sprayberry Road as she hurried to Promiseland.

"Well, well," the Reverend Goodlow looked up at her and smiled as she knocked haltingly on the frame of his office door. "How goes the battle?"

"Hello, sir," she said, wondering if he already knew about her struggle. Perhaps he could see it in her eyes.

"Going to be a cold one tonight, isn't it?" he said. "Have a seat."

In the morning light the church office had an otherworldly look, but the aroma of fresh coffee emanating from one corner gave Tammi a feeling of comfort and intimacy.

They made small talk for a little while, until the reverend rubbed his chin in a manner of contemplation, beckoning to her with a nod. "What's on your mind today?"

"I've been wrestling with some spiritual matters."

"Is that a fact?"

Tammi gazed over his shoulders at a narrow band of sunlight filtering through a split in the curtains. "It all began October of '74," she said, "and it's reached the point where I don't know what to do. I hardly know how to start."

"Start at the beginning," he said, studying her. "I've got all the time in the world."

"Well, I disobeyed Granny," she said hesitantly, "and I led Orry down the wrong path, too. I carried him trick-or-treating, and we ended up with this big stack of novels in our pillowcase, and I didn't know, I mean I didn't realize, how much they'd come to mean to me. I absolutely crave them, Reverend. I'd have to say I *adore* them. It's like they mean more to me than Jesus does. You should see me when I haven't had a chance to read in a while. I guess they must be idols." She twisted the hem of her dress. "It's all I can figure, anyway. And like you always say, 'What agreement hath the temple of God with idols?' "

He nodded.

"I think about the folks in the novels all the time. And I don't want to have to stop. The novels bring me so much pleasure."

"Books can be a fine diversion," he said. "The Lord knows we need our pastimes and our escapes." His eyes crinkled as he smiled. "But it is wrong to disobey our parents, Tammi. That's your spirit, your conscience, telling you that."

"She's not even my real blood grandmother."

"Right, I knew that," he said, slapping the heel of his hand to his forehead like he was adjusting his thoughts. "But Constance Elco *is* your elder. Your guardian. And you should obey her. Go to her and confess what you did, and get it off your conscience. You'd be surprised. Make all the difference in the world."

"Mmmmm," she said.

"What kind of books did you get?" The reverend kicked back in his chair, lacing his fingers across his belly.

"Romance novels," she said.

The reverend shifted in his chair. "Romance novels," he said flatly. "Are these graphic or fluff?"

What did he mean by "graphic"? The books definitely didn't leave a lot to the imagination. "Maybe." She shrugged.

He cleared his throat. "You read these to Orrville?"

"Yessir." Tammi gazed at her knees, a twinge of guilt gripping her heart as she recalled the vow of secrecy she'd made. But surely confessing things to a preacher didn't count. It was like telling it to God! "I started this book club," she said. "This *secret* book club."

He coughed. "There aren't many things more powerful than pornography."

"Pornography?!" Tammi said, appalled.

"Yes, things that objectify people. Some of those books are readable pornography."

"Really?" Tammi felt her face color. She looked away. They sat without talking as the sounds of passing cars drifted into the office.

"Lots of those books are just women's pornography," he said at last. "Gets them all heated up. And it's addictive, you know."

Tammi felt her heart seize up. She could not speak.

"I believe the act of reading those women's romances titillates and encourages illicit relationships," he said gravely. "They blur the lines between right and wrong. It's the lust of the flesh that First John warns us against giving in to. We're also admonished to flee youthful lust in Second Timothy 2:22—to do battle with our own flesh."

Tammi swallowed hard. *Flee youthful lust.* Wasn't that Leon's mantra?

"The evil fiend in sex is lust, Tammi. True sexuality, the way God planned it, leads to humanness. But lust pushes toward dehumanization. Lust *possesses* rather than frees a person."

Tammi frowned, picturing an image of herself desperately clawing at a stack of romance novels just out of reach.

A long silence, then the Reverend Goodlow said, "A certain libidinousness becomes accepted, even desired, behavior, and we're to make no provision for indulging the flesh—to put a stop to thinking about the evil cravings of our physical nature. We cannot gratify its lusts. Romans 13."

Tammi tucked both hands between her knees, squeezing her palms together. How could she argue with this? She looked at the floor, then up at the Reverend Goodlow's eyes. "What should I do?" she asked sheepishly. "I'm really hooked on these things."

"My advice is to pray. It's hard to break an addiction of any kind. Pray and then wait for the truth to come into your mind." He put his right hand atop a faded black Bible and smiled. "Prayer will move what you know in your head into your heart. Truth can hardly be discovered by human intellect. It must be disclosed by God. Sometimes we can't even put our real requests into words. We've always got a gazillion things we need, and it's impossible to simplify all of them down to mere words.

"What David did is he prayed, 'Give me an undivided heart.' He wanted to love God with his whole heart, but he just couldn't do it on his own, so many affections pulled him in so many different directions. What he did was ask God to guard his heart."

"I'll pray!" Tammi assured him, jumping to her feet.

"In the meantime," he said, "keep yourself busy. Give no opportunity for temptation. I'm sure you've heard this plenty, 'Idle hands are the devil's workshop.' " The reverend folded his hands together and in a gentle voice he said, "I've found that pouring myself into Christian service keeps me from temptations of the flesh. Christmas being just a bit over a week away, we could always use an extra heart and some hands to visit the homebound of Promiseland. And of course I'll be praying for you and your addiction."

The Reverend Goodlow is happy, Tammi thought as she slammed the door of Promiseland behind her. *He's serene and he's happy. Why shouldn't I be able to achieve this?*

The next morning dawned clear, with skies a purplish blue, everything sparkling in the bright morning sun. Tammi opened her window to take a deep breath. She'd slept peacefully, the expectation of deliverance a soft bed.

Her spirits were high as she dressed, then flew across the dew-covered grass to the barn, where Leon was refinishing a Queen Anne highboy. The maple highboy lay on its side, and Leon was bent over in intense concentration, scraping a sludgy paste from a cabriole leg. A Pepsi sat on the floor next to a half-eaten ham biscuit.

"Morning, Leon," Tammi said demurely. "Sorry to interrupt, but I've got a little favor to ask." She could see the muscles in his jaw tense. "I want to pour myself into Christian service, and I wondered if you might carry me to visit the homebound of Promiseland. Spread some Christmas cheer."

Tammi loved the look on Leon's face as he laid his scraper on an old pie tin. "What brought you to this decision?"

"Oh, I'm doing battle with the flesh."

"Wonderful." He closed his eyes. "Meet me after we eat supper."

After supper, Tammi waited at the shed beyond the rose trellis as Leon had instructed. She leaned against a cement wall, the low angle of the waning sun making her shut her eyes. She kept her fingers on the handles of a canvas tote that held felt stockings that one of the ladies' circles at Promiseland had made. They were filled with small packets of tissues, notepads, and candy canes. She knew nothing about the homebound; she had merely glanced at their names on the sheet of paper the Reverend Goodlow had pressed into her hands as she left his office.

Would she even know what to say to these folks? Suddenly she couldn't wait till this was over and done with, checked off. Then she felt ashamed of her ulterior motive. All she really wanted was Leon's attention. And boy, this had gotten it.

Maybe it would just take time for her motives to get pure. Maybe after she'd ministered to these folks, after she'd prayed some more, she'd lose her selfish ways. *I'm paying penance*, she thought. *This will set things right with God.*

Leon's black hair fell slightly over his eyes as they sped down the drive. When they neared the highway, his lips curved into a smile. "Which way, Pilgrim?"

Tammi glanced down at the paper in her hands. "Fambro Village," she said. Fambro Village was in the middle of a run-down area on the outskirts of Rigby. Dozens of tar-paper shacks lay scattered like dominoes in a weedy acreage full of rusty cars and mangy dogs. Not many upstanding citizens ventured near Fambro Village. The police, mainly. Maybe a preacher or two. Besides, it didn't seem that the residents *wanted* any interaction with folks outside their community, as if they all but announced, *We have each other. Leave us be.*

Tammi's heart boomed as Leon pulled up along the curb and cut the engine. "I won't be long," she said, stepping out to cross a patch of dirt and climb a few steps to a shaky redwood deck. She knocked.

"Ain't locked," came a man's gruff voice, and Tammi walked into a dim room off the side of a tiny kitchen, where she saw the top of a wiry gray head and the back of a Barcalounger. Strewn all over the floor were yellowed newspapers and drink cans. She choked at the smell, forcing herself to walk through the debris and stand before him.

"Hi," she said, goggling when she realized he wore only boxers. "I'm Tammi Lynn Elco, and I brought you a Christmas stocking. I . . . I go to Promiseland." She placed the bag she was carrying on a table. "The Reverend Goodlow says to tell you you're in his prayers."

He looked her over hungrily. "Come here and bring me that there treat, little lady." He smiled and she saw his empty gums.

Tammi pinched the top of the stocking between her forefinger and thumb. Sidling over a tiny bit nearer to him, she held it at arm's length.

"Ain't a-gonna bite yel" He laughed as his hands fumbled with his fly. "You're a purty lil' thang. Come closer to Daddy."

Tammi looked quickly away, dropping the stocking before stumbling out the door to the tune of his laughter.

The next two visits, one to an ancient woman laid up in bed, who called Tammi "Mother," and the other to a plump woman with no legs who only cried and cried, pushed Tammi even further into the depths of depression. When she returned to the Jaguar after the last visit, she made a disgusted noise in her throat and sank wearily into the dark passenger seat.

"You okay?" Leon's voice was tender.

"Um, sure," she said, trying not to cry. "I'm fabulous."

Nothing more was said, and when they reached home Tammi crumpled the list of shut-ins and threw it in the trash. She ran upstairs, tossed the remaining stockings into the back of her closet, then knelt in the dark at the edge of her bed and tried in vain to pray. The course had seemed so clear to her, and now she was totally confused. Sometimes it seemed the romance novels were indeed fleshly, sinful, while at other times they were only beautiful expressions of love.

She was suddenly very tired of being on this roller coaster. "I just don't care anymore," she whispered, pulling *Hot-Blooded* out from under her mattress and setting it across her knees.

Could she picture life without this sweet escape? This passion?! When she contemplated being without the romance novels, the club, it cut her to the heart. She could not give them up. What in heaven's name had she been thinking?

In two days, Tammi finished reading *Hot-Blooded,* sighing in relief and exultation as Desirée lay happily enfolded in François' pulsing embrace, her desperate yearnings satisfied.

She read it again and again, and each time the words salved Tammi's frayed edges a bit more. The steamy, sensual worlds of

Desirée and François were, Tammi acknowledged, on some level, fiction, but she continued to find joy in their story.

The book became her defense against Leon's avoidance of her, against Granny's growing agitation over the deepening drought. Whenever her conscience or the Reverend Goodlow's face threatened, Tammi had only to bury her thoughts in the steamy words that had become her world.

And, at last, she simply set her teeth and told herself that spiritual riches could not compare to the joys of the flesh.

She could not admit this to Leon, however. She loved appearing pious in his eyes. He treated her differently now that he thought she'd stopped reading the books: held the chair for her at mealtimes, helped her with chores. But it was not passionate, not charged with sexual energy, and the sheen of this wore off quickly. *Oh well, he'll be gone to Fort Worth soon, anyway,* she admitted to herself bleakly.

CHAPTER 22

"Happy 1976, sweetie!" Minna threw open her front door. "How ya doin'?"

Tammi trudged in and slumped down onto the sofa. "Terrible. It's not like this was sprung on them out of the blue. *Granny's* the one who wanted Leon to go to seminary. Nanette, I can understand. But now they're both tearing around up there like raving lunatics while Leon packs. Hollering. Mainly at each other."

Minna lit a cigarette, inhaling deeply and then letting smoke drift luxuriously from her nostrils. "How do *you* feel about Leon leaving?"

"Scared." Tammi felt herself shrink even further inside.

"Howdy!" Parks barreled through the door and LaDonna followed, a bag of Doritos and a two-liter of Pepsi in her arms. "We pick us a new book today, huh? I don't know if I can pick between *The Sheik's Temptress* and *Sweet Bride of Revenge*."

Tammi had skipped breakfast and lunch and was suddenly starving as she made her way over to where LaDonna was filling four cups with ice. She helped herself to a great mound of chips and a cup of Pepsi, sitting back down carefully, listening to Parks's rich laughter as Minna confided that she'd already blown her annual New Year's resolution to look like Farrah Fawcett.

"Let's get started," Tammi called, and they all took their places, kicking off shoes to tuck stocking feet up comfortably, the crunch of Doritos resounding.

"This meeting of the Romance Readers' Book Club will now come to order." Tammi patted her lips with a napkin. "Who wants to go first in the discussion of *Hot-Blooded?*"

"I will," LaDonna said. "Let me see . . . I have to say I was glad to find out that neither François nor Desirée were sleeping with other people. Still, I don't feel it was honest for Desirée to wear that white gown when they got married. After all, they'd done it with each other, every which way. *Everywhere*, too."

Parks snorted. "I think they deserve gold crowns for all those temptations they made it through! Look how Bettina flung herself at François!"

"You do have a point," LaDonna admitted.

"I was totally impressed with Desirée when François' horny handsome brother, the one with all the gold, tried to buy her that castle," Parks said. "She stuck by her pauper!"

Tammi could think of little to say to all these comments. Her mind was consumed with Leon's imminent departure.

Like she could read Tammi's thoughts, LaDonna turned to her and asked, "How's *your* romance going, girl?"

"Not too great." Tammi's voice quavered. "Leon's separating himself from worldly things. But I love him with all my heart, and sometimes I feel like I could just literally *die!*" She turned her stricken face to Minna. "All those boys I kissed at school, you know? Like you suggested? Well, it was awful. Felt no different from kissing my pillow. Worse! Wasn't one bit like kissing Leon. I thought if I just waited it out, he'd . . . ." The words died in her throat.

"Darlin'," Minna crooned, wrapping her arms around Tammi as if she were a child, rocking gently. "Don't worry. We'll help you. Won't we, girls?" Minna looked beseechingly at Parks and LaDonna.

"Sure thing," Parks said. She frowned into space a moment. "This puts me in mind of the discussion topic we were s'posed to do *last* meeting. I'd been studying on it, too, so let me see if I can remember how it was I figured you could land a reluctant man . . . I remember now! I'd show the boy some *skin*! As we've learned, men are defenseless when it comes to a woman baring her naked flesh. Remember old François?"

LaDonna groaned, looking fiercely at Parks as if her glare could pierce her cousin. "You're disgusting! We're talking love here, not lust!"

"Don't you know by now?" Parks shook her head in wonder. "You can't go fishing without a worm. You've got to get over this wholesome crap. Everyone knows we're just animals."

LaDonna folded her arms, gazing off into the distance like she was trying to gather her patience. "We're *not* animals," she said loudly.

"What do you think, Minna?" Tammi murmured.

"It can't hurt to cover all your bases, hon. You never know what might be just the ticket for a particular man."

Tammi smiled as Parks's words rang in her ears. Sometimes people *did* act like animals. Maybe she could corner Leon before his departure and bare some flesh. Skin would ignite his passion and convince him to love her! This would be her last-ditch effort before he left for seminary. Hey, maybe he wouldn't even go to seminary! Surely he was no more immune to bare-naked flesh than Mikolo, Cody, Running Bear, and François.

After the pledge, Parks put her hands on her hips. "I say we pick *The Sheik's Temptress*, on account of that sexy hunk on the cover. I'll read first, and let's cover the first fifteen chapters! I'm also gonna pick the discussion topic: 'What and What Not to Touch to Get His Loins Throbbing.'" Parks guffawed when she saw LaDonna's exasperated expression.

The smell of woodsmoke hovered in the air the next day as Tammi made her way out to the barn. Temperatures had fallen to the 30s, and she wore a thick sweater with no brassiere underneath, acutely aware of the giddiness in her knees and her bare nipples against the wool.

The barn reeked of turpentine as Tammi stood in the shadows, drinking Leon in, all the way from his blue stocking hat to his rump-hugging jeans. "Morning," she breathed.

Leon jumped. He turned, narrowing his eyes at the deliberately tousled mane of hair hanging loosely around Tammi's expectant face. "Good morning," he said tersely. "You'll have to excuse me, but I've got to finish this before I leave."

Tammi eased into the stall. It looked like a tornado had touched down. The floor was carpeted with newspapers and stained rags. A wooden door propped up on sawhorses held a jumble of clamps, drills, and steel wool.

"Got to finish," Leon said more firmly, sliding a putty knife along the top of a Sheraton drop-panel chest until he had a gooey pile of residue waiting at the edge. He bent to get a rusty can to scrape the glop off into.

"That piece certainly has nice lines," Tammi said, parroting what she'd overheard a million times from Granny.

"Yeah," he said. "Sometimes, when you get the veneer off of some-thing, you can see the beautiful wood grain underneath like this cherry here, with bird's-eye maple and mahogany banding on the drawers" Leon's eyes were shining as he ran his fingers along the chest. Tammi shivered; it felt as if he were running them all over her body.

There was good energy around Leon right now, a feeling of satisfaction in the work he was doing, and she moved closer, watching while he worked as precisely as a surgeon. He knelt to inspect something on the side of the chest, and said to Tammi, "Mind handing me that razor knife there?"

She moved quickly, eager to please him. "Here," she said throatily, pressing the knife into his palm, letting her hand linger on the warmth of him beneath the rubber glove. Her fingertips began tingling, and she used them to yank her sweater over her head, tossing it to the floor. "I love you, Leon!" she uttered in a wild, breathless cry, thrusting her naked breasts forward.

Leon jumped to his feet and turned his back to her. "Put your sweater back on, Tammi." Fury coated his words. "You don't love me. You lust me. You'll forget me when I'm gone. I bet you're reading those romance books again, aren't you?"

Tammi gave a small gasp of hurt and sank to her knees, palms cupping her breasts to offer them the way Desirée did. "I swear I won't forget you! We're meant to be together, Leon. I knew it the moment we first kissed and you swept me up in tumultuous passion. You changed me, Leon, and I became *this!*" She pulled her hands away from her breasts to gesticulate wildly. "A person madly, madly in love with you!"

Shaking his head, Leon kept his eyes averted from Tammi. "Passion is not love," he spit. "It's just hormones. Purely responding to stimuli! This is only youthful lust."

Fury shook Tammi's soul as the wind rattled the weathered boards of the barn. "I know it's not only youthful lust!" she cried, struggling to her feet, every hormone in her body firing as she moved toward him. Leon remained a statue when she wrapped her arms around him from behind in one last attempt at seduction. She pressed the tip of her tongue to his vulnerable neck, her hardened nipples jutting into his back. "Oh, please, Leon," she breathed into his hair.

Leon shook his head. Firmly he unhooked Tammi's arms and pushed them down to her sides. He bent to pick up her sweater, keeping his eyes on the floor as he placed it in her hands. "Put this back on," he said in a strangled voice.

Leon turned away from her quickly to stride out of the barn, but not before she'd seen the hunger, the animal longing in his dark eyes.

Tammi ran out of the barn and up to her bedroom, where she wrapped herself in her quilt, silent tears of mortification rolling down her freckled cheeks. She lay there through lunch and afternoon chores, until she fell into a fitful nap, startling awake when Granny's voice floated upstairs, "Tammi Lynn! Come set the table for supper!" The last thing she wanted to do was show up for Leon's farewell supper, but she knew Granny would ask way too many questions if she stayed in her room any longer. She got up and stumbled down the hallway to splash her face with water and went downstairs.

At supper, the space between Tammi and Leon felt monstrous. It was like Tammi was on one planet and Leon on another, floating in opposite directions. He spoke to her in a brisk, offhanded tone that cut her to the quick.

Granny had pulled out all the stops; candles flickered down the center of the long mahogany table, which was set with heavy ornate silverware, crystal glasses, and linen napkins embroidered with Es.

"I'm really going to miss you, Leon," Granny said over baked ham and yeast rolls. "I imagine we've had our best months ever at Elco Antiques! It's hard to believe our finds: the Duncan Phyfe table, the Windsor chairs, the Sheraton drop-panel chest. And don't forget the mahogany Pembroke table!" She paused for a sip of iced tea. "I knew you'd refinish everything just like a professional! Beats all I ever saw, the way you can transform furniture. If I didn't know you were destined to be a man of God, I'd think your calling was antiques." She leaned into Leon, closing her eyes in an enraptured smile.

Tammi shot him a look in the flickering light. He was more gorgeous than ever, in a navy turtleneck, his sideburns neatly trimmed.

He didn't say a word, and they ate in silence for a space of time, until Tammi blurted out, "I'll help with the refinishing now that Leon's leaving." She smiled at Granny.

"You've got no experience."

"Everybody has to start somewhere." Tammi looked steadily at the old woman, her pulse throbbing at her wrists and neck like tiny hammers. "I'll bet I could learn quick. I'll study all those books about stripping and refinishing you've got out on the porch."

Granny pushed her cut-glass bowl of ambrosia away. In the dancing flames, she looked different; the hard angles of her face softened somewhat. "I never dreamed you'd take a shine to the antique business, Tammi Lynn," she said at last. "But maybe you'll have a knack for it."

Chapter 23

All through the days of January, Granny immersed herself in the world of antique collecting. It was as if, now that Leon was gone, she was possessed with acquiring rare pieces, scouring the countryside like a tornado, trailing equal parts of exhilaration and exhaustion in her wake.

Everyone tried to stay out of her way, except Tammi, who had embraced the idea that keeping busy was critical. "Put me to work," she begged.

"We'll go soon," Granny kept assuring her. "I'll teach you the business from the ground up."

The Sheik's Temptress was a glorious escape when it made its way to Tammi, but mostly it felt to her as if she were merely existing, marking time until who knew when. It was as if she were walking around with her outer layer of skin peeled off—every thought of Leon was like being splashed with lemon juice. She tried not to recall the image of the Jaguar's taillights fading to nothingness as Leon left for Texas, a scene so heinous Tammi felt panicky every time it crossed her mind.

"He'll be home for Easter, and Easter will be here before we know it," Minna remarked cheerfully one afternoon as Tammi trudged through her yard on the way home from Viking Creek. "I'm sure absence will have made his heart grow fonder. Time apart clears up a lot."

Tammi hugged herself against the chill in Minna's side yard. Which would it be? Her to forget him, or him to want her?

They left the house together the first Saturday in February, Tammi following Granny out to the Cadillac underneath an overcast sky. Granny settled a red plaid thermos on the seat between them, and looked over at Tammi, a slow smile warming her sharp features. "Well, dear," she said, "I promised I'd teach you the business from the ground up."

Tammi goggled. She'd never been called "dear" by Granny in her whole life! She was warmed as she couldn't remember being in a long while. The feeling inside the car was chummy and conspiratorial as they sped along, slowing to a stop for gas on the lower outskirts of Rigby at Tabor's Stop 'n Shop. Tabor's was festooned with cheap red and green tinsel along the roof overhang, plastic poinsettias affixed to the gas pumps with black electric tape.

"Christmas decorations in February! There's some tacky folks out this way," Granny said when she returned from paying. She took two cups from the glove box and poured coffee from the thermos, handing one to Tammi. "Now, lesson number one: to find treasure around here, you've really got to know the backroads. The prime opportunity is at the very end or very beginning of each month, right before rent payments are due.

"Last month folks were desperate for money to pay Christmas bills, and I got a sterling silver tea service for twenty-five bucks, and an Empire lyre-back armchair, underneath layers of Dutch-blue paint, for fifty bucks! Just a little elbow grease and I quadrupled my investments."

Tammi listened wide-eyed.

"Now, February is good, too. Folks are still trying to pay off Christmas." She took a long gulp of steaming coffee and gave a satisfied nod. "Save your cup," she said, starting the engine once again.

The Cadillac bounced along the rutted parking lot and back onto the road. "Rather have a brand-new vinyl Barcalounger than a Regency carved armchair!" Granny shook her head in disbelief. "All they want is the new stuff."

Tammi was silent.

"I said *new* stuff. Mass-produced junk, like Formica dinettes, glass-and-chrome coffee tables, velour sofas. Tacky, tacky. Has no lines!" This thought caused Granny to sit up taller, straighten her skirt, and pat her handbag on the floorboard next to Tammi's feet. Her handbag was shiny black patent leather with a big gold clip shaped like a horseshoe. When Granny began easing her way along the shoulder of Landrum's Road looking for somewhere to park, Tammi slugged down the last of her coffee.

Granny locked the Caddy up tight, and they walked along the shoulder of the road for a quarter mile or so, coming to a halt between two rows of shotgun shacks in various states of disrepair. Granny toed a white tire sticking halfway up out of the dirt, then took hold of Tammi's arm and strode along between two rows of river stones.

"Don't act excited about a thing you see." Granny lowered her voice. "Act like you think it's worthless junk." She knocked briskly on the door. "To them it is," she whispered.

Presently the door opened a crack. "We don't need nothing," a woman's husky voice said as two little children's faces squeezed between her hip and the door frame, edging it open. "Get on back in there!" the woman barked and they scurried away.

"Hello, Nita." Granny pushed the door open wide to reveal a dark woman with a red-checked dishrag in her hands. Behind her four small children were clamoring around a tiny black-and-white TV set on the floor.

"Hello, Miz Elco," she said, wiping her forehead.

"How you making out?" Granny asked.

"I be tired," Nita said, looking at Tammi with a frown.

Tammi smiled warmly at her.

"I'm sorry to hear that," Granny said, peering around Nita to look at a man stretched out on a rug behind the door. "This be my granddaughter, Tammi Lynn Elco," she added, unaware of how affected she sounded.

"It's a pleasure to meet you." Tammi offered her hand.

"Nita, darlin', do you need some money?" Granny dipped her chin to her chest. "Do you, hon?" She patted the woman's forearm. "You could buy yourself one of those chrome daybeds down at Paley's Furniture. I imagine that would be a lot more comfortable than him laying on that old rug on the floor." Granny reached into her handbag and pulled out her wallet. "Give you thirty dollars for that old rug, Nita."

"I told you last time you was here, Miz Elco, when I sold you that old pot, that rug were my gramma's and it was give to her by her master when he free her. She give it to my momma, who done left it to me when she died. That rug's got history."

Granny shook her head. "You got sentimental value for a rug that was a *castoff* from white folks?!" She slid inside the house, fingering the rug. "It's bare in a patch or two," she said. At this the man on top grunted and rolled over onto his back. His mouth hung open to reveal a few brown teeth.

"I don't know . . ." Nita looked down at the rug. "That rug has history."

"Threadbare!" Granny sighed. "I don't know *why* I'm even wanting to give you any money to haul it out of here for you. Help you tidy up your home for the new year. I reckon it's just that I'm still in the holiday spirit. And because of that holiday spirit, I'll give you forty dollars. You can buy yourself one of those pretty store-bought Christmas trees they got on sale at the Kmart."

In the uneasy silence, Tammi crept over to the rug. She lifted one corner. It was an Oriental pattern in maroon, navy, mustard, and cream. Tammi recognized it from one of the books she'd been studying on antiques. "Looks like a hand-loomed Persian!" she whispered close to Granny's ear. Immediately Granny laid a rigid finger to her lips.

"I don't know," Nita said again, shaking her head.

Granny was now over in one corner of the kitchen rubbing the top of an old trunk that served as a storage shelf for jars of beans and tomatoes. "Oh, Nita, honey," Granny said, her voice rising as she bent down to feel along the bottom of the trunk. "What do you mean? Surely you want the finer things in life!"

"Never had no daybed before." Nita's jaw was thrust out.

"Doesn't mean Jerome wouldn't be proud to own one. They're shiny gold and have a nice foam pad on top. Mmmmm, feel a lot better'n that old rug on the floor."

Nita stared at the sleeping man. He stirred, sat up, and looked at Granny with his mouth open. He rubbed bloodshot eyes with his thumbs, breathed out a "How-do" in Granny's direction.

Granny's nostrils widened. "Drinking," she said sharply.

Nita hung her head. Tammi looked away.

"What's going on?" The man gestured so excitedly with both hands that he lost his balance and flopped over.

"Nothing you need to worry over, Jerome," Nita said wearily.

"I say what's going on, woman?"

"Miz Elco want to buy that rug you on."

Jerome looked down.

"Your sweet Nita wants to buy you a fancy new golden daybed with a soft pad on top, sir," Granny said excitedly. "I'm aiming to help her raise the money by buying that worn-out rug."

Jerome looked up suspiciously.

"Looks like your young'uns need some new shoes, too," Granny added, a look of sympathy washing over her face.

"Then why don't you just *give* us some money?" Jerome exaggerated each word. "You wanting us happy?"

Granny leaned in to whisper conspiratorially, "Your beautiful wife is a proud woman. I'll pay her forty dollars, get that old rug out of your way, and put you, sir, on a fine new daybed fit for a king." Granny strode to her purse, removed her wallet, and pulled out four crisp bills, holding them up in a fan shape.

"That right?" Jerome said, inspecting the rug once more. He shrugged, struggled to his feet, and snatched the bills from Granny.

Tammi was on Granny's heels as she carried the rolled-up rug outside, stopping to give it a good shake, scattering the children who followed behind.

It was six o'clock when they finished, almost dark. "Thanks to us, those four little families will have themselves a nice new year," Granny said.

Tammi did not reply.

"Don't you think they'll have a nice new year?" Granny prompted as they turned into the driveway. The skin on her nose seemed to draw up tighter. "Don't you?"

"Well," Tammi said, measuring her words carefully. "Those were some valuable things we got."

Granny's eyebrows flew up. "Those folks needed money, Tammi Lynn. They needed cash right now. We performed a service." She pulled underneath the shed and cut the engine. "The fact of the matter is," Granny said, sitting erect, "it would never cross their mind that they could do that! They'd never have the get-up-and-go to carry their rug or their plate or their vase or their candlesticks to an appraiser.

"You don't think it would ever occur to them to do that, do you? To find out how valuable what they consider to be an old hand-me-down is? Do you?" Granny jangled the car keys.

Tammi gave a weak shrug.

"Of course it wouldn't!" Granny snapped. "Those folks are ignorant. God *made* them to be ignorant. It's part of His plan. He made the likes of *us*, those with the brains, to *help* them. That's God's plan. That's what He likes to watch down here."

"Oh," Tammi said.

Granny carried the rug, and Tammi carried a pasteboard box full of the rest of the items into the house to set them on the dining room floor. Granny sat down with a contented sigh.

"All this for under a hundred!" she said. "When we get the rug cleaned and these other things spit and polished, you'll see how good we did!"

Tammi didn't respond, and Granny leaned forward to touch her shoulder. "Think of those little pickaninny faces, Tammi Lynn! Thanks to us, they'll have new shoes. If their sorry daddies don't drink up all the money, that is. Yessum. For all we know, their sorry daddies would've fallen asleep with a lit cigarette and burned their valuable antiques slap up! Maybe the young'uns, too. Burned up, I mean. Don't you see?"

Tammi laughed nervously. "Oh, well . . . yes!"

Granny's determination and enthusiasm were wonderful distractions for that wounded part of her.

Tammi sat on the couch in the parlor the next afternoon, visiting with Nanette and Minna. Granny was gone to a meeting at Promiseland, and Pepaw was turning the soil in the cotton fields.

"I believe I'll fix us some Cajun-spiced popcorn," Nanette said. "It's this great little recipe I used to do for my bridge club."

By the time the big yellow bowl was empty, Tammi was beginning to feel drunk on the popcorn, light conversation, and warm feelings.

Suddenly Nanette said, "I heard from Leon yesterday. He's doing well, learning a lot, he says. Asked about all of you."

"That's nice. We sure miss him around here." Minna looked pointedly at Tammi, whose heart had moved up to her throat and was hammering like crazy.

"Yeah," Nanette said, "me too. But it sounds like the environment is good for him. He got to talking so about his classes he didn't even mention his father."

"How is poor Finch?" Minna's face was pinched with concern.

Nanette shrugged. "Still recuperating."

"Maybe that near-death experience will be a real wake-up call for him, and he'll give up the drinking."

"If he'd give up the women, Minna, I'd go back to him. I mean, the drinking's bad, but I can handle that. Ever since he started running around on me, I've wondered if it isn't just me. If I couldn't change somehow, and he'd stop. If I couldn't be prettier, or more fun . . . because I know how much it hurts my boy to see us like this; it tears him up. Leon's a sensitive soul, you know. Things affect him so much more than they do most people. He just seems to go inward somehow. He won't *talk* to me about it. I say to him, 'Leon, honey, let's talk it through, you and I.' Wouldn't you think the boy could talk to his *mother*? You should see him. So stoic. Won't say a word. But it hurts him, I know."

"Before we left for Rigby, we were packing up our things, and Leon came up on a stack of Finch's girlie magazines, and he just went ballistic. Screaming and yelling and, I don't know, berserk. Ripped them all to shreds."

Nanette slumped forward and said, "I know my boy needs help."

Minna handed her a crumpled napkin. "He'll be okay, Nan," she said softly, though she didn't sound at all convincing to Tammi.

CHAPTER 24

Parks brought refreshments to February's meeting. "Got us some frozen pizzas, plus a six-pack of ice-cold Pepsi," she said, sprinting up Minna's front steps with LaDonna by her side.

A thrill spread through Tammi when she spied the cover of *The Sheik's Temptress* jutting out from underneath Parks's arm. She'd been holding her breath till today's meeting, longing for her turn to read again. She'd never needed anything more in her entire life.

There were still waves of pain and mortification whenever she recalled the scene with Leon in the barn. She was going to call Parks on the bare-naked theory.

Minna appeared as Parks was sliding the pizzas into the oven. "Ooh whee, pizza!" she squealed. "Believe I've got a loaf of Velveeta in the Frigidaire."

"Well, guess we better pig out first then." Parks dug around in her shoulder bag, lit a Marlboro, and sank down at the dinette. LaDonna and Tammi joined her for cold Pepsis while Minna stirred a boiler of melting Velveeta and popped in an 8-track of Neil Diamond singing "Sweet Caroline."

Parks began describing an office romance at the Zenith Insurance Agency, where she worked afternoons as a receptionist. "They're both of 'em married," she said. "And when Mrs. Dendrick calls, I have to cover for Preston, and when Mr. Hogan calls, I have to cover for LuAnn. He would just *die* if he found out."

"Who?" asked LaDonna.

"Mr. Hogan. He thinks his wife LuAnn hung the moon. He's in blissful ignorance."

This struck Tammi as sad, and she closed her eyes to sigh.

"Hey!" Parks slapped the table so hard her Pepsi can jumped. "LuAnn informed me that Mr. Hogan don't melt her butter no more. Okay? Don't you go getting all hangdog on me. We got a party going on here!"

What a perfect phrase! Tammi's mind wandered to Leon, and she whispered soulfully, "You melt my butter, Leon."

Parks took a drag off her cigarette. "You still got it bad for old cuz, huh?"

"Yeah," Tammi admitted. "Bad thing is, I don't believe we parted on a very good note."

"Tell!" LaDonna's voice lilted with eagerness.

Tammi leaned forward, forgetting to blush. "Well, I flashed my bare-naked titties right up in his face."

LaDonna's mouth dropped open, and Minna let out an astonished poof of breath. Parks got to her feet. "Way to go, girl!" she yelled.

"Oh, for heaven's sake." LaDonna looked sharply at Parks. "Didn't you hear Tammi say things aren't rosy between them?"

Tammi cleared her throat, and in a small, quiet voice described the entire scene in the barn. "That blows your whole theory on no man being able to resist bare female flesh, huh, Parks?"

"All depends on who's doing the flashing!" Parks laughed herself into snorts, then straightened up and looked seriously at Tammi. "You know I'm kidding. I can't believe he didn't take the bait."

"Well, he didn't, and it was so weird around him after that. I felt like dying."

"Bet it was tough, darlin'," Minna crooned. "But remember how I said I think absence will make Leon's heart grow fonder?"

"Leon told me that separation would make me realize that it's not love. That I'll realize it's only lust."

"What if it is only lust?" Parks said. "Is that so terrible?"

"It's *not* only lust!" yelled Tammi. Then after a bit, "At least I don't think so."

"You mean you aren't *sure*?" LaDonna's eyes grew huge. She clutched her Pepsi tightly.

"Stop!" Parks shook her head as she rose to pull the pizzas from the oven. "I told y'all, none of this serious crap. What *is* love, anyway?"

Her words hung in the air as everyone devoured the pizzas, dunking each bite into the pot of bubbling Velveeta Minna sat in the center of the dinette. When they finished, Parks stood, burped, and said, "Let's move to the comfy den. For our *fun,* lighthearted meeting!"

No fair! thought Tammi. *If Parks won't let me discuss my personal romance issues, A club should support the members!*

"Okay, who'll start us out on *The Sheik's Temptress*?" Parks said, plopping down heavily into the wing chair. "I personally found it very scrumptious. Got me hot when it described Abdul . . . those little indented places on the sides of his muscular brown butt? I swear I felt like crawling into this book and biting them!"

LaDonna's mouth twitched into an involuntary smile. "He does sound cute."

"'Too bad he's betrothed to that Najat woman," Minna said. "He barely knows her. They've only talked once, and he certainly doesn't love or desire her."

"Arranged marriages are to produce an heir," LaDonna said. "It may seem like a barbaric custom, but I'm hoping he'll fall in love with Najat after they're married. It could happen."

"Abdul loves Rosemary!" Tammi's whole body felt tense.

"Maybe," LaDonna said, "but he's known from the day of his birth that he's to be king. Every little thing, from his education to them picking Najat as his fiancée, is geared toward that destiny."

"Listen to this!" Tammi grabbed *The Sheik's Temptress*, flipped it open, and began to read:

Abdul's throbbing loins wouldn't let him sleep. He desired to drink in every little thing about that fair American beauty, Rosemary, who lay sleeping beneath the Sahara sky. The way her golden hair curled about her shoulders, her rose-tinged lips, the sound of her breathing like water over rocks. He'd never known anything with the perfect clarity that he knew he loved this creature, desired her.

Abdul was naked from the waist up, and his chiseled muscles shone in the moonlight as he placed a quivering hand on Rosemary's creamy forearm. Never before had he been tempted to shirk his duty, to turn from his destiny. "I long to sheathe myself inside you, Rosemary!" Abdul screamed silently through the darkness. "I have known it since I first saw you." Frustration and helplessness drained the life from him. He couldn't fight desire, or his turgid member, even if this country would soon be his responsibility. He could not marry Najat, a woman he did not love. Could not turn away from Rosemary.

"Don't y'all see?" Tammi asked, her eyes filled with tears. "Isn't it sad?"

"Uh-uh! None of that!" Parks said. "Let's move to our topic. Who wants to begin?"

"I will." Minna smiled. "What and what not to touch to get his loins throbbing," she mused. "Now, with Franklin, all I had to do was pinch his nipples."

LaDonna's mouth fell open.

"Oh, honey. Even on men, nipples are an erogenous zone. Now, with Charles, it was nibbling his neck . . . and let's see . . . Petey was a toe man. Sucking his toes got him hot."

"Disgusting!" LaDonna breathed out.

"Tell about that," Parks begged.

"I had to pretend they were hot dogs." Minna giggled. "You know, go somewhere else in my mind? He'd yank off those boots, peel off his socks . . . he had really big, hairy toes with sock fuzz stuck on, so that took a lot of imagination! Eventually he got to where he'd let me run a wet washrag over him first. He loved me to drag my teeth along his insole."

LaDonna gagged.

"Don't knock it till you try it," Minna said simply.

"Okay!" Parks said robustly. "I'll tell about what *not* to touch. There's this guy, we went out some, and I just couldn't resist his hair! He had this sexy mullet, see? Man oh man, I couldn't help myself. I'd reach out and run my fingers down his long gorgeous hair the color of rum. First time, he asked me not to touch it. He took great pride in that hair of his. Later, though, he got to slapping my hand away. I'd hit him back, of course, and things got nasty. Now he's losing his hair."

"Serves him right," Minna teased. "What else?"

"Oh, ain't nothing much else a man doesn't crave for us to touch. Except maybe his wallet. And memories of his dear mama. Don't say *nothing* bad about a man's mama. Hear?"

"You're right about that," Minna said. "LaDonna?"

"Me?" she squeaked. "I can't say. But maybe I can soon. There's this certain fellow I've got my . . ." She blushed deeply.

"Ooh whee!" Parks clapped her hands. "You got yourself a crush?"

"Maybe," LaDonna peeped.

Tammi's curiosity burned, but she knew enough not to dig at the girl. LaDonna would reveal things in her own sweet time.

"Alrighty," Tammi said. "Time for our pledge. But first, read the next ten chapters of *The Sheik's Temptress* for next meeting. Anybody got a suggestion for a topic?"

"Let's tell our fantasies, girls," said Minna. "Let yourselves go wild! Pretend you live in a world where nothing's considered sinful or taboo."

"No moral absolutes?" LaDonna squeaked.

"None."

When Tammi carried *The Sheik's Temptress* down to Viking Creek, she found that it was dog-eared and scuffed, crumbs dribbling from the book's seam as she turned pages. She'd planned to read only the next ten chapters and send it back around, but somehow, when she sat down on the cool pine straw and began reading, the rest of the world grew distant. It faded away to nothing as she walked the wide, sandy stretches of Arabia, following poor Abdul and his unquenchable yearnings, until the very end, where at last they were quenched in Rosemary's passionate embrace.

It startled Tammi when she got to the last word in the book, and she began absentmindedly flipping through the last pages, blinking at advertisements for a half-dozen other selections in the Exotica Erotica series.

First she felt a twinge of disloyalty to the club, reading ahead like that, but when she stopped and considered, she realized that reading the entire novel was necessary. It was like a drug, like insulin to a diabetic. The author, Daphne Cherrisse, might have been writing of

Tammi. The heartbreaking words spilling from Abdul's mouth mirrored her own.

"I'll never settle for anyone else, either," Tammi whispered. "I do love Leon, and if he won't have me, I'll just live a life of sad frustration."

Days went by, and Tammi spent hours shut away in her room, broody and distant. Her growing anguish began to frighten her when a few brave irises made their appearance in early March.

It was the driest spring in recorded history. There were no puddles spawning wiggletails, no dogtooth violets carpeting the riverbanks, and folks sat around talking longingly of the past. Of lush green lawns sprinkled with forsythia and azaleas.

One early evening dusk drifted down like a shroud over Tammi as she lay in bed listening to the noise of cicadas. Her thoughts turned to LaDonna, and she realized all of sudden why they called it a "crush." It was pure, unadulterated agony, the way your heart physically ached. Tentatively she placed one hand over her chest and pressed.

"Got . . . to keep . . . busy," she mumbled, wincing as she stepped into her work jeans, pulled her hair back, and made her way downstairs.

The barn held its arms out to welcome her. She pulled the string on a forty-watt bulb, and the back stall flooded with light. There among the piles of dusty furniture she felt the presence of Leon. She cringed at the memory of shamelessly exposing her naked breasts, at the fervor in those dark eyes that twisted her gut.

But, oh, mercy, how she ached for him still. She pulled a Duncan Phyfe window seat from the tangle of furniture and placed it on the newspapers spread out in the stall. She pulled on a pair of stained rubber gloves, and, biting her lip, poured a thick coating of remover onto the window seat, spreading it evenly with a brush.

Tammi stayed at the barn all night. The moon was full, and she glanced out the rough boards of the window every now and then to admire its silvery shape. Her hope and prayer as she scraped away the old finish was that she could push from her mind all the despair hovering like a tidal wave.

Close to dawn, Tammi heard footsteps. A shadow fell over the window seat as Granny eased her stringy frame into the stall. "There you are," Granny said. "I've been looking all over for you. What are you doing out here at this hour?"

"Working." Tammi's heart hammered as Granny sat down on an overturned bucket.

"Tell me what's the matter, Tammi Lynn."

Words gushed out of Tammi. "I miss Leon, Granny. And—I never meant to—I didn't plan it, but—but I love him! We've kissed. And there's definitely passion between us! Now it feels like I'm possessed—"

Granny's mouth made a straight line. "I might have known," she said at last.

"I'm sorry," Tammi said in the deafening silence that followed.

"What fellowship hath righteousness with unrighteousness?" Granny looked at Tammi, fury in her eyes. "And what communion hath light with darkness?" She paused for a ragged breath. "Wherefore come out from among them, and be ye separate, saith the Lord, and touch not the unclean thing, and I will receive you."

Tammi's chin trembled. Did Granny mean she was the unclean thing? Crazy images whizzed through her mind: there was the Reverend Cotton, and Jesus, then Leon, beckoning her to flee youthful lust.

"This was going on under my nose?" Granny's arms were crossed so tightly across her chest they were quivering. "I thought something was up. I said to Nanette that you've been acting mighty strange.

More secretive even than usual. You'll plan to put Leon out of your mind now, won't you?"

Tammi nodded. She felt like an insect pinned to a velvet display board.

"Leon is one of the chosen. Do not impede the work of the Lord," Granny continued. "Don't hurt *us*."

Tammi gave a small gasp of hurt. "What?"

"Do I have to spell it out for you?" Granny's jaw hung slack. "This drought! I *knew* there was unconfessed sin. Just didn't know it was in my own household. You're hurting Rigby with your unbridled lust."

Tammi's insides shriveled. Tears hung hot on her jawline.

"Don't cry now, child," Granny said, softer now. "Come on in the house. Got you a ham biscuit and grits ready. Coffee too. From the first pot."

Tammi stood at the sink, both hands in sudsy water as she washed the breakfast dishes.

"Careful!" Granny yelped as an orange mug slipped from Tammi's exhausted fingers and crashed against the bottom of the sink.

"Sorry," Tammi said quickly, pulling dripping pieces of the mug up from the water. "I'm sorry."

"You broke it, you little strumpet!" Granny's harsh words stunned Tammi speechless. Pepaw, too, was quiet.

"No harm done, Constance," he said gently, after a bit.

"Melvin," she waved his words away. "You know that mug is one of the few personal things I have left that belonged to my father."

As she left for Elco Antiques half an hour later, Granny was still bristling.

"There you are, gal," Pepaw said, coming around the door frame of the dining room, his cap in his hands. He sat down at the table across from Tammi. "Listen, you deserve to know some things about Constance Elco. I know they won't make the things she says and does any easier to swallow. She's a hard woman to live with, I know. But when you hear where she came from, her terrible childhood, what she's endured, you'll understand."

Morning light washed through a row of windows in slanted golden shafts, and Tammi hunched her shoulders protectively. For some reason, Pepaw's mention of Granny's childhood unnerved her. She couldn't imagine the woman as a fresh-faced girl, engaging in innocent games, wishing on a star . . .

"She came into this world a sickly little thing," Pepaw began slowly. "Her mother was a call girl. You know what that is?"

Tammi felt a warm flush bloom in her cheeks. She nodded almost imperceptibly.

"Well, her mother wasn't but a child herself, and she passed on some type of venereal disease to her baby. Wasn't married to Monk Childers, either, as you might imagine. Well, when that girl saw her baby, all frail and skinny, crying constantly and needing so much, she just turned tail and ran. To some brothel in Mississippi, and she passed away before she even turned twenty. Well, Monk Childers, he didn't know what to do with a sickly baby. He already had a pile of other children by different women. Plus, he stayed drunk, in and out of jail." Pepaw shook his head.

"Heck, they were so poor the children had to pick through the dump on a regular basis. Eating trash, wearing whatever folks passed along to them out of kindness or pity. One day a Welfare fella went out to the Childerses' place, wasn't nothing but a tar-paper shack, and found those children roasting a dog for their supper. Can you believe that? All they had to eat. I heard someone say they ate rats, too. Just fighting among themselves for food! Isn't that sad?"

Tammi answered with a slow nod.

"All the other kids," Pepaw continued, "they were a good bit older than Constance. They just took off one day. Flew the coop when they found out they were fixing to be put in foster care. Monk, I believe he was just oblivious to it all. So one day they came to take your granny— she was around four by this time—and they put her first with a lady who lived way out in the sticks. Made Constance work like a dern slave. I guess she must have thought it was heaven, though, because there *was* always food on their table. She started school and studied hard. Had a good head on her shoulders. Made straight As.

"Well, come to find out, this big woman beat on her. The third-grade teacher saw bruises and welts all over Constance's arms and legs, and soon she was taken in by the Reverend Graves and his wife. Must've been way up in their sixties by then. Never had any children of their own. They were old-school Baptists, hellfire and brimstone. Didn't hold with any foolishness. Scared your granny to death with all that talk about death and sin and Satan. It can't have been easy to be a teenager under that roof. But Constance, she took it all in stride, and she stuck to the straight and narrow path. I guess that's what she found to be her ticket out of starvation and violence." Pepaw rubbed his chin.

Tammi blinked, wondering if he expected a response. But after a moment, he started in again.

"Those two, the Reverend and Missus Graves, they changed her name to Constance. She told me her real name once. It's still on her birth certificate: Dee Lishus Childers. She claims Dee Lishus is the name of a floozy, and she saw herself, sees herself, as the absolute embodiment of purity and uprightness. It hurts her, that name. She'd be mortified if she knew I'd told you."

"I'll never tell, Pepaw."

He smiled sadly at her. "Story gets harder. Old Missus Graves passed away when Constance wasn't but thirteen, and then the reverend, he got feeble with Parkinson's. Bedridden for years. Constance, she took care of him: cooked, cleaned, sat by his side holding his palsied hand to the very end. Made her old beyond her years. I guess she felt very alone when he did pass."

"But what about her real father?"

"Oh, she went to visit Monk Childers in the jailhouse a time or two. She worked at forgiving him, but I don't think she ever really has completely. For his philandering ways and his laziness. He's dead now, of course." Pepaw gazed down at his hands. "Anyhow," he said, and it seemed to Tammi that the tone of his voice had changed to one of matter-of-factness, "it's made your granny who she is today. I think she's just scared to death we might run out of food. Or water, as the case may be. Or something else essential. Scared we won't have *enough*. I think she's also terrified of something evil taking ahold of those she loves. She's so scared, and the only way she can have any peace is to be in control. In control of the finances, in control of the spiritual climate . . . But regardless of how it seems, she really loves you, gal. I know it doesn't seem like it sometimes—"

Tammi scoffed. "She hates me! Blames me for Junior's death."

"No," Pepaw said mournfully. "She blames herself. Believe me, I've heard her cry her heart out about it a thousand times."

"But she wasn't even there!"

Pepaw cleared his throat. "She didn't say her prayers that morning."

"So?"

"Every morning Constance prays down God's angels, His ministering spirits, she calls them, to protect her loved ones. She said she didn't get around to praying that morning of Good Friday. Got busy with her tomato seedlings and plumb forgot to pray."

Tammi stared at Pepaw, struck by the arrogance of Granny's guilt. Like *she* was the one keeping them all safe. On the other hand, she felt somehow irreverent, like who was she to say Granny's prayers didn't touch the heart of God? Finally, she felt relief. Whether Granny's assumed guilt was warranted or not, she was glad to be off the hook, and she knew that the strangling roots of guilt wrapping around her own heart were much looser now. "What did you tell her?" she asked at last.

Pepaw smiled. "Well, I told her I said my prayer that day."

"What did she say?"

"She said, 'Maybe you didn't have enough faith.' "

Tammi's eyes widened. "You're kidding."

He shook his head.

"So she blames you, too?" Tammi's breath caught in her throat.

Pepaw turned to stare out the window, his face lined with pain. "Only heaven knows," he said softly, but with all the authority of a person who understands that some things are best let be.

That night Tammi lay in bed thinking about her conversation with Pepaw. Dee Lishus. The name was simply unthinkable for Constance Elco. She wondered whether if she called it out the old woman would turn to answer, if her face would register shock, then horror over the awful memories. Tammi's heart felt tender and she bowed her head.

First she asked God to help her be sensitive to Granny's load of pain, then she drifted off to sleep whispering another prayer, asking Him to please let Leon love her.

Chapter 25

Overnight Granny seemed much older. The drought was still her favorite topic of conversation. She liked to point out her wizened spider lilies and the fact that there was not adequate topsoil moisture for a vegetable garden. Deep-soil moisture was lacking, too. According to the county agent, Rigby needed at least twenty inches of rain to end the drought, but the weatherman said that wasn't likely to happen anytime soon. The water table was so severely depleted that any quick bursts of rain they might receive would not soak in but would run quickly off the top of the ground.

Farmers were taking fire-sale prices for their cattle, and vitamin A deficiencies were causing blindness and stillbirth in calves. There was no hay put by for winter, as the farmers cut what little hay they had to feed their cattle immediately. To ease the farmers' financial plight, the U.S. Department of Agriculture was making low-interest drought-relief loans available.

"Still got to pay back a loan!" Granny remarked to Pepaw at lunch, her eyes on Tammi. "I've said it till I'm blue in the face: it's unconfessed *sin* that's the root of this drought."

Tammi held her breath, picturing the years passing by dry and achingly slow. Was she destined to spend the rest of her life mourning for a love that would never be? She could hardly wait for the next day's club meeting.

The following March afternoon was warmer than anyone could have imagined. Temperatures crawled up over 70, and the air was thick with drifting pollen. The heat made Tammi feel droopy, and she pulled her long hair up off her neck for the walk to Minna's.

Priscilla, crouched in the shade, merely lifted an ear as she spied Tammi and the approaching dust cloud from Parks's Trans Am.

"Hey, girl!" Parks called through her open window. "How's it hanging?"

"Fine." Tammi waved.

"I reckon we're going to have to eat first again!" Parks said as she bounded into Minna's den wearing a wide grin, holding up a grease-splotched Krispy Kreme bag. "They're fresh out of the fat! Got milk, Minna?"

Minna nodded, looking amused as Parks reached into the bag, grabbed a doughnut, and mashed the entire thing into her mouth.

"He'p yo'selves," Parks garbled around a mouthful. "Three apiece." She bounded over to Minna's radio, fiddling with the dial until loud rock 'n' roll throbbed throughout the house. She wiggled her big rear end to the beat, throwing her head back to sing along, throaty and off-key.

Tammi felt fluttery and a little wild. She longed to be as carefree as Parks, and she sang along with the Rolling Stones to "(I Can't Get No) Satisfaction."

Parks clapped. "Attagirl, Tammi! Let it all hang out!"

They finished their warm doughnuts and adjoined to the den, where Parks lowered the volume. "Ladies," she said, eyes sparkling as she lifted *The Sheik's Temptress*. "This is one hot piece of lit-er-a-ture! I know we're all itching to see if Rosemary will get Abdul to dishonor himself. Pick desire over duty."

Tammi fingered the fringe of the zebra pillow. "Confession time," she said slowly, feeling all their eyes piercing her as she paused for a breath. "I . . . went on and read the whole thing. I'm sorry." She was pleading now. "Please forgive me."

At last Parks bent double laughing. "Hell, girl. That's okay, 'cause I did too!"

"So did I," LaDonna said in a near whisper.

Minna looked amused. "I also finished *The Sheik's Temptress*."

Now they all leaned in, giggling, slapping each other's knees, giddy with the relief and thrill of a common weakness.

"Well, since we've all done read the entire thing," Parks said, "I believe we can all agree we're mighty tickled that Abdul picked Rosemary!" She lit up a cigarette and blew a stream of smoke out one side of her mouth, saying, "Now let's talk fantasies. You first, Minna."

Minna laughed, a tinkly sound. "Well, I hate to disappoint you, but I'd be lying if I said I wanted a fiery, hormone-ravaged man like Abdul to fetch me away. Or any of our other studly sex machines smothering my protests with his mouth and quenching my desire with the primal thrusts of his loins." A look of serious contemplation crossed Minna's face. "Shoot, my fantasy is for a loyal man who'll just *cuddle* me! Hold me tenderly on a cold winter's night while we listen to Elvis! Walk along Viking Creek with me and make my coffee in the mornings. Now, wouldn't hurt if this fantasy man still had all his own teeth!" She laughed, tears in her eyes. "I know I must sound ancient to you gals, and, *honestly*, I love reading about these hot young bodies doing it, but my fantasy is so G-rated now."

LaDonna's face registered surprise in every young curve. She smiled shyly as she said, "Mine aren't G-rated! I wish Patrick Presnell would lay eyes on me in the hallway at school and ravage me like some savage beast!" She ended with a high-pitched sigh, then immediately blushed at what she had revealed.

"Lord have mercy," Parks breathed. "Girl, *you* ought to write one of these romance novels!"

"If Patrick Presnell were the lead man, I sure could," LaDonna said.

After a spell, Parks said, "Tell us your fantasy, Tammi."

Tammi's alarm system went off. "Me?! I um . . ." she mumbled, twisting her fingers together. "Look," she admitted at last, "I want us to be honest with each other. Totally open. And I came to the club today intending to confess everything, so I'm just going to answer this question as truthfully as I can. My fantasy is two syllables—*Le-on.*"

LaDonna nodded. "I totally understand now. It just kind of takes you over, doesn't it? Blocks all rational thought."

"Yeah," Tammi said, gratitude and empathy flooding over her. She had, she realized, misjudged LaDonna immensely.

After a spell, they turned to look at Parks.

"It's my turn, I reckon," she said, throwing up her hands. "I'm a little scared to say mine out loud, 'cause I don't want to jinx it. But I'm living out my fantasy."

"Tell!" they begged.

Parks smiled smugly. "His name's Dale Crumpett, and he drives a wicked GTO, and he's fallen hopelessly head over heels in love with me. He appreciates a *big* girl. Keeps me in fried chicken and beer. Smokes, drinks, chews, ain't possessive. His mama lives away up north somewhere."

"But that's not a fantasy, dear," Minna said. "That's reality. I told my fantasy, LaDonna told hers, and we've known poor Tammi's for quite a while."

Parks carefully shook out a Marlboro, lit it, and blew a long stream of smoke. "Right. I know that. I can't say I've got any steamy sex fantasies, any wild act, 'cause y'all know I've already tried everything in the book. Know what my fantasy is?"

They were literally on the edge of their seats.

"I want to get hitched, settle down, and have me a house full of babies!"

Silence.

"Doesn't sound like the steamy plot of one of our romance novels, does it?" Parks grinned. "Well, I'd just have to keep me a stack of them on my nightstand, wouldn't I?" She laughed uproariously.

The mood was light as they stood for the pledge, then decided on *Knights of Desire* as their next selection. LaDonna came up with an idea for discussion that they all agreed on—titles and plot ideas for their own personal romance novels.

"Minna ought to call hers *All His Own Teeth to Kiss Me With*, Parks guffawed, slapping her generous thigh. "I'll call mine *Nights of Steamy Fried Chicken.*"

When April came, the county agent warned constantly of the increased chance of wildfire. The dogwoods were still proclaiming the drought as well, refusing to unfurl their white blooms, but there was a sprinkling of snapdragons and larkspurs in riotous hues all around the big house, no doubt a gift from the dishpans full of water that Granny carried outside and flung on them each evening.

Granny stood in the kitchen in the early dawn of Easter Sunday, fretting about dinner preparations. "Got the ham in," she told Tammi. "Peas shelled and potatoes ready to slide into the oven. Tea's made. We'll steam the asparagus when we're home from Promiseland." She paused for a breath. "I don't understand why Leon said he might not be here for Easter. Wouldn't you think Easter's a big enough holiday? Friday week I went on and sent him money to fly home, but I've heard nary a word. Still, he could be coming. Don't you suppose?"

Tammi drew in a quick breath at Granny's pained tone. "I don't know," she said. "Guess Easter's a pretty big deal at the Baptist Theological Seminary."

The air was sweet and cool that afternoon as they returned from Promiseland. Tammi sat tensely in the backseat of the Caddy, eyes peeled for any sign of Leon's arrival. She felt her heart plummet as they entered the quiet house.

"He's not here," Granny remarked in a small voice. Pepaw patted her shoulder and disappeared with Orr into the front parlor as the women stowed their Bibles and purses and went into the kitchen to finish fixing dinner. Tammi stood at the sink, quietly snipping the tender ends off asparagus stalks, but Granny slammed the cookie sheet full of biscuits into the oven. When Onzelle and Carson arrived she slammed ice into the glasses.

"Orrville! Melvin! Minna Lee!" Granny commanded and soon the long dining table was full.

After the blessing Carson let out a whistle. "Corn prices sure have shot sky-high!"

"Need to sell those cows," Granny said firmly, slathering jelly over the top of a biscuit. Tammi watched her stare down Pepaw.

He drained his tea glass. "Made it through over two years of drought, thanks to Carson's generosity with his hay. Now I'm gonna get me a government loan and buy an irrigation system of my own." Pepaw turned to Carson. "Son, how're your hay pastures coming along?"

"There's enough hay to get hundreds of cattle through the winter," said Carson.

"Got to change with the times," Pepaw said.

Granny looked stricken. "Man made rain, irrigation, whatever you call it, the water's got to *come* from somewhere! It'll run out well dry! Then *we'll* be the ones shriveling up!" She looked sideways at Tammi. "I know what it says right there in First Kings! 'When heaven is shut up, and there is no rain, because they have sinned against thee, if they pray toward this place, and confess thy name, and turn from their sin, when thou afflictest them, then hear thou in heaven, and forgive the sin of thy servants, and of thy people Israel, teach them the good way wherein they should walk, and give rain upon thy land.'

"Don't you see, Melvin James?" she pled. "God is judging Rigby. Cursing us until we have the sense to repent and turn."

"Well, I do believe this drought makes us realize Who we're dependent on down here," Pepaw said in the reverent manner of someone giving a careful nonanswer.

At length the somber mood at the table lifted, and they talked lightly and lazily in the lemon-yellow sunlight seeping through the venetian blinds.

Late the following evening Minna knocked on Tammi's bedroom door. "Mind if I come in, hon?" she whispered.

"Okay," Tammi said. She was in bed, wearing her nightgown.

"Nanette says Finch has taken a turn for the worse," Minna said, stepping inside, running her fingers through her frosted hair. "He's developed a real serious infection, and things don't look good."

"He could *die?*" Tammi asked.

"Any day now."

Tammi wasn't surprised by this news, but she did feel strangely sad for knowing the man as little as she did. "Does Leon know?" she asked suddenly.

"Nanette thinks it would disrupt his studies."

"But it's his father! He *deserves* to know! And besides, he told me once that Uncle Finch never got saved! Leon said his dad's going to

be the first person he preaches to when he graduates from seminary!"
Tammi swung her feet out of bed. "I'm going to call him right now!"
She ran down the hall to Nanette's room.

Nanette sat in the center of a king-sized bed, a little silver flask
open on her nightstand. "Hey, darlin'," she said, beckoning Tammi
to come sit beside her. There were dark circles under her eyes, and
her skin was white as the Easter lilies on Promiseland's pulpit.

"I'm sorry about Uncle Finch," Tammi said, patting Nanette's
arm.

"That's real sweet, Tammi Lynn," she sniffled.

"Minna says Leon doesn't know how bad off his daddy is,"
Tammi said softly. "He wants his daddy to rise up to be with Jesus
when it's his time to fly, you know."

Silence from Nanette.

"He does! You should hear how it breaks his heart! And if Finch
were to die before—"

"Don't *say* that!" Nanette took a swig from the silver flask.

"Please, let me call Leon!" Tammi looked pleadingly at her
aunt.

"Honestly," Nannette said in a weary voice.

"*Please,*" Tammi said. "We're talking eternity here. Now what's
his number?"

Nanette peered closely at Tammi, hiccuping every second or so
from behind a cupped hand she held to her mouth.

"Leon's number?" Tammi urged. "I'm going to call him."

"Don't bother. I'll call him for you." Nanette closed her eyes,
sinking wearily against the headboard, trilling her fingers in a little
half-wave, dismissing Tammi.

Morning light brought the sound of Nanette's voice raised in a
piercing wail like Tammi had never heard. The mournful sound

grew like the flames of a bonfire as Tammi opened her bedroom door and stood rubbing sleep from her eyes. She knew without asking that Finch had passed on.

Over the next hour, the big house pulsed with the news of Finch's death. Minna, Orr, and Pepaw gathered at the dining table, drinking coffee and speaking in somber tones. Granny was on the phone with the Reverend Goodlow. Nanette was draped across the settee, her shoulders shaking as she wept.

Nanette was to fly out to Nevada for the funeral. She did not speak of Leon, and all questions fired at her went unanswered.

Later that evening, when the supper dishes were washed, dried, and put away, Tammi walked down the back steps to look at the sunset. The night was steamy hot, and heat lightning danced on the horizon around the sinking orange ball of sun. She sat cross-legged in the shadow of a rose of Sharon tree, trailing her fingers in the grass, wondering whether Leon would be at his father's funeral. Whether Finch had made his peace.

At last she stretched full length, surrounded by the thrum of cicadas, thinking of the nighttime things she had to accomplish before Promiseland tomorrow: washing her hair, ironing her dress, and studying her Sunday school lesson.

You would have to say it was her faith that was keeping her anchored to sanity at the moment. Sunday was a peaceful day. The big house woke up more slowly. Everybody lingered at the breakfast table. There was the smell of Pepaw's aftershave, the sight of his fresh pink cheeks above his suit coat, his leather Bible waiting on the table at the front door, spilling over with church bulletins and strips of paper.

Tammi's own Bible was plumped up now, too, the result of hours spent riffling through its tissue-thin pages as she hunted passages to give her strength and assurance through her struggle to love Leon without missing him to death. The battle waxed and waned on any given day. At times the ground beneath Tammi trembled and quaked, and she felt literally crushed by the unquenchable longings. Sometimes there was also the paralyzing sadness of missing her mother mixed in with her Leon heartache. Tammi had underlined two verses in Revelation that promised that God was going to wipe away all tears, that there would be no more death nor sorrow nor pain in the eternal bliss of heaven.

But it wasn't easy to wait for heaven.

She'd been pondering the title of her romance novel for the next club meeting and had decided to call it *Waiting for Heaven. Why?* she wondered. *Why does God make us wait like this? Our earthly life so tragic and tinged with unfulfilled desires . . .*

A car engine roared up, disrupting Tammi's thoughts. She turned her head to see the ancient blue pickup of Eugene Watley, a deacon from Promiseland. He hopped out, striding toward the front door.

"Evenin', Mr. Watley," Tammi said, getting to her feet.

Mr. Watley startled a bit and turned toward the dusky shadows where Tammi stood. "How do," he said, removing his hat. His face reminded Tammi of a pug, his red hair buzzed flat across the top. "Miz Elco here?" he asked.

"Yessir. She's making a pie."

"Uh, I see," he said. "Mind fetching her for me?"

"Come on in," said Tammi.

Mr. Watley entered the parlor.

"Have a seat," Tammi said, watching him pace nervously along the hearth.

Granny was peeling apples at the sink. "Eugene Watley's here to see you," Tammi said, touching her elbow gently.

"What?" Granny spun around, her mouth falling slack.

"He's in the parlor," Tammi said.

Granny stood still as death. The smell of cinnamon and nutmeg rose up to meet Tammi's nostrils, and something else, something hard and dark and somehow terribly wrong. Tammi was about to go tell Mr. Watley that Granny was ill-disposed, to lay the old woman down on her bed with a damp washrag on her head, when his heavy step sounded at the doorway to the kitchen. He cleared his throat meaningfully.

"Evening Miz Elco. Something has come to the attention of the Standards Board at Promiseland."

Granny's face blanched white. She reached over and twisted the dial to turn the oven off, leading Mr. Watley silently into the parlor. Tammi crept along at their heels, lingering outside the door frame. His words were too low for Tammi to distinguish, but their ominous tone made her stomach muscles contract.

"I'm not sure I understand," Granny was saying in a strangled voice. "You'll have to say it again more slowly. I've been accused of *what?!*"

Sunday morning came, and the house was hushed and still; Pepaw and Tammi crept about awkwardly.

Minna and Orr appeared at nine o'clock, coiffed and dressed in their Sunday finery, their faces registering shock when they saw there was no coffee made, no biscuits on the table.

"Where's Mama?" Orr looked wildly about.

Presently Pepaw spoke. "She's in bed. Go see about her. She's not feeling well."

Orr galloped off. When he was out of earshot, Pepaw turned to Minna. "Something we need to discuss, gal," he said. "Mind making us some coffee? Tammi Lynn's just got in from feeding the chickens, and she needs to get dressed."

Minna set to work furiously, measuring coffee, getting cups and saucers from the cabinet. She plunked the cream and sugar in the center of the table. "Alrighty," she said when there was a cup of steaming coffee in front of Pepaw. "Time to give us the nitty-gritty."

Pepaw hung his head. "Dear God," he said, "I just can't hardly believe it, but Constance has been accused of taking folks' things. Their valuable antiques."

Minna's eyes began to tear up, and she reached over and put her hand on Pepaw's back. "What happened?"

"Eugene Watley says she took some kind of a fool thing called a sucket fork, and a tankard, from Minnie Washington's residence."

"No." Tammi shook her head emphatically. "Granny would never steal!"

"Tammi," Pepaw said gently, "there's apparently been lots of talk among the parishioners. There are more things they say she's taken, too." Pepaw gulped his coffee now, his Adam's apple flying up and down. "They want her to repent in front of the congregation."

"Tammi, were you aware of any of these shenanigans?" Minna's voice was abrupt.

"No," Tammi whispered in a strangled voice.

The silence spun out.

"Are you sure?" Minna asked. "Because you've been with her a lot lately."

"No!" Tammi said. "I didn't see her steal!"

"Did you ever get this *feeling*? You know, this uncomfortable feeling that Mama might be hiding something? No one's blaming you, sweetheart, but the only way we'll ever get to the bottom of things is for everyone to open up and be completely honest."

Tammi's temples were pounding. A hovering gray shape, like a rain cloud, filled her heart and mind. *Careful now. Don't spill out any false accusations.* "I mean, she got things cheap. Yeah," Tammi said.

"Too cheap, maybe. But I never saw her *take* anything. She may be a little greedy, may have given folks too little for their things, but she lives by the Bible, and she would not go around stealing!" Tammi gulped coffee, its searing heat drowning the painful words. *Please, God,* she prayed silently, *don't let Granny be guilty.*

Tammi was curled up on Minna's couch that next week when Nanette burst in.

"Sister?" Nanette called and Minna appeared in the front hall wearing a curve-hugging black slip and fluffy pink bedroom slippers, her hair up in rollers from a Toni home perm. "Yeah, darlin'?"

"I just did something real stupid."

"Sit down," Minna said. "Let me go blot this mess and we can talk."

Nanette slumped down at the dinette.

"What did you do?" Minna asked when she'd returned, plunking a can of Fresca down on the glittering Formica at Nanette's elbow.

"I let it slip about Mama when I called Leon." Nanette sighed deeply as she popped the pull tab on her drink, sending a small burst of effervescence into the air. "He got all worked up, totally lost it when I told him she refused to get up in front of the congregation and repent."

"It's been a shock to all of us, Nan."

"Yes. But it seemed to take the wind right out of Leon. He just kept going, 'No! Tell me it isn't true. Not Granny!' "

Minna frowned and patted a roller at her temple.

"He said he's coming home." Nanette blinked. "Dropping out of seminary."

Minna patted her hand. "It wouldn't be so awful, now, would it? To have your boy home? You didn't really want him to go, anyway."

"You don't understand," Nanette said. "When Leon flew into his tirade, he sounded like some old codger who lost his hound dog."

"Well, I'll bet it was just a quick and momentary reaction, dear. He'll calm down."

"I don't think so," Nanette said miserably, taking a swig of her Fresca. "His mind is made up. He'll be home directly."

"Tell him not to worry. That Daddy's giving those pitiful folks some money for their stuff." Minna checked her watch and patted a roller at her temple. "Gotta go take these out of my hair, darlin'. Hang around and we'll chat some more."

"I better get back to the big house." Nanette yawned. "I'm exhausted."

Tammi's head was reeling. Leon was coming home! Leaving seminary! This opened up all kinds of possibilities. Maybe he wouldn't be so holy now, wouldn't be fleeing youthful lust.

CHAPTER 26

Leon Dupree came back to Rigby on May first. He drove up in a battered 1969 Ford—sun-scorched silver with a torn vinyl roof—and parked in the scant shade of a parched butterfly bush. Orr galloped out to welcome him, and together they toted two suitcases and a trunk into the big house and up the stairs. Leon collapsed on the bed after his long drive. Minna, Nanette, Pepaw, and Tammi all stopped by his bedroom to say "Welcome home," but there was no friendly chitchat about the weather, no questions about where the Jaguar was or about the Baptist Theological Seminary.

Granny stayed shut in her bedroom, silent, nodding only occasionally when Pepaw or Orr spoke to her. She did not go to Elco Antiques. "I'm scared for Granny," Tammi had whispered into the cotton fabric at Pepaw's shoulder one evening early on. "Don't be," he'd said, wrapping her in his arms. "With the Lord's help we'll get this mess straightened out."

Tammi was worried about Leon, too. He had the mark of a wounded soul on him from the moment of his arrival: stooped shoulders, a continual sigh, and a brow constantly knit in puzzlement. Pepaw whispered to Nanette that there was no doubt in his mind that what the boy needed was some good old-fashioned work. After several days, in which Leon mostly slept, Pepaw clapped him on the shoulder and said he sure could use an extra farmhand.

Leon donned blue jeans and boots, and tramped outside to the barn. It was as if he were determined to prove himself a real man's man, a man who came back to the house evenings covered in cuts and bruises, drenched in sweat, with red Georgia clay a permanent color beneath his nails. Within a week's time his hair and beard grew out, and the sun gave his face the tawny glow of an Indian.

Tammi watched all this from a distance. Leon seemed, she thought, like an actor, cast in a role that had somehow taken him over. This man had no connection with her, and she poured herself into schoolwork, working extra hard at Elco Antiques on afternoons and Saturdays to help Nanette hold down the fort.

Tongues wagged incessantly about Granny's escapade and her subsequent withdrawal. Minna maintained that Granny just wasn't in her right mind when she committed her so-called crimes, but the talk that careened around Rigby was more in the nature of legend: Constance Elco was ripping people off so she could sell their valuable objects and get money to buy drugs; Miz Elco was a kleptomaniac and would need to go to the state mental hospital in Milledgeville for treatment; Miz Elco hated black folks and wanted to keep them poor . . .

Late one evening in the middle of May Tammi heard a male voice singing out on the lawn. She rubbed sleep from her eyes, eased out of bed, and crept to her window, pulling the sheers aside. There was a slim scythe of moon, and it was too dark to see anything but a murky shape moving near the salvias. It was a plaintive song, a "my baby cheated on me" song.

Tammi bit her lip and raised the window high enough to press her forehead against the screen. It was Leon! Exultation bloomed inside her as she pulled on shorts and tiptoed downstairs.

Leon was barefoot and shirtless, singing B. J. Thomas's "(Hey Won't You Play) Another Somebody Done Somebody Wrong Song," playing an air guitar, and grinning like a Cheshire cat.

Stunned, Tammi cried, "Leon, it's two o'clock in the morning!"

"Hi, Tammi! How ya doin'? I been getting crazy out here."

Tammi's nose was assaulted by the reek of booze and stale sweat. "Now, Leon—"

"Don't you worry," he said in a pleading voice. "I just thought I'd cut loose a little. Let it all hang out, ya know? Closed down the Lucky Lounge." He belched and swaggered unsteadily a bit before lying down on the grass.

Tammi raised her eyebrows, drinking in his luscious shoulders, then his back, which swooped long and lean to his taut rump. "You're drunk," she said. "Let me help you up and inside. I'll perk some coffee."

"Aw, come on, Tammi. I'm all right. See?" He held out trembling hands. "I'm fine." His face flopped forward into the dirt.

"You're wasted," she wailed, kneeling beside him.

He grabbed her shin. "C'mon, pretty baby. Lay down beside me."

"Please come inside." She patted his back awkwardly.

"Tammi." Leon's voice trembled. "I dropped out of seminary. I'm not a worthy vessel for the Lord. I harbored evil in my heart toward my father, and I didn't point him to the way of salvation. Now he's perishing . . . " His words trailed off. His shoulders began shaking.

"Stop talking like this!" she cried.

"He was a womanizer," Leon said slowly. "You can't know what that's like if you never lived with one. He lusted after anything in a skirt. My poor mama . . . it was terrible for her. For us. We had to get out of there. It was hurting her so bad. You understand, don't you, Tammi, why we had to leave him?

"Only sometimes, now, I think I should've stayed. Offered to him Christ's compassion. He needed, he deserved, forgiveness . . ."

"Oh goodness, Leon!" Tammi said. "Y'all were in the poorhouse because of Uncle Finch's drinking and carousing. You weren't but seventeen. You couldn't have done anything!"

"You really believe that?" Leon said doubtfully. "He's dead now, Tammi. Dead. My daddy's dead, dammit!" He pounded the grass with his fist.

"Things'll be okay," she crooned, focusing on a winking star close to the moon.

"I sold the Jag," he said.

"I know."

He smiled. "I've got the money to buy Pepaw's irrigation."

"That's nice," she said, "but if Granny hears about it, she'll be spittin' nails! She—" As soon as the words were out of her mouth, Tammi knew she'd said the wrong thing.

"She stole from those poor, pitiful folks. So poor they sometimes go hungry! I thought the woman was righteous; I didn't know she . . . was a *hypocrite! dirty rotten thief!*" Leon managed to get onto his hands and knees, wobbling, a furious look on his face.

"Leon, it's okay," Tammi said soothingly. "Pepaw made it all good. He gave money to those families. More than the stuff was worth."

"My granny is a stealer!" Leon said, laughing and getting shakily to his feet. "Granny is a stealer!" He hung an arm around Tammi's neck. "You ever think, babe, that our Granny would *steal?*"

"Quiet, Leon! You'll wake everybody."

He looked around as if people were hiding in the bushes. "Tell me something hot and steamy," he said, leaning closer to her face. "Something lusty!"

"Stop!" she said. "We need to get you in bed."

"Ha ha! Only if you get in bed with me!" He kissed her on the lips fiercely.

"You're drunk," she said, shaking her head and sliding her hand in his pocket, moving it around to hunt for his car keys.

"Yeah, baby," he said. "You're getting frisky now!"

"I'm going inside, Leon," she told him, jangling the keys victoriously.

"Wait—"

Tammi strode into the big house and climbed back in bed, trembling, holding his keys on her stomach and crying silent tears until she went to sleep.

It was a Tuesday morning toward the end of May. There was a weeklong Elvis celebration in Memphis, and Minna was all decked out to go in a neon-orange sundress and big white sunglasses. She had come to the big house to say bye to everyone.

Nanette had gone early to Elco Antiques. She had been managing things while Granny stayed away. Tammi was dressed for school, standing at the stove boiling grits and frying ham, while Leon, Orr, and Pepaw sat drinking coffee at the table.

Tammi had managed to steer fairly clear of Leon since their nighttime encounter. It hurt her too much to witness his behavior, for anybody with eyes in their head could see the lonely struggle between his heart and his calling, the way he made a beeline to the Lucky Lounge each Friday and Saturday till the wee hours, then scrambled wearily and red-eyed out of bed on Sunday mornings to stagger into Promiseland, where he sat on the front pew, listening intently and tossing out an "Amen, Brother Goodlow," every now and again. He went forward to kneel at the altar rail at the end of each service.

Pepaw had moved Granny's radio to the kitchen windowsill, and some days the signal came through loud and clear. "Our dry red clay is holding its fragile breath," the booming voice of an announcer was saying. "Temperatures every day this week will soar above 98 degrees. This extreme heat will only aggravate dry conditions across Rigby. The twenty-six-month battle with drought is forcing officials to impose water restrictions."

Pepaw sighed loudly.

Leon slammed down his coffee mug. His cheeks held high spots of color. "Sir? I sold my Jag and I aim to buy that irrigation!"

"Well, that's—really something," said Pepaw. "Thank you kindly, but you heard the fella—water restrictions."

Minna settled herself at the table. She wrapped her arm around Leon's shoulder. "I been meaning to talk to you about selling your Jaguar."

"You have?"

"Yessiree. Boy like you needs some fancy wheels! You don't need to be tooling around in that ancient Ford!"

"I don't care about that! I don't need material possessions. All I want is to help out. Do my share."

Tammi turned from the stove, where she was flipping ham in the skillet. There it was, the sound she dreaded most, that edge of desperation in Leon's voice.

Minna shook her head. "She's poisoned your mind, and I don't know how she still does it, her in trouble for stealing! What you need, darlin', is a trip to Memphis. Papa? Can't you spare him for a spell, Papa?" Minna spun the lazy Susan in the center of the table with one Day-Glo orange fingernail.

Pepaw scratched at his whiskery chin. "I reckon, gal."

Tammi still hadn't gotten used to the more relaxed life they were having without Granny around.

It was 3:00 A.M. that following Sunday, and Tammi sat downstairs in a puddle of lamplight, working a crossword. When the front door opened and Leon appeared, suitcase in hand, she went cautiously to his side. He stood in the foyer, frowning. His hair hung lank on his head, and there were dark circles under his eyes.

"Hi!" she said. "Have fun?"

There was a small silence, and then Leon said, "Memphis is a really wild place, and those Elvis fans are crazy. They worship him. Act like he's God or something."

"Well," she said, smiling. "He is the *King*. I can't wait to hear all about it."

Leon was silent, and then he said, "Not now. I'm beat. What are you doing still awake?"

"Oh, I couldn't sleep. I was thinking so hard about stuff." She met his eyes. "I was worried about you, mostly, Leon."

"Listen, I—I'm sorry about that night when I attacked you . . . I don't know what came over me, but I shouldn't have acted that way. Forgive me?"

She shrugged. "It's okay."

"I did a lot of soul-searching when I was in Memphis, and I guess I'll just have to steer clear of the alcohol. I don't seem to be able to handle it. Take after my old man that way. I've decided to mend my ways, sure enough," he said, and Tammi saw the determined flash in his eyes before he trudged upstairs.

Leon came downstairs the next morning wearing his baby-blue suit, holding a Bible.

"Don't you look nice, son." Nanette offered him a doughnut from a Big Star bakery box.

"Thanks," Leon said. "Believe I'll carry one of these to Granny and have my breakfast with her. Care to join me, Tammi?"

"Uh, sure," she said curiously, looking first toward Granny's closed door, then at her aunt.

"Good luck," Nanette said, shaking her head. "She won't talk to anybody."

"She'll talk when she hears what I've got to tell her! I'm not leaving till she does!"

Tammi could see how tightly wound Leon was as he walked down the hallway, and she wondered what kind of sensation he was about to create.

Granny sat in the center of her massive bed, hands on her hips. Tammi was shocked when she saw her. She must have been eating everything she could get her hands on; her face was plumped up so much that the angular planes of her cheekbones and her chin were gone. Her tight bun was gone, too, her hair spilling out around her face like a wiry gray fright wig. Only her cat's-eye glasses with the sparkling rhinestones remained to remind Tammi of the old Granny.

"Good morning, Granny dear," Leon said brightly. "Grace, mercy, and peace from our Lord and Savior Jesus Christ be with you!"

Granny scowled.

Leon was undeterred. "Maybe you've heard that I'm planning on staying in Rigby for a while, and you want to know why I dropped out of seminary?"

Granny fished around in the covers and stuck what looked like a Baby Ruth in her mouth.

Leon didn't miss a beat. "Well, Elco Antiques is why I'm back! Figured you might need some help with the shop and whatnot, while you're, uh . . . otherwise occupied. Now, I *want* to do it, so don't you say a word about it." He held up a hand like Moses parting the Red Sea.

"Elco Antiques will flourish," he continued, "like the cedars of Lebanon."

Granny stared to the left of them, unblinking, her jaws working as she finished the candy bar.

"Listen, I've figured out a way we can double our business!" Leon said, slapping his hand down on the cover of his Bible. "Legally!"

Granny's eyes zoomed in on him. "Is that so?" Her voice held a note of suspicion.

Goodness gracious, Tammi thought, *he's getting her to speak! But, more important, what* was *this brilliant idea of his?*

"We'll do trade-ins!" he said. "You know, like a used-car lot! Folks will voluntarily bring in their old pieces—their dining tables, sideboards—and we'll give 'em trade-in value toward another piece. Or cash, if that's what they want. Then, if need be, we'll restore their old piece before we sell it. It's a win-win situation! Won't have to go around hunting antiques anymore."

Granny was sitting forward now, her jaw set square.

"Whaddya think?" Leon urged. "Doesn't it sound fabulous?"

"I 'spect it might do." Granny couldn't contain her smile.

Leon sighed happily, pressing his long, slender fingers together. "There's something more I'd like us to talk about," he said. "Besides antiques."

Granny gave him a confused look.

"Eternal matters," Leon told her in a somber tone.

"Uh, well—I," she said, her face like a little drawstring purse.

"I'm talking about *your* earthly pilgrimage," he said. "Specifically, your recent escapade. God will forgive you only if you repent."

"Well, I never!" she flared, turning away. "It's time for you both to leave."

"Please!" Leon said, jumping to his feet. "If you'll just hear me out . . . doughnuts! I've got doughnuts here! Look." He lifted the Big Star box.

Granny studied it, licking her lips, and sank back against the headboard.

"When my daddy died," Leon said slowly, "and I didn't take the opportunity to lead him to salvation, I vowed—"

"Finch Dupree was a lowlife!" Granny hissed. "I can't forgive him for what he put you and your mother through! Now, give me those doughnuts and I'll . . ." Her face looked old and sad in the overhead light.

"God don't make no junk," Leon said firmly. "It's one of my greatest regrets, and I *promised* myself, I vowed, that I'd never, ever, let another opportunity to witness, to point souls—"

"Don't keep on with me, boy!" Granny's eyes flashed. "Finch Dupree is right where he belongs!" Her jowls were trembling with fury. "He got what he deserved!"

Leon's shoulders drooped forward noticeably. "God's mercy and grace is for everyone," he said softly. "Most of all the vile sinner— and every single person who walks this earth is by nature a sinner, stands guilty and condemned by God until they accept forgiveness." He ran his hand through his hair. "Think about Jesus as a furniture builder. *The* Carpenter. He doesn't get rid of us when we're old or broken or scarred. He's patient, working carefully and lovingly to smooth away the stains and scars of sin. He restores us, so we're new again. He *refinishes* us just like a valuable antique!"

"That's absurd!"

But Tammi knew by the way Granny thrust herself forward to clasp Leon's wrist that she didn't think it was absurd.

"I'd like to lead you in a little prayer," Leon said simply.

A holy, hushed kind of silence fell as Granny dipped her head almost imperceptibly forward, and Leon began: "Let us then fearlessly and confidently and boldly draw near to the throne of grace—the throne of God's unmerited favor to us sinners—that we may receive mercy for our failures and find grace to help in good time for every need."

Tears shone in Granny's eyes as she began a tumble of words asking God's forgiveness for deceiving folks about their antiques, for judging and despising Finch Dupree, and finally for the foolish and stubborn pride that had kept her from repenting sooner.

Late that afternoon, just before supper, clouds began to gather and the sky darkened. Thunder rolled across the pastures, and rain soon followed. Thumb-sized drops smacked the earth and softened the crusty ground. Pepaw shucked his dusty work boots and began dancing outside near the well house. Tammi smiled from the kitchen sink, where she stood gazing out the window and peeling potatoes.

It rained nonstop for the next seven days, and on Granny's radio the county agent said, "Folks, I can't believe it! Looks like the bottom's done dropped out on us. But, hey, you won't hear me complainin'!" Even the deejay's voice was edged with delirium when he returned to the microphone.

Tammi stayed keenly aware of Leon's every move. He was flying high, elated over the rain, staying away from the Lucky Lounge. Instead, the wet evenings found him out at the barn, refinishing. At last Granny emerged from her room. She walked the house, straightening and adjusting things, nodding out each window at the downpour. She unplugged her radio from the kitchen and carried it back out to the porch, where she sat down on her wicker sofa, smiling as though she was expecting a guest.

Friday evening Tammi ran from the big house to the barn, through sheets of rain, to call Leon to supper. She found him bent over a mahogany card table, and she stood dripping at the stall door to watch him work.

Tonight he seemed possessed, working with a vengeance as he sanded one leg with all his strength, his lips pressed in a straight, hard line.

"What's the matter, Leon?" she asked.

"Nothing."

Something in the back of his voice prompted Tammi to shed her raincoat and take a seat on the floor in the corner. She ground her teeth hard because being near Leon still hit her every time like a jolt of the strongest coffee, got her heart jittery, buzzed her loins, and set her off throbbing in ways she couldn't control.

Leon turned to face her, and the deep circles under his eyes caused her to draw an unconscious gasp of breath. Oh, he was definitely up to something out here! Tammi felt she had to be terribly careful, to pick exactly the right words. "Come back to the house with me," she said softly. "You missed supper, and you need to eat."

At last his eyes met hers. "Can't you see?" His voice was raw. "I'm wrestling not against flesh and blood, but against principalities, powers, against the rulers of the darkness of this world."

"What?!"

"Ephesians 6," he said chidingly. "I'm working through some things."

"Tell me," Tammi insisted gently.

He shook his head.

"At least let me bring you a pork chop and butter beans."

He winced. "I'm *fasting*. Denying bodily appetites so I can hear more clearly."

Tammi had no idea what to say back to this. Should she act like she understood? Get him to elaborate?

"It's what I have to do." His voice sliced through her thoughts. "And I really need to be alone. I've decided to go up on Pickle Rock for forty days after I finish this. Mama probably won't understand. She never has. Granny, I don't know. I'm being led to do this by the Spirit, Tammi. I can promise you that. It feels like a river just rushing through my soul, telling me I need to be in prayer and fasting so I can hear and fulfill what He has for me." Leon paused for a long breath. "I can't tell you yet what I'm supposed to do. All I can do is obey the Spirit's call. If you really love me, you'll support me."

A lump rose in Tammi's throat as she turned to go. In her mind she saw him, running from the demons that dogged him. Leon with his dark wing of hair hightailing it up to Pickle Rock on some sort of desperate quest.

CHAPTER 27

It seemed that Leon had dropped off the face of the earth. The refinishing stall at the barn was desolate. He didn't make his usual managerial appearances at Elco Antiques. He didn't attend meals at the big house. The covers on his bed remained tightly tucked between mattress and box spring.

For three days Tammi managed to rein in her hysteria, though she did fret about the ongoing rains. What if a sizzling bolt of the sporadic lightning found his vulnerable frame? She had to admire Leon. Had she ever known such a determined and purposeful pilgrim?

Tammi sat in the parlor late Tuesday evening with Nanette, distractedly leafing through a magazine. "You think Leon's okay?" Tammi asked.

"He's an intelligent man," Nanette said, removing a silver flask from her apron pocket and taking a long swallow.

Tammi persisted. "Don't you think we should go up there and at least check on him?"

"Let him be," Nanette said firmly. "If you only knew what a peculiar child Leon was. He's always needed his alone time, and I believe he's needing it now more than ever."

Concern and love in equal measure flooded Tammi. How could someone's *mother* be so offhand? "We could sort of spy on him. Make sure he's okay."

"No! I know what's best here. To step in now would be disastrous. I assure you . . . he needs his space."

When thirteen days had passed and still Leon was gone, Tammi thought she might go crazy from the worry. It was as if Leon's struggle had sliced right into her heart. Everything she did or saw put her in mind of him. There had not been so lush a sprinkling of daylilies or azaleas in her memory, and she longed to share their splendor with Leon. The burgeoning sights and sounds of summer, from the first pulses of the lightning bugs to the throbbing of the cicadas, almost took away her resolve not to visit him.

She marveled at how Pepaw, even Granny, everyone but herself, in fact, seemed so nonchalant about his absence. "When do you think he'll take a notion to come home?" she whined to Orr one evening as he stood at the sink beside her, drying dishes while she washed. For the first time she thought perhaps she preferred the wild, drunken Leon. At least he was around then.

"Papa says to keep saying our prayers." Orr shrugged. "Things'll be okay."

Tammi didn't feel like a bold and fervent prayer-warrior anymore. She'd grown weary of playing that part. It was hard work to keep faith alive, and over the past weeks she'd even had moments of pure doubt, entertaining the idea that humans were merely animals, like Parks claimed—brute beasts with a finite end—who ought to try and lap up every ounce of pleasure this world had to offer. Her prayers were merely rote and said from force of habit, her moments at Promiseland spent daydreaming of Leon. She felt no hopeful stirring of faith, no constructive purpose underneath all her troubles.

Strolling along the sidewalk in downtown Rigby on her Saturday lunch hour from Elco Antiques, Tammi mused that the seventeen days Leon had been up on Pickle Rock seemed an eternity. There had to be something to take her mind off the pain.

Gazing in the window of Trade-A-Back Books, a cozy nook next to the courthouse, she all at once recalled the feel of the surf at her ankles, the balmy air bathing her shoulders, the passion of Tatiana and Cody in *Island Pulse*.

It was such an intense, flooding feeling that she stood transfixed for a moment. Taking a deep breath, she ducked in the door.

A radio played soft classical music as Tammi stood between two islands of spinner racks marked ROMANCE BOOKS. Dazzled by the sheer number of enticing titles, she asked Sue Jenkins, the owner, for help.

"Set in Hawaii, huh?" Sue said, strumming her fingers across a row of spines on a shelf behind the counter. "Let me see . . . that strikes a chord somewhere."

"Now I remember!" Sue looked up, smiling. "Last week, this peculiar little old lady, Dell Terhune, I believe her name was, came toting in an enormous sack of books, and I do recall her telling me about one set in Hawaii. 'Bout had it memorized! She was a real character. Let me run in the back and hunt it. I haven't set those out yet."

Tammi swallowed hard. A wave of nostalgia swept through her. She saw herself and Orr that long-ago Halloween night, walking along the trail in silhouette against the edge of a full moon, swinging a flashlight and an empty pillowcase. It was a picture of their innocence, those carefree days.

By the time Sue returned, Tammi was so far back in her memory that she half-expected Orr to come bounding up, wearing his scarecrow costume and begging for candy. Instead she accepted a copy of *Honolulu Heaven* from Sue and held it against her chest. At length she stroked the glossy cover, fixing her gaze on a dark-haired demigod standing waist-deep in a glassy blue ocean with his arms encircling an ebony-skinned maiden. This was what Tammi needed! A trip to Honolulu.

After supper, Tammi sat cross-legged on her bed as *Honolulu Heaven* sucked her in. She followed breathlessly as Jennifer Balfour watched the sun sinking over Mamala Bay in the opening scene, feeling Jen's loneliness and longing so vividly it eclipsed her own.

When it grew late and Tammi could barely sit upright, she lay down with her head on her pillow and propped the book open on the bed. It was too good to put down.

Jen Balfour was wandering along a hot stretch of beach at Kupikipikio Point, sand shifting beneath her feet. She was hungry for passion, and Tammi was hungry in the pool of lamplight, breathing Jen's frustration along with the tropical breeze.

Tammi *was* Jen now, and she could feel the abrasion of sand on her toes as she slipped out of her sandals, threw off her batik wrap, and plunged into the balmy waters of the ocean.

> *Jen emerged from the water. A sound interrupted her quiet reverie, and she glanced toward a distant grove of jacaranda trees. The bright moon splashed down on the form of a man in swim trunks. Unkempt hair fell to his broad shoulders. Was it Liam?*
>
> *It was! A flicker of anger ran through Jen. Just who did he think he was—and why did he think he could show up here again—arrogantly strutting along the shores of her beach? She had to be strong enough to turn away from her utmost desire.*

"What are you doing here?" she demanded.

"Looking for you, babe."

Jen drew in her breath sharply. Liam was even more gorgeous than she remembered, his long, muscled torso plunging to that perfectly ripped six-pack, then down to those sculpted hamstrings.

Just for a second she let herself meet the mesmerizing gaze of those amber eyes that she remembered so well. "This is unfair, Liam," she said, more forcefully this time. "You've haunted my every waking thought since I first laid eyes on you. Since you left me for the third time." Jen stood trembling, her heart so heavy in her chest that she felt bound by its weight. She was angry, but at the same time she felt a little tremor of anticipation rippling through her body.

"C'mere, babe," Liam said huskily.

Should she take the chance and kiss those wandering lips of his until they were bruised and swollen with desire for her? Would the man ever understand that they were meant to be together always? She moved toward him, close enough to smell his earthiness. His fingers reached out to brush the full, velvet swell of her lips. His steady, warm hands wandered along her bare forearms, teased at her breasts, sending shivers down into her stomach and delicious tremors between her legs. He covered her mouth in a probing kiss that sent her over the edge.

The all-consuming hunger she'd imprisoned for months surged free, and they fell slowly to their knees in the hot sand. Wantonly Jen arched her back, releasing cries of rapture, her breasts rising to Liam's delicious torture.

At 6.00 A.M. Tammi groggily rubbed one short hour of sleep from her eyes as she went downstairs in the darkness to perk coffee. She was satisfied to a degree, as the close of *Honolulu Heaven* had Jen and Liam's destinies surrendered to each other in a marriage ceremony on Kawaihoa Point.

But now Tammi longed for passion with every atom of her being.

I will *go to him!* she thought, *because love must triumph, must come out victorious in the end!* Love was the most potent force in the universe and would conquer the deadliest of rivals. There were bound to be struggles and blocks to *prove* that it was real and true. Hadn't the Romance Readers' Book Club taught her that the end of the story *always* had love satisfied?

Desperate and cast down, the heart's future had to look bleak. Look at Jen! Wasn't her heart broken and trampled three separate times before her glorious fulfillment at the close of *Honolulu Heaven*? Wasn't her favorite saying, "It gets darkest just before the dawn"?

The best part of *Honolulu Heaven* was when you totally despaired that Jen and Liam would ever get together. Things looked totally bleak, and Jen was threatening to throw herself from the top floor of a tall building in downtown Maui. But love stepped in, and she wound up in Liam's arms, poised on the edge of unbelievable bliss.

You knew in your heart of hearts that it just wasn't worth a thing, the story, that is, and maybe even the love, if it came easily.

As soon as she'd guzzled a cup of coffee, Tammi ran back upstairs to throw on shorts and to grab her empty backpack. Pausing briefly in the kitchen, she wrapped a day-old biscuit in a napkin and poured the rest of the coffee into a thermos. These she placed in the backpack, and she slid it over her shoulders.

With the peaty smell of damp moss and the squawking noise of blue jays surrounding her, she drew a deep breath and took off running hard down the narrow path beyond Viking Creek. Early dawn fog hung in the branches of the trees so that it looked like smoke hovering above the damp trail. Happily, the rain was only a slight drizzle.

She reached the ravine, and, recalling Leon's last words to her, her heart tightened like a fist. She felt for him, yes, but she couldn't let him give up passion, the juice of life!

Breathlessly she sprinted through the ravine and crested the hill, spotting his shape on Pickle Rock, lying down on his belly, spread-eagled, along the edge of the boulder's broad flat surface. Two large black golfing umbrellas lay angled on their sides, their domes set against the northwest. A blue nylon book bag was bunched underneath one and a gallon jug under the other.

Her step snapped a twig and he lifted his head.

"Hi!" she warbled.

Leon merely stared at her, unblinking in the misty morning.

Without hesitation Tammi scaled Pickle Rock, crawling along its damp surface toward him, feeling slimy patches of lichen on her palms and knees. She came close enough to smell his ripe scent and sat very still. From the looks of his rumpled clothes and his bearded face, the eighteen days had taken their toll. Just from his stringy hands, she could tell he'd lost a good deal of weight. His eyes were huge and otherworldly.

He watched her set the thermos near his elbow. She unwrapped the biscuit and set it on the flattened napkin, poured coffee into the plastic lid of the thermos. A thin wisp of steam escaped along with the nutty aroma.

"Leon?" She sat quietly, listening to her own blood as it thundered in her ears.

"Hm?" he said at last.

"Why don't you come home and forget all this religious stuff? After all, you dropped out of seminary!" It took all of her self-control to keep from flinging herself on Leon, but a cautious voice piped in with *Don't, Tammi.*

"Paul wrote almost half the New Testament, and he didn't go to seminary or Bible college, either. He went out into the desert to pray and seek God. Among other things, it's been revealed to me now that I'm to pastor Holy Faith Full-Gospel Church right here in Rigby, Georgia."

Tammi watched an amber-colored ant scurrying along a crevice. "But you said you were going to manage Elco Antiques."

"Well," he said solemnly, "who am I to tell *God* what I'll do?

Tammi imagined Leon behind a pulpit, preaching and serving and ministering to the flock of rough hillbillies and blue-haired old women who attended Holy Faith Full-Gospel Church, folks who would suck up all his energies, his earthly passion poured out for their eternal good.

Tammi picked up his hand, searched his face. "I suppose you realize what you're getting yourself into." Heaviness strangled her voice. She sat staring vacantly out across Taylor's Gap, listening to a cardinal's cry of *purty-purty-purty.* "You're gonna be stuck here in this little podunk town! *I'm* going to Hawaii. I've been dying to go to Hawaii." Regret squeezed her heart so tightly her chest hurt. "Drink your coffee," she said, passing him the warm cup.

He waved it away.

"Hawaii's a tropical paradise, Leon! Just imagine!"

He raised his chin and struggled to put his palms flat on the surface of Pickle Rock, hoisting himself to a sitting position. He looked out at Taylor's Gap through the misty clouds of morning. "Tammi, there's something you need to realize. *Rigby* would be exotic to folks from Hawaii. Look at this!" He made a magnanimous sweeping gesture with his hands to encompass earth and sky. "It's spectacular!"

Tammi let herself gaze outward for a moment with a stranger's eyes. She watched the wind blow through sycamore trees in the valley below: soft, fluid, certain, undulating the boughs as bits of the rising sun reflected off individual leaves like a myriad of tiny prisms. She drew a quick gasp of air and sat motionless. *If I hadn't been born here,* she thought, wouldn't *I think this was gorgeous? Wouldn't I be content to stay here? But what about passion?* she reminded herself just as quickly. She reflected on the fact that she could live nowhere without passion! She tried to swallow her frustration as she thought of that afternoon at the reunion when Leon had kissed her and she had felt the world opening up. She recalled his face as they pulled apart. He'd looked happier than she'd seen him since. He did not look happy now. He looked like some kind of tortured soul.

"Well," she said without looking at him, tears teetering on the rims of her eyes. "It is kind of pretty."

"Aw. You're crying," he said, pulling Tammi's hand over into his lap.

"I love you, Leon Dupree." Tammi swallowed hard. "And I love your goodness. Really, I do. But I hate it at the same time! Why does God have to go and make you a *preacher*? Who will there ever be in my life to match our passion! And what a dull life you're gonna have here in Rigby. It's a crying shame."

Leaning back on his elbows, Leon narrowed his eyes thoughtfully. "Who said a man of God can't be passionate?" he said at last. "You think a man of God can't feel passion, Tammi? Is that it?"

"Well, no," she said quickly. "I *know* you do. But you're always talking about fleeing youthful lust and all that other religious stuff. I just don't know if . . ." Awkwardly she made to pull her hand away, but he grasped her fingers hard.

"Do you want to hear what Paul said in First Corinthians?" Leon's gaze was on her face now, pale and intense. "He said, 'But if they cannot contain, let them marry; for it is better to marry than to burn.' "

"What?!"

"Burn with lust, he meant. To be married would help a man 'flee fornication.' "

Tammi felt a stirring of curiosity. Leon must have been pondering these matters; he was so quick with all the scriptures.

"Listen," he said, running his tongue across his upper lip, "I've been doing a lot of thinking up here, and I realize now that we were made for each other." He shifted, leaning closer to her. "Will you wait for me, Tammi Lynn Elco?" he said wetly into her ear, his bearded lips sending shivers to join the tangle of excitement growing now between her legs. "When you're of age, we can marry, if you'll wait for me."

Tammi pulled away quickly. She drew her knees up underneath her chin, and wrapped her arms around her legs, raising her eyes to a hawk circling above them. Did she want to miss out on Hawaii and be a preacher's wife in Rigby, Georgia? The part of her that said she shouldn't, that recognized all too well the restlessness waiting if she did was grappling with the voracious desire that had been pulling her toward Leon since that first kiss at Viking Creek. "I don't know," she whispered at last, looking out across the valley, rubbing her palm across the rock she loved so much. "I know you're absolutely sure of your destiny, Leon, and I hope you're totally happy as a preacher here. It's just that . . . I don't know what the next chapter of my life holds, and . . ."

There was a long silence. Then Leon smiled. "Well, I hope your dreams come true. That every single page holds happiness no matter what you choose to do, where you go. I only pray your life never turns into one of those trashy romance novels."

Tammi unfolded her body from its tight knot. She lay back on the cool surface of Pickle Rock and began to laugh. She heard echoes of her laughter bouncing off the fluffy morning clouds hanging above Taylor's Gap.